IF THESE WALLS
COULD TALK

A JOE BOYD SUSPENSE NOVEL - BOOK 1

DAN WALSH

BAINBRIDGE PRESS

PRAISE FOR DAN'S JACK TURNER
SUSPENSE NOVELS

When Night Comes (Book 1)

"Though Walsh steps into a different genre, fans will not be disappointed. He continues to infuse historical facts into his books, bringing history to life in this character-driven tale. The pace quickens as events unfold, making it challenging for the reader to predict the twists and turns." – *RT Book Reviews, 4.5 Stars*

"Dan Walsh surprises with his new novel, *When Night Comes*. This engrossing mystery/thriller is a break from his normal superb Christian fiction and proves Walsh is more than one-dimensional." – *New York Journal of Books*

Remembering Dresden (Book 2)

"Few authors can straddle multiple genres successfully but Dan Walsh is proving he is in that elite group as he releases his second suspense novel...Remembering Dresden gripped me from start to finish. Once again, Walsh weaves together historical and contemporary events, resulting in a compelling tale...He fills the book with believable personalities well-suited to the story, as well as a plethora of heart-wrenching and heart-pounding moments, making it impossible to set aside." – *Mocha with Linda Blog*

"Walsh has another suspense-filled hit, proving that his flair for an engaging tome spans genres. History buffs will love his latest, which could be read as a standalone, though it is second in the series. The past and present scenes seamlessly blend together to create a fast-paced, intriguing story which will leave readers anticipating the third book."
– *RT Book Reviews Magazine, 4.5 Stars/Top Pick!*

(Also Available, Books 3 and 4 of the Jack Turner Suspense Series)

For a look at these and more of Dan's books, go to Amazon and type "Dan Walsh Books," or visit his website at:

http://danwalshbooks.com/books/

If These Walls Could Talk

Joe Boyd Suspense Series – Book 1

Bainbridge Press

Editor - Cindi Walsh

ISBN: 978-0-9979837-7-7

Cover design by Bainbridge Press

Cover photo Licensed through 123rf.com:

Image ID : 76935715

Copyright : Steven Gaertner

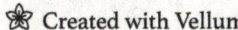 Created with Vellum

1

"I'll be right there." Sergeant Joe Boyd hung up his desk phone. "This can't be good."

He was alone in the same office he'd occupied since first joining the Culpepper PD four years ago. Nothing fancy, but at least he had his own space. He hadn't had a raise or promotion since that first year, either. But then, he hadn't moved the family down here from Pittsburgh to move up the ladder. He did it to save his marriage, get a chance to become a real dad to his two kids.

And it worked.

But now this.

Guess the rumors were true. Why else would his boss—the Culpepper Chief of Police—interrupt Joe in the middle of the day, ask him to come to his office ASAP? He'd never done that before.

Not in four years.

Joe rolled his chair back from the desk and stood. He

wondered how much time they'd give him once they let him go. Hopefully, there'd be a decent severance package. The HR gal had said something about that when he got hired four years back, but he couldn't recall the details.

Whatever it was, his finances were about to take a nose-dive, no doubt. Wished he hadn't bought that pop-up camper three months ago. Five more years of payments. That was stupid. He'd have to sell it quick, probably get half its worth. Kate and the kids would be heartbroken. They'd only taken the one trip in it last month. Everyone had such a blast.

He remembered, the kids were asleep in the camper. He and Kate held hands by the campfire, gazing at the moonlight's reflection on the lake. Talked about all the memories they were gonna make with this thing.

He sighed, started walking down the hallway to the open cubicle area. There was Hank Jensen, his partner, talking on the phone at his desk. Smiling, enjoying another low-crime day in Culpepper. Joe wondered, would Hank be next? How far would these budget cuts go? Then again, maybe it was just Joe getting the ax. Hank liked to always rib him, when Joe got stuck doing some crap task: "That's why you get paid the big bucks."

Maybe now those big bucks would be Joe's undoing. He not only got paid the most out of all the detectives, he had the lowest seniority. You know the saying, last in, first out.

If that happened, Joe would be genuinely happy for Hank. He liked Hank. Maybe they'd even give Hank Joe's job. For a fraction of the pay, of course.

Joe walked past his cubicle.

Hank noticed. "Hey Hon, gotta go. See you at dinner." He hung up the phone.

Joe stopped, peered over the cubicle wall.

"What's wrong?" Hank said.

"Who said anything's wrong?"

"Your face. Something come up? You feeling all right?"

"See what I mean, Hank? Sometimes with you it's like I'm talking with Kate. Always trying to read my moods."

"Maybe if you didn't wear your moods on your face you'd get less attention." Hank spun around in his chair, faced Joe.

Joe laughed.

"No, really Joe. What's going on?"

Joe looked around, made sure no one was within earshot. "Just got a call from Captain Pendleton. Wants to see me right away."

Hank's expression instantly changed. Probably matched the look on Joe's face. "That never happens, right?"

"Nope, never does. The Captain's got something to say, he usually comes out to you to say it."

"He must want privacy," Hank said. "For whatever he wants to say, I mean."

"I know what you mean. And that can't be good."

"You think it might be about...?" Hank leaned forward in his chair, whispered, "The budget cuts?"

See, Joe thought. Hank gets it. "What else could it be?"

"I wonder who else he's going to call after you. I mean, you know. You're kinda at the top of the food chain around here."

"Guess it depends on how far the cuts are gonna go. Maybe you'll get lucky, and it'll stop with me."

Hank had no quick comeback. What could he say? Better

you than me? Then he said, "Maybe, Joe, it's something else entirely. Maybe the rumors are just that...rumors."

"Maybe. Anyway, I better get in there and face the music."

Joe walked slowly through the halls between Hank's cubicle and Pendleton's office. More thoughts, more memories. Besides the havoc a layoff would play with his finances, the truth was, Joe really liked it here in Culpepper. It had taken him a few years to really adjust to the slower pace. Well, the extremely slower pace. But he did get there.

Now, he didn't see himself ever going back to fighting crime in the big city. Maybe he could find a detective job in some other smallish town in the South. See, even that. The South. Joe had been born and bred a Yank. Lived up north his entire life until four years ago. Never even took a vacation in the South. Even when they went to the beach, they always went to the Jersey shore.

Since moving here, they had vacationed twice in Destin, Florida. They all liked that beach way better. He and Kate had even talked about taking the pop-up and going camping down in the Keys. He'd seen pictures of it on the internet. Like a tropical paradise down there.

Joe reached the doorway to Pendleton's office. No, wherever he wound up, he would limit his job search to somewhere in the South. Another town in Georgia, maybe Florida.

He knocked on the door, opened it a few inches.

"That you, Joe?" Pendleton's deep voice. His strong southern drawl evident even in a few words.

Joe opened it the rest of the way. "It's me, sir."

"Come on in, Joe. Have a seat. Want me to fetch you a cup of coffee?"

"No, I'm good, sir." Joe came around and sat in one of the cushy office chairs, glanced up at the Captain's face. Not the look Joe had expected to find. The man was smiling. No seriousness in his eyes.

Joe felt a flicker of hope.

Maybe this wasn't the end after all.

2

_____

Captain Pendleton sat back in his office chair, propped his feet up on the corner of his desk. Again, not the posture of someone about to lay you off. Joe was further encouraged. He began to relax a little.

"So Joe, thought we'd have a little chat about your future," Pendleton said. "You like your job here, right? I mean, mostly. I know things are way slower here than they were in Pittsburgh, but that was part of the reason you came down here, right?"

"That was most of the reason, Cap. And yeah, I like my job around here mostly."

"We got pretty good people here for a small town operation, don't you think?"

A few good ones, Joe thought. Probably not the right answer. "Yeah, I'd say so. Hank especially. I can see him doing pretty good back in Zone 5, the precinct I worked in." He wondered where Pendleton was going with this.

"You know I took off for a week. Just came back in yesterday."

Joe nodded.

"Something interesting happened on my vacation. We didn't go anywhere. Had a bunch of home projects the wife wanted to get done. But in the evenings, we mostly stayed home and watched TV."

At this point, Joe was pretty sure he wasn't getting a pink slip.

"I started watching this series on Netflix. You get Netflix?"

"Yeah, we do."

"It's pretty nice. Can watch all these shows in a row, no commercials. Anyway, I started watching this series about cold case murders in small towns. Can't remember the name of it. There were several seasons, so apparently it's kind of a hit. So, I started watching. They got these towns spread out all over the South and Midwest. Really small towns. Smaller than here. Most of them only had four or five law enforcement personnel working in their offices. I just checked. We got eighteen working in here, not counting the guys in patrol cars."

A regular metropolis, Joe thought. Where was this going?

"Most of these fellas, these sheriffs and deputies and whatnots, seemed like decent people. But—how can I say this—none of them seemed very bright to me. The stars of the show were these retired homicide detectives from big cities. Again, don't remember where. There was a lady detective and a guy, the two of them worked together like partners. They'd come into these towns to help them solve cold case murders that happened ten, twenty, even thirty years ago."

"I've seen shows like that," Joe said, just trying to connect. "Not that one though."

"I don't know how they got these assignments, but some way or another, there they are, going over these old cases with the full cooperation of the local law enforcement folks. As the episode goes on, they start re-interviewing everyone remotely involved in the case. The cops who worked on it, any witnesses, family members, even the potential suspects. And this is where it starts bugging me. You know, as a career law enforcement officer myself. I don't have a degree in this, do you? I don't remember when I interviewed you, if you did."

"No, sir," Joe said. "Just the academy, some in-house stuff they offered along the way. Mostly learned through experience and working with some really smart guys."

Pendleton slid his feet off the desk, sat up a little straighter in his chair. "So, we've got a similar background. I don't know if the big city detectives on this series had college degrees, but they knew what they were about. But these local guys? In one show after another, I'm thinking, how do some of you people even function in society? In almost every case, these outside detectives were asking the kind of questions any detective solving a murder should ask. But you could tell, it's like, no one had ever thought to ask any of these questions before. And before long, just by applying some normal crime-solving detective methods, they'd have the big mystery solved."

Joe found Pendleton's review of this detective series interesting enough, but he still didn't have any idea why he'd asked him to come in here.

"After I'd watched about four of these shows, I got to

thinking. Culpepper has never had a cold case department. Apparently, you've got hundreds of small towns spread out all over this good ole US-of-A, all of them with a pile of murders that happened years ago, in their town, and not a one of them ever been solved."

"Which means," Joe added, "you got a whole slew of good ole boy murderers walking around free as you please, with no fear of ever facing justice."

"Exactly," Pendleton declared. "That's my point. That ain't right. And in some ways, it's downright embarrassing, to think such a thing is going on all across this country. And then I started thinking some more...I can do something about this. Not everywhere else, but here in Culpepper I can."

"You can, Cap?" Joe decided to play along, keep the momentum going. He was starting to like where this conversation was headed now.

"Yes, I can. And that's where you come in, Joe. That's why I asked you in here."

"Me, sir?"

"Yeah, you. You and maybe Hank."

"So, you're thinking of setting up a cold case squad here? In our department?"

"That's exactly what I'm thinking. Like I said, it came to me about four shows into this series. So, I got on my phone and called the mayor and several of the City Council members, enough so that we'd have a majority. These are all friends of mine, mind you, golfing buddies or fishing buddies or both. I told them about this series and what I was thinking. Asked them as a personal favor to me to watch the show, at least a couple episodes. Then, let's talk. They did. In the meantime, I put together a little proposal, laying out how this idea could work. Give them something they could vote on. Well, the short version is, all but one of them agreed. For some reason, Councilman Rhodes voted no. But he was the only one, so it was approved. It's about time a town like Culpepper had its own Cold Case Squad."

"And you want me to be a part of it, sir?"

"A part? Joe, I want you to run it. Lock, stock and barrel. It won't be much of a squad starting off. Could only get funding for you and Hank. But I figure, since these are cold cases we're talking about, not like anyone's paying attention. No press breathing down our necks. No family members calling us every day, demanding we solve the case. I figure you guys could fit this in, you know, between your regular duties."

"Fit it in, sir?"

"Yeah Joe, well, it's not like I can hire two detectives to come in here and replace you. You've probably heard all the talk about budget cuts. It took some real horse dealing to get this thing to happen. But hey, listen, the Council members realize it ain't right to just give you more work without compensating you. Don't muzzle an ox while he's threshing and all. There'll be a raise in it for you, both you and Hank. And a promotion. You'll be made a lieutenant, and Hank a sergeant."

Joe sat straight up. "Really?"

"I take it you're interested then?"

Joe couldn't hold back a smile. "Definitely, sir. I'm pretty sure you can count Hank in on this too." Joe figured with Hank just getting married a couple months ago, starting up house payments, he could say that with certainty.

"Good then," Pendleton said, standing up.

"So, when do we start, Cap? What cold cases did you have in mind?"

"I'll get into all that just as soon as I get back from the little boy's room. You sit tight."

Professor Jack Turner sat at a table at a Starbucks staring at the door, anticipating his wife Rachel to walk in any moment. She'd called a few minutes ago telling him to order her usual—a breve latte, grande size. She was that close.

Jack had gotten himself the same, fixed it up and was sipping it now. This Starbucks wasn't the closest one to the University, which was always packed with students. Jack had driven to the next one on Google Maps, about ten minutes further away.

As the Dean of Military History at the school, he pretty much set his own hours. He'd just finished giving a lecture that morning for one of the professors in his department who'd called in sick. He really enjoyed it. The money in this new position was so much better but sometimes Jack wondered if he shouldn't just give it up and go back to teaching full-time.

He looked up. There she was coming through the glass

door, as beautiful as ever, even now being seven months pregnant. Of course, he knew he needed to say it more often these days, not just think it. He didn't know why she was still so self-conscious about her looks.

She glanced at him, smiled, then looked at her latte and smiled even more. "You got it. I'm so glad. Is it already fixed?"

"Just the way you like it." He leaned toward her and they kissed.

She instantly grabbed her latte and took a sip.

"Careful," Jack said. "Mine was pretty hot."

"It's perfect. Thanks for getting it." She sat down. "I really needed it today. For some reason, the kids were just awful this afternoon." Rachel still taught at the same private school she'd been teaching at since last year. She'd be doing it for a few weeks more.

"My kids were a little better behaved," Jack said. "You look great, by the way."

"Thanks. This might be the last time I wear this blouse, though. I could barely button the last two buttons." She took another sip. So, what did you want to talk to me about, something that couldn't wait until dinner?"

"It's not that. It could have waited till then. I just wanted to see you. We hardly ever get to do this in the middle of the week anymore. Figured since the class I taught ended at three-thirty, and I knew you'd be off by then..."

"Then I'm glad you suggested it. And I'm glad my doctor said I can still have these." She held up her drink. "As long as I don't have too many."

"But there is something I did want to talk about," Jack said. "Now that you mention it."

"What is it?"

He slid his tablet out of his brief bag.

"Something you want to tell me or show me?"

"Both. I'll start with the tell-you part. I know we kinda decided not to go on anymore vacations or getaways until after the baby."

"It's just we're both going to want to take off so much time."

"I know. And your folks will be coming in for a lengthy visit."

"Well," she said, "my mom will. Not so sure how long my dad will stay."

"Anyway, I've been thinking a little more about our property out by the lake," Jack said. "Thinking maybe we should sell it. In fact, one of the other professors at the school asked me about it this morning, shortly after I got in. I told him I wasn't planning on selling it, but then he offered me several thousand more than we paid for it. And it got me thinking about another idea."

Rachel took another sip. "Before you tell me what it is, I'm totally fine if you want to sell that lakefront property. I don't think we're ever going to build a cabin on it. With how busy you are, you haven't even begun to design a place yet, and we've owned it for almost a year."

"I know. That's part of what I was thinking. But the thing is, even after all of our...misfortune with cabins by the lake, I still like the idea of having one. It's so beautiful out there, and whenever we do get out there, it's so easy for me to relax. Right now, we have the money to get a place. Between what the property will sell for and the money still in savings from selling the last cabin."

"I'm not sure *misfortune* is a strong enough word to

describe our experiences with cabins by the lake, Jack. The first one you inherited because Professor Thornton was murdered there. And the second cabin you leased for your doctoral research retreat wound up being the home base of a Nazi serial killer. Have you forgotten that?"

"No, I haven't forgotten. But nothing happened on the lakefront property we bought. Except for all the Civil War relics Joe and I were able to dig up with our detectors."

"Okay," she said, "technically, nothing happened on our property. But how about the shooting that took place on the property right next door? Those two New Jersey guys and the buried treasure?"

Jack set his latte on the table. "I haven't forgotten."

"To tell you the truth," she said, "I wouldn't mind if you sold the property to your professor friend, and we bought something else entirely different. Someplace that had nothing to do with lakes."

Jack reached for her hand. "I didn't bring this up to upset you. It's just...it seems like maybe you're getting a little superstitious about this. Lake Sampson has nothing to do with any of these circumstances. And lakefront cabins, in general, are perfectly safe places. Think about it, Rach, there are literally hundreds of cabins and cottages around the lake. And nothing ever happens on any of them. Families make crazy-good memories on these lakes every year. Swimming, fishing, canoeing, sailing, roasting hot dogs or marshmallows on a fire down by the water. Can't you just see us doing that with our kids down the road? I know I can."

She sighed. "Yeah, I guess. It's just..."

"I'll tell you what," Jack said, "you don't need to be involved in this at all. Unless you want to be. I'll sell the

property and do all the legwork with the realtor to find a
new place. And I'll make sure two things are true on whatever lakefront place I pick out for you to see. First, it'll be big
enough to fit all the kids we're planning to have. And second,
I'll make sure no one's ever been shot there or killed there, or
even on any of the properties on either side. Is that a deal?"

She smiled. "Okay, that's a deal."

4

Joe sat in the middle chair at a gray metal table in a dimly-lit room of the Culpepper PD basement. Two cardboard storage boxes sat at one end. He was surrounded by floor-to-ceiling utility shelves filled with countless more cardboard storage boxes, each containing files, documents and evidence saved for a particular crime. They all had some kind of label on the front, or else words written on the box with a black marker, including someone's last name, the type of crime and a date. Some of the dates were just the month and year.

A quick scan of these labels told Joe two things: First, they were grouped together by the year the crimes had occurred and, second, some were very old, dating back decades. But compared to what he was used to in Pittsburgh, the place was a mess. Clearly, it was no one's job to maintain this room. Probably never had been.

Captain Pendleton had warned him not to expect much,

so Joe lowered his expectations accordingly. He hadn't ratcheted them down nearly enough. There wasn't even a separate shelf or even a separate section for homicides or other major crimes. Everything was all thrown in together, separated only by date.

Joe was also used to using a "Murder Book" in Pittsburgh. He'd already known that wasn't a practice followed here from the handful of murders he'd investigated. Apparently, the ones he'd created for his homicides were the first ones ever made. Murder Books were generally thick notebooks containing all the files, reports, witness statements, crime scene photographs...literally, everything that had anything to do with a homicide from the moment the case opened to its final conclusion.

The Captain had explained they'd never created them because they'd hardly ever had any murders. Sometimes, they'd go three or four years without one. And when they did occur, most were usually solved within the first few days. Not well-thought-out premeditated sorts of things. Wives shooting husbands. Husbands shooting wives. Husbands shooting a wife's lover or vice versa. The killers around these parts, he'd said, were too stupid to even try and get away with it. Nothing ever happened that would've made for a good episode of Perry Mason or Matlock. Really, the Captain had said, the homicides Joe solved the last few years with that history professor, Jack Turner, were the most complicated things he'd ever seen in this town.

Except...for a series of unsolved murders Pendleton remembered from his high school years in the mid-80s. At first, the police thought they were all committed by one killer. Later it became clear, the nature of these particular crimes couldn't possibly have all been connected.

Joe heard loud thumps coming down the stairs. Had to be Hank.

"This is how they treat you for a promotion?" Hank said. "Feels more like being banished to a dungeon."

"I'm in here, Hank. Watch your step. Some stuff on the floor between you and me, and the lighting is terrible." He heard Hank's feet land on the floor then make his way through the maze of shelves.

"We gotta do something about this. Pendleton can't be expecting us to work down here." Hank made it to Joe and sat across the table from him.

"What did he tell you when he gave you the news?" Joe said.

"Almost nothing. He said congratulations, I'm promoting you to Sergeant. And that I'll be working with you on some new cold case squad, that I'll get some more money but still have to do all my old work besides. At least for a while. Then he got a phone call that he absolutely had to take and closed with, 'Ask Joe, he'll explain everything.' So, I'm here. What's going on?"

"I'll tell you. But hey, you don't seem all that happy. An hour ago, you and I were talking about whether I was the only one getting laid off or whether you were going to join me. Now, neither of us got a pink slip. Besides that, you're a Sergeant, and you got a raise. How's about a little gratitude?"

"I should be thanking you? Did you make this happen for me, Joe? The Captain didn't mention that."

"No, I had nothing to do with it. I mean...well, I don't

know. Maybe being grateful to the Man Upstairs? It's just...
right off the bat, you're complaining about the dingy room?"

"I am grateful. And you're right, this is a good thing. The
new title, more money. And I'm even grateful I get to be
working with you more. But seriously, are we really
supposed to be working down here?" He took a strong sniff
with his nose. "It even smells bad."

"The captain didn't say anything about where we work.
I'm fine if we just come down here to get the files and boxes
we need, then take them into my office. You have the key to
the lock on my office door, right?"

"Yeah, I think so. You gave me one, but I've never used it."

"Well, dig it out. Because if we bring anything up there
and leave for the day, or really, leave for any length of time at
all, we should lock my door from now on."

"I'm sure I can find the key. So tell me, what's going on?
What are we going to be working on? All he said was, they'd
be cold case files."

"Well, he didn't tell me a whole lot more. I guess he saw
some true crime series on cable about some big city homicide detectives coming into these little podunk towns to
solve their cold case murders. Because the people there
weren't smart enough to figure them out for themselves. He
figured you and I were smart enough, but he realized
Culpepper had never done anything like this before. He
thought it was about time he fixed that. So, here we are."

Hank pointed to the two cardboard boxes on the table.
"Are these the cases he wants us to work on?" He started
reading the labels.

"Maybe. Maybe not. He left that up to my discretion.
Well, sort of. Basically, he wants us to dig out any boxes from

the eighties that involve murders that don't have the word CLOSED written on the front. These two on the table are the first ones I found before you got here."

"Why the eighties?"

"I guess it's because Pendleton joined the force in the early nineties, so he pretty much remembers what happened after that. He said the few homicides that occurred since he became a cop got solved pretty quickly. Not so much by him, but because they weren't big mysteries. He wants us to focus on the eighties because he remembers a whole bunch of murders that happened during his high school years that never got solved. When he became a detective, he'd asked whoever was the chief at the time if he could work on some of those murders from the eighties but was turned down flat."

"I wonder why there were so many murders around here in the eighties?"

"I don't know," Joe said. "Culpepper was even smaller than it is now. But there were a bunch of serial killers back then. Even more than there seem to be today."

"Wasn't that the era of guys like Ted Bundy, the Zodiak Killer and that Son of Sam guy in New York?"

"Close. That was the seventies. It kept going on in the eighties, too. You had guys like the Night Stalker out in California. That creep Jeffrey Dahmer. And the guy who killed that poor little kid, Adam Walsh. You know, the guy who did that show *America's Most Wanted*? It was his son. But nowadays, it seems like we have more mass shootings. Either terrorists or else guys going nuts, killing a whole bunch of people in one sitting."

"Then shooting themselves," Hank said. "I never get that.

What do they think God's going to do the second they reach the other side? Congratulate them for breaking one of the Ten Commandments a dozen times, as their last act on earth?"

"Yeah, right?" Joe said. "But back in the seventies and eighties, you'd have all these serial killers taking people out one at a time, or sometimes two. Then they wouldn't kill for days, sometimes weeks or months. And some of them didn't get caught for years."

"I guess," Hank said, "some got away with it for good. I mean, aren't these cases all unsolved?"

"Yeah, but that doesn't mean the bad guys got away with it," Joe said. "Could be. But it could also be they got away with the murders committed here but got caught somewhere else."

"And no one ever connected the murders here to the bigger case," Hank added.

"Something like that," Joe said. "There was no internet back then. Nobody was connected with anybody else. Now, some of these cases might not have anything to do with a serial killer. That's what you and I are supposed to find out, I guess."

"So, where do we start?" Hank stood. "Want me to start finding more homicide boxes from the eighties?"

"Yeah, do that. I'll start making a list in this notebook here. See if I can start making any sense of this. Since there was one specific instruction Pendleton gave me about where to start."

"What's that?"

"He said to pick a case that looked like the easiest one to solve, not one that might take months or years. He wants to be able to brag about this new cold case squad idea in the papers? Get some positive publicity for the department."

"Gotcha," Hank said. "But Joe...you know nobody calls it the papers anymore, right? Everybody gets their news on TV or on the internet."

"I know that. Get outta here."

5

J oe had finished up going through the storage shelves with Hank, making sure they'd gotten all the homicide boxes from the eighties. And he'd made a reference list of each one, with a few columns of details. But not much else. At quitting time, they'd locked everything up in the cage and headed home.

Joe was just pulling up into his driveway now. As soon as he'd gotten in the car, he'd called Kate, told her it was time for a celebration. Put the dinner on hold or in the fridge. He was calling in pizza for the kids and taking her out someplace nice. She wanted to know what was going on. Of course, he'd said it was a surprise. For the most part, Kate hated surprises.

But she wouldn't hate this one.

As Joe got out of the car, the pizza guy showed up. "A large pepperoni?"

"This the Boyd residence?" the delivery guy said.

"Yeah, that's a large pepperoni, right? One of my kids won't eat anything else on their pizza."

"That's what I got here. Nice and hot."

Joe paid the guy fifteen bucks. "Keep the change." He walked through the front door. You'd think he was Santa Claus on Christmas Eve the way Joe Jr. greeted him.

"Is that it? Mom said you were bringing home pizza." Joe Jr. wrapped his arms around his dad and squeezed.

"Hold on now, don't wanna drop this thing."

"It's pepperoni, right?"

"What else? Here, you bring it in the kitchen. You and your sister can say grace yourselves, then dig in."

Joe Jr. took the pizza. "What's going on? Mom said you were taking her out to celebrate."

"Just something good that happened with my job."

"I'm glad for whatever it is. You saved us from having to eat baked fish and spinach." He hurried into the kitchen.

Kate came walking down the stairs.

"Well, look at you," Joe said. "All dolled up."

"You said you were taking me out someplace nice. Were you making that part up?"

"No, I meant it. And you look great." She reached the bottom of the stairs and they kissed.

"So, what's the big news? And second, where are you taking me?"

"How about I tell you in the car? The kids are all set. They got their pizza. I told your son to say grace. Did you remind Kristin not to be bossy?"

"I did. She said she had no idea what I was talking about."

"Okay, you wait right here. Don't get sucked into

anything with them. I'm going up and change my shirt very quickly and grab my sports coat."

"You mean the blazer? You're taking me someplace where you need to wear a blazer?"

Joe started up the stairs. "How's the River Bend restaurant sound?"

"River Bend? You're taking me to River Bend?"

"That's why I gotta change. Be right down."

Ten minutes later, they were in the car and on their way.

Joe apologized for all the rush when he got home, but normally you can't get reservations at a place like River Bend on such short notice. The gal on the phone had said they'd be able to get a seat only if they got there within the hour.

Kate said, "Okay, so can you tell me now what we're celebrating?"

"Only if you start calling me Lieutenant Joe Boyd from now on."

"Lieutenant? They made you a Lieutenant?"

"They made me a Lieutenant. Starting today. And I'm getting a raise. Not sure how much yet. Hopefully enough to at least pay for this dinner we're about to have."

"Joe, that's so wonderful." She leaned over and gave him a kiss on the cheek.

"Man, don't you smell good."

"If I'm dressing up, I'm putting on the good stuff. So, what brought this on? Were you expecting it at all? Because you haven't talked about making lieutenant for months."

"It was totally unexpected. To tell you the truth, and I can tell you this now, when Pendleton called me in I was totally convinced I was getting a pink slip."

"Really? You thought you were going to get laid off? How long has that been going on?"

Joe stopped at a red light. "A few weeks, maybe a month. There were rumors of budget cuts. Well, the budget cuts weren't rumors. They're still happening. The rumors were, there were going to be layoffs. I figured being one of the newest guys in there and one of the highest-paid, I was a goner for sure."

"I'm sorry you had to carry that around by yourself for so long. Why didn't you tell me?"

"I figured, why tell you when they're just rumors? All you could do was worry."

"No, I could've also prayed, been a support to you. You know how I worry about your blood pressure."

"See what I mean? You worry about things. I didn't want you to worry. Anyway, the whole thing is moot now, right? I didn't get a pink slip. I got the opposite, and we're on our way to River Bend restaurant. Let's focus on that."

"So, what do we have to give up for you to get this new lieutenant badge and raise? Is it going to start getting like Pittsburgh, where we never see you anymore?"

"No, nothing like that." Joe spent the rest of the drive filling her in on the captain's new cold case squad idea. He was still talking about it when they pulled into the restaurant parking lot.

When he'd finished, the first thing Kate said was, "Well you know me, Joe, I always love watching cold case murder mysteries on TV. I don't think I'm gonna mind this new position at all. Know how you never want to bring your work home with you? Maybe now you can. I mean, since these are all cases from the 1980's, it's not like there's going to be anybody breathing down your neck to get it solved."

"Well, maybe nobody from the family. But the Captain wants some positive results pretty quick. He's kind of sticking his neck out making this change when everyone else is getting their budget cut."

"Well, you know what I mean," she said. "When you're working on homicides that just happened you can't ever talk about it with me, because it's an ongoing investigation. But it won't be that way with these cases, right? I mean, maybe I could even help. I've watched so many of these things."

"We'll see. But yeah, I won't have some of the same restrictions about what I can say or can't say on these. Even still, just scratching the surface today on some of these cases, things could get a little creepy. I don't mean ghost-creepy. I mean creepy perps. You know, the guys that committed these crimes were pretty screwed up. Some of them, downright perverted."

He pulled the car up to the valet parking area. "I don't see that kind of thing making for particularly good dinner conversation, if you catch my drift."

6

Saturday, Mid-morning
Three Days Later

Jack hoped she liked it.

Since he'd first introduced to Rachel the idea of buying an already-built lakefront place a few days ago, Jack had spent all his spare time on the internet looking at properties on Lake Samson. Based on what they'd discussed, he'd narrowed it down to three. Yesterday, he'd taken the afternoon off to tour those three places with a realtor. After seeing them in person, he'd been able to quickly rule out two of them.

So now they were driving Jack's blue BMW sedan along the familiar winding roads that weaved around the lake area toward the one remaining cabin he felt had the most promise. Well, cabin wasn't exactly the right word. Cottage might better describe it. But even that wasn't quite right. It was too big to be a cottage. Jack had shown Rachel some pictures from his tablet that morning at breakfast. She'd liked it enough to agree to drive out there and see it together.

The thing she liked most about it was that it reminded her of the houses they'd seen last year on Cape Cod when visiting Jack's grandmother.

"This is the road," Jack said. "It's only about a block more down this dirt road."

"I like how many trees there are out here," she said. "I'm not seeing hardly any other cabins since we turned off the main road."

"That's one of the things I liked right off when I came out here yesterday. It's really quiet. I guess whoever originally built this place wanted some serious privacy. The realtor told me he'd actually bought the properties on either side of the house, just to leave them as woods."

"You mean, all the way down to the lake, too?"

"Yeah. You'll see. It's cleared out pretty nice right around the house itself. But on either side of it, there's just thick woods going all the way down to the water."

"Isn't that going to make this thing a little pricey?" she said. "Compared to the other cabins we've seen out here?"

"A little. Maybe...even a little more than a little. But it's not too much of a stretch. And it's a big part of the reason I liked this place more than the others. It makes it feel like we've got our own private lake." Jack saw the clearing up ahead on the left. He looked at her face. It would be so nice if she liked it. Then he could stop searching and shift his focus on making this place into the kind of place they both would really love.

Another fifty yards and they were there. He watched to catch her expression as the house and property came into view. Her eyes brightened and a smile appeared on her face. Exactly what he'd been hoping. "So, you like it?"

"From what I can see so far, yes. It really does resemble a Cape Cod house, minus the cedar shakes."

"I thought the lap board siding kind of gives it the same effect. And see how the porch wraps around the side, so you can face the water or the woods? I know Cape Cod houses don't typically have wraparound porches. That's kind-of a southern thing, but I still love the way it looks." He pulled the car up to the front and stopped.

"I like the porch," she said. "And I especially love those dormers in the front. Does it have a second floor like your grandmother's place?"

"Yes and no." He turned the car off. "The roofline is a little less steep than my grandmother's house, so there's not as much usable space up there. It's really more of a partially finished attic. But I was up there yesterday, and you can stand perfectly straight in the middle area in either direction for at least twelve to fifteen feet. I figure we can easily convert it into a couple of bedrooms down the road. Or one bedroom and a play area."

"How many bedrooms does it have downstairs?"

"Two, but they're both pretty big. The biggest one comes with a bathroom, but there's another bath off the main hallway." They got out of the car. "Of course, the master bathroom isn't anything special. This place was built in the sixties, way before the idea of master bath suites."

Rachel walked around the car and took Jack's hand. "Do we have to wait for the realtor?"

Jack pulled a set of keys from his pocket. "Nope. We have the place all to ourselves. I asked the realtor for a favor, told her it would be a lot easier for me to talk you into it if we were alone."

"Talk me into it? Is that what's going on now?"

"Not at all. Well, maybe a tiny bit. But that's not why I said it. I could tell she was really set on being here with us, maybe hoping to close the deal with both of us here. But I knew you and I really couldn't talk about things unless we were alone. But seriously, Rach, if you don't love the place, we'll just keep looking."

"Well, I've got to say...I like what I see so far." She turned and glanced out over the water. "You really can't see too many other places from here, the way this part of the lake is shaped. I am a little sad there isn't any fire pit or deck by the water, like that one cabin had. That was so nice."

"That wouldn't be hard to add. I could do that over a weekend." They climbed the few steps up to the porch. Jack unlocked the front door. "This place didn't come furnished. And before I open the door, I should say, I really love everything about this on the inside...except one thing. Which I really don't like at all. But I've asked about it, and it's something that can be easily fixed."

"That doesn't sound very encouraging. I thought you were going to look for a turnkey kind of place, Jack, because of how busy you've been at the school. Now you're talking about remodeling the attic, building a fire pit and deck outside. And now there's something on the inside that's pretty big you need to fix."

Jack's hand was still on the doorknob. He didn't play this one very well at all. "It's not really like that, Rachel. You'll see what I mean when I open the door. At least I think you'll see it. Maybe it won't bother you, and we can leave it alone indefinitely. And as for the attic idea, that's for something way down the road when we have our second or third kid. The second bedroom downstairs is ready to go. And seriously, if I need to, I can hire somebody to build the fire pit and deck."

"Wow, I can tell you're really wanting this place," she said.

"I do like it, but I'm totally serious. If you don't, I'll give the key back to the realtor, and we'll just keep looking."

"All right. Then I guess you better open the door. Let's see if I figure out the big thing you don't like on my own."

He swung the door open, and they stepped inside. Jack decided to keep his mouth closed and just walk around with her, let her take things in her own way. It wasn't a huge place, so it didn't take very long. When they came back into the living room, he said, "You want to go upstairs and see the attic?"

"Maybe. I think I figured out the big thing you don't like, though."

"Okay, what is it?"

"All the walls," she said. "There's way too many walls in here. Makes everything feel small and closed in. I'm used to cabins having big open areas, at least in the living space."

"You got it," he said. "That was my big thing, too. In fact, at first it was a deal breaker for me. The realtor could tell I was discouraged, and she said it really wasn't that big of a problem."

"Seems pretty big to me."

Jack walked over to the wall dividing the living and dining rooms. "Apparently, back in the sixties when this was built, people liked having more rooms. That was kind of a bragging point, how many rooms a place had." He banged on the wall. "See this? It's not load-bearing. In fact, she said none of these interior walls are load-bearing, except maybe the ones around the bathrooms. She said you can knock down walls like this one, and that one over there pretty easily. People do it all the time on those house-flipping shows on TV. Then this whole area would open right up and feel plenty big enough."

"I guess that's possible. Do you think that's something you could do? Maybe we should hire somebody, like a handyman or a carpenter."

Jack liked hearing what she just said. She was talking like this place could work. "I know I could do it. I watched a bunch of YouTube videos about it. I could get it done over a couple weekends. I might need to hire somebody to patch up the ceiling and floor, but these walls? I can definitely knock down these walls."

7

Saturday - One Week Later

J ack was pretty excited about this project. In one way or another, he'd only been doing white-collar work since his college days. Today and for at least the next couple of weekends, he'd be working with his hands. Manly work. Smashing into walls with a crowbar. Ripping out drywall. Knocking out studs with a sledgehammer.

But before that, there was some prep work that required careful thought.

"I can't believe we're out here already doing this," Rachel said. They were standing inside the living room of their newly-purchased lakefront house. "You're sure the owner is okay with this? You told him what we're actually doing today?" She was looking at his array of also newly-purchased wall destruction tools from Lowe's, spread out on the living room floor. "We haven't even officially closed on the place yet."

"Everything's fine, Rachel. I spoke with the old owner myself. The realtor was there, too. He knows we'll be paying cash. I told him it'll just take about two weeks to get everything together. In the meantime—so he'd know we're totally committed to this place—I gave him a five-thousand-dollar, non-refundable down payment in cash."

"Non-refundable? Yikes."

"Are you having any second thoughts?" he said.

"I guess I better not be."

"Rachel, I thought we were in total agreement about this."

"We are. I'm sorry. It's just...I guess we're moving so fast on this. It was just last Saturday we saw it for the first time. Well, first time for me. And now we're ripping down walls."

"I know," he said. "It feels a little rushed. But I was looking at my schedule. I only have this weekend and the next two completely free. Then I've got that speaking engagement in Richmond and something else happening the weekend after that. I thought if I could get on this right away, I could get everything done before that Richmond trip. And while I'm gone, pay some guy to patch up the ceiling and floors. We could be using the place in a month."

"All right," she said. "Then a month after that, this little guy'll be here." She pointed at her belly.

Jack came over, gently put his hands on her belly and said, "And we can't wait to see you little guy."

"So, what's that gizmo in your hand?"

"This...this is a stud finder. Supposedly, behind this drywall, about every sixteen inches, there should be a 2 x 4. I run this thing across the wall and it beeps and lights up whenever it detects one. Here, let me show you." He demonstrated how it worked.

"That's pretty cool."

"Yeah. So, I'm just going to mark all the studs on all the walls that are coming down. Who knows? Maybe we'll get lucky and discover a fortune some previous owners had unwittingly stashed behind the walls."

"What are you talking about?" she said.

"A news story I read when I was researching how to do this project. There was this couple demolishing some walls in an old house and they uncovered a hidden fortune. The house had been built by a couple in the 1940's who did much of the work themselves. To save money, instead of buying insulation the guy filled the space in between the studs with movie posters. Apparently, he'd managed a local theater and had plenty of them stacked in a storage room."

"So, this couple tears out the plaster and finds all these now totally collectible movie posters in mint condition."

"Something like that," Jack said. "Some seventy years later, the total worth of that poster collection, after an auction, was over a half-million dollars."

"That would be amazing," she said. She looked down at Jack's collection of tools. "What's that other gadget?"

"That thing is a wire detector. It will actually help me trace all the electrical wires running behind the walls."

"Jack, tell me you're going to turn all the power off before you start smashing into these walls with that crowbar."

"I promise. As soon as I trace out the wires and mark where they are on the wall, I'll shut off the breaker."

"What if you accidentally shut off the wrong breaker?

Who knows how they wired things back in the sixties? Why don't you just shut the power off for the whole house when you get ready to start smashing away? Just to be safe."

"Okay, that's what I'll do. How about you do something while I'm marking up the walls? I'm kinda hungry, and I could really use another cup of coffee, maybe some kind of snack to go with it. There's that convenience store we passed on the way here. It's only about six or seven minutes away. Could you set up the coffee maker we brought in the kitchen and maybe take a quick drive down there for a snack?"

"Sure, I could use another cup, too. And I wouldn't mind getting something to eat. Maybe I'll pick up a few other things for lunch since the fridge is working. But...there's no way you can get hurt doing any of this stuff while I'm gone?"

"Not unless I trip over my own two feet."

By the time Rachel got back with the snacks and made the coffee, Jack already had the studs all marked on the three walls that were coming down. He had just switched gizmos and was now getting ready to start tracing the electrical wires.

"Wow, that went pretty quick."

"I know. Can't imagine how people used to do projects like this back in the day."

"Well, take a little break and split this nice big banana nut muffin with me. And the coffee is nice and hot. That's actually a great little store. It was super-busy."

"I can imagine," Jack said. "The next closest one is about twenty minutes away."

"They have this nice baked goods window case, kind of

like Starbucks has. The lady behind the counter was the owner, she and her husband. She said everything in there was baked last night."

"See? It's like a sign from God, saying we picked the right place. Right on the lake, plenty of room for a future family, and fresh baked goods only five minutes away."

Rachel shook her head in mock disgust. Using a plastic knife, she cut the muffin in half. "You take the bigger piece."

After finishing his snack, Jack spent the next half-hour tracing and marking down all the electrical wiring behind the walls. Rachel sat in a comfy fold-up chair with her feet propped up on a box and read a book on her tablet.

He came over and put the electrical tracer back in his toolbox then reached for the crowbar and grabbed the dust mask. "Now, it's time to start hacking away."

"No, now it's time to shut off the electricity to the whole house."

"Yes, that. And then I start hacking away at the drywall."

"How do you know it's drywall? Didn't they use plaster back then? It could get pretty messy in here."

"It's going to get messy, but it's not plaster. I looked it up. Starting in the 1950s, everyone switched to drywall. But even so, I don't think it's a good idea for you to stay in here with all the dust I'm gonna make. It looks like the sun's shifted a little. Might be warm enough to sit out on the porch. Or if there's something you want to do for the next hour or two. Maybe some shopping, or something."

"No, I want to stay. I'll just sit on the porch. I've got my hoodie in the car if I start getting chilly." She stood. "But you really be careful. You're not used to doing this kind of work."

"I will. But nothing I'm doing is dangerous. I'd have to

really do something stupid to get hurt." He kissed her on the cheek and put the dust mask on. He carried her folding chair out and set it up on the porch where she wanted it. Then headed back inside to start hacking away.

He decided to just go all out and take all the drywall down on all three of the walls. Just to refresh his memory, he re-watched the YouTube video on how to get it done quickly and safely. To his great surprise, the whole job went pretty smoothly.

The living room floor was an absolute mess with big chunks of drywall stacked on top of each other and white gypsum dust covering everything. But it took just over an hour to get it all done.

Jack was amazed at the result. There were all the wires attached to the bare studs, just like they had been marked. He could already see how much nicer and more open things were going to be at this stage. Walking out to the porch, he tapped Rachel's shoulder. "I'm not done yet, but you gotta see this."

She set her tablet down on a little table and looked up. "Jack, your hair. It's covered in white powder." She stood up. "It's giving me a glimpse, though, of what I can expect growing old with you."

"Come on in and see." He led her back in through the front door.

"Wow, I can't believe how much you've gotten done. Are you ready to stop for lunch?"

"Not yet. I'd like to get a little more done. Maybe get all the wires pulled and capped. Knock out that first wall of studs separating the living and dining rooms. I'm sure I'll be ready then."

"Okay. You've turned the power off?"

"Already done. Head back out to the porch, and I'll start cutting away these wires."

Again, following the directions of the handymen gurus on YouTube, Jack was able to add all the electrical wiring and outlet boxes to the trash pile in short order.

Now it was time for the sledgehammer.

He started smacking away at the studs. Most of them came out with a few good whacks. Only a few cracked and split as he pried them loose. He decided to make a separate pile for the studs on the other side of the living room.

After making his way through the intended first wall, he was feeling some soreness in his upper arms and shoulders. Not to mention feeling totally beat. Now it was time for lunch. Maybe even time to quit for the day. For one thing, he had no idea he'd have gotten this much done on the first morning.

Before going out to the porch for Rachel, he decided to clean up a little. Make the stack of drywall straighter, so it wouldn't fall over. And make the stack of 2 x 4 studs a little neater. Then he swept all the white powder and small chunks of drywall into a pile to be picked up later.

He stood back to admire his handiwork when something about the 2 x 4 studs caught his eye. Walking over, he bent down to get a closer look. "That's odd," he said aloud.

He took his gloves off and reached down to one of the studs. It appeared that someone had carved something into the side of it. It almost looked like a group of letters. He traced the cuts with his finger. They were fairly deep and looked like something done by hand, not by a saw.

"What in the world?" he muttered. It looked like the letters U, C, I and D. "UCID?" Never heard of it.

He stood back to look at it again from a few feet away. Yes, they were definitely hand-carved letters. Then he noticed, several other studs in the stack also had sections where it looked like someone had carved into them. Quite a few, in fact. The carvings were mostly in the center section of the studs. Some looked like complete letters and some just parts.

"Hey Rachel," he yelled. "You've gotta come see this."

8

J ack heard Rachel walking on the front porch, watched her walk through the front door.

"What's the matter? Are you okay?"

"I'm fine. Come on over here. You gotta see this." He faced the stack of 2 x 4's and bent down.

"Why? What is it?"

"Come see. These are the 2 x 4's that used to be behind the wall I just knocked down. Look at the top one there first. Tell me what you see."

She did. "What am I supposed to see? Looks like an old piece of wood to me."

"Look in the center. See those carved-in marks in the wood?"

"Okay, yeah I can see them."

"Do those look like letters to you?"

She bent down also. "Yeah, I guess they do."

"The letters U-C-I-D, right? That's what I'm seeing."

Rachel didn't immediately respond. She kept staring at the letters.

"Isn't that what you see?" Jack said. "Looks pretty clear to me."

"I see what you're saying. But do you see the carved marks that keep going vertically down on each of the letters?"

"No, what do you mean?"

She pointed out each one. "See? On each side of the letter you're calling a U, see the carved marks? They keep going vertically down, right to the edge of the stud. It's the same with the C. I guess the I is still an I, but look at the last letter, the D. The vertically-carved line keeps going down."

"So, what do you think it means?"

"I'm not sure. Do we have any paper here?"

"Yeah, I always keep a scratch pad in my toolbox. There's a pen clipped to it."

She walked over and got them. After staring at the letters a few more moments, she pulled a blank sheet out, held it up to the first stud, so that the paper hung below the etched letters. She pulled it back and began writing some vertical marks on the page. When she got to the third letter, the I, she drew a short horizontal line at the bottom. "Okay, let's see if this solves the mystery." She held her marked-up page to the bottom edge of the stud.

Jack gasped. With the carved letters on top and Rachel's paper on the bottom, the word "HELP" could be clearly seen. He read it aloud. "Why would someone carve the word HELP into the side of a 2 x 4?"

"Into the side of two 2 x 4's," Rachel said. "We're only

looking at the top half. We need to see if there's another 2 x 4 with carvings that match this paper."

"I'm sure there must be," Jack said. "Look at the rest of the pile. I found several more with carved-up letters." He bent down and pointed them out. "Some are easier to see, some are probably like the word HELP. Half of the letter on one board, the bottom half on another."

"Well," she said, "Let's first see if we can find one that matches this paper."

Jack walked over, pulled a flashlight out of his toolbox. "Might make it easier to see the letters."

It took them a while to find the match, but that was because when they did, another string of letters had been etched below and to the right of the word HELP. Clearly, this new string of letters was the top half of at least a few more words.

"I wonder what's going on here?" Rachel said. "Why would someone carve parts of a message sideways on 2 x 4 studs that were going to be covered up behind a wall? You think it was just to mess with us? You know, freak the people out who'd take the walls down someday, like we did, when they'd see the carved letters and wonder if it's something sinister?"

Jack thought a moment. "Maybe. But what if the message wasn't carved into the wood sideways? I mean, that would be pretty hard to do. And the message wouldn't ever make any sense unless you did what we just did. But what if the message was carved into the wood when all the studs were stacked together? Like they would be at a store...like Lowe's? That's how they get delivered to the job site, not individually but in a big stack. I've seen them, eight or ten rows high.

Stacked that way, all the sides are flat and make like a short wall. It wouldn't be hard to carve a message into the boards then. Of course, our house was built in the sixties. Lowes wasn't even around then. But the point is—"

"I get the point," she said. "And I'm sure that's how this carving job was done. I can't believe I even thought what I said."

"Don't feel stupid. Hey, I brought you over here to show you U-C-I-D. You figured out it was the top half to HELP."

She stood up. "Why don't we use two of those saw-horses and re-stack these boards, so we don't have to bend down the whole time. My lower back is starting to hurt."

"Good idea," Jack said. "In fact, we can make two groups. We'll put these studs on the first set of saw horses, then use the other set to create the puzzle."

"What do you mean, puzzle?"

"The puzzle of words carved into the wood. Like we did with those first two studs to form the word HELP. If the message was carved into the side of the stack of 2 x 4's, it stands to reason that it got all jumbled up whenever the stack was delivered to this house, back when it was under construction. The carpenters building the house never saw the message. They just cut the bands holding the studs together and started using them, one by one, to build the walls."

He looked down at his small pile of studs. "I've only taken down the studs for one of the three walls we're tearing out. There's at least four or five with carved letters. I'll bet if we look at these two other walls where the studs are still in place, we'll find more."

He brought the flashlight over to the two remaining

walls. Rachel followed. The first three studs were blank, but on the fourth Jack hit pay dirt. "See? Here's another one."

They turned their heads sideways to read it.

"Definitely more letters," Rachel said. "But like the others, they're only top-halves and bottom-halves. Can't really make out what they're saying. And I'm getting dizzy with my head looking sideways."

Jack walked back to the first stack he'd already taken down. "Let's start here. I don't want you to lift anything. I'll put all these studs on this set of saw-horses, except for the two that go together. We can work out the rest of the puzzle once I knock the rest of the 2 x 4's down."

Jack did what he'd suggested then they both walked over to the first two studs. You could clearly see the word HELP with them stacked in the right order.

Then Rachel noticed something else, as she stared at the bottom of the two boards. "Jack...look at the first two letters on this. The ones that look like V and C. These are only the top-halves. In my head, I imagined drawing the vertical lines down like we did with the word HELP. Can you see what I'm seeing? What the first two letters really are?"

Jack did what she said. "Oh, man. M-E," he said aloud. "HELP ME."

9

"**T**his is starting to get weird," Rachel said. "HELP ME. Jack, this has to be some kind of joke, right?"

"A joke? Rachel, you think I carved these letters in the studs when you were out there reading? Why would I do that? Considering what you said about our shaky history with lakefront cabins, you think I'd prank you on something like this?"

Rachel looked back at the two studs and the HELP ME message. "I never said *you* were pulling the joke. I know you'd never do that. But what in the world is going on, Jack?"

"I don't know, Rach. But I promise you, I am as clueless as you are about this. Maybe it's nothing sinister at all. But now that we've uncovered it, aren't you curious? Don't you want to try and figure out what it means?"

"Yeah, I guess I do. But it's just so crazy. I wish you had called me in here to show me a bunch of priceless movie posters."

Jack laughed. "Me, too. But this is what we've got to work with. I don't mind pulling on these threads myself, if it's going to upset you."

"No, I don't want that. I really do like this place. I guess no harm can come from figuring out the mystery, since these studs were put behind these walls so many decades ago."

"That's what I'm thinking, too," Jack said. "I think it might be kind of fun, like solving an archaeological puzzle or a riddle."

"So, what should we do next?"

"Well, I don't have any grand strategy forming in my head. But if we start from the premise that the entire message was carved into a complete stack of 2 x 4's, when they were still banded together in some building materials' warehouse, that would mean only the boards on the side would have been carved on. Which is why so many of the boards don't have letters on them."

"And that's what we find," Rachel said, "in this pile of boards you've already knocked out, and on the ones still in place. Most are blank, only a few have letters."

Jack didn't want to share the next thought. Which was, even after he knocked down the remaining two walls, that wouldn't mean they had found all the ones with letters carved into the sides. It just made sense that a whole bunch more of the carved 2 x 4's would be hiding behind some of the walls they had no plans of tearing down.

"Jack, where'd you go?"

"I'm sorry. Just thinking. How about this? Let's separate out all the boards with carved letters into a separate pile. We really don't need the others. Then I'll take a few minutes and smash out just the boards in the remaining two walls that also have carved letters on them."

"Okay," Rachel said. "Since I can't swing a sledgehammer, you do the second part and I'll do the first part, separating the boards."

"How about, Miss Pregnant Lady, you'll do no such thing. I'll do both parts while you make us some lunch. You're really not supposed to be lifting things like 2 x 4's."

"Okay. But I want to help solve the puzzle, so don't start moving the boards around until I get back."

"I won't."

It didn't take too long for Jack to knock out the boards. He only found five more with carved letters on them. He set them aside momentarily, removed the blank studs from the main pile then added the new ones to form one pile, all of them with part of the message carved into one side.

"Your lunch is ready," Rachel said. "Why don't we take a little break and sit outside, enjoy the nice weather, some food, and drink our coffee while it's hot?"

"Good idea. I could use a break. Since this mystery's been locked behind these walls for fifty years, I guess it can keep for a few minutes more." He took the mug from her, put his arm around her shoulder, and they walked out to the porch.

As soon as they sat down, Jack was reminded of why he'd picked this place. What an amazing view. There was no wind, so the lake's surface had that glassy look normally reserved for early morning. "I can already see where I'd like to put the fire pit," he said.

"Right over there?" Rachel said, pointing. "That flat area just beyond the big willow tree?"

"Yep. That makes it official." He took a sip. "Perfect as always. Thanks for making it and the sandwiches."

"You're welcome." She reached over for his hand, closed her fingers gently over his. Neither one said anything for a few moments.

"Help Me," Rachel finally said. "It's so crazy. That we'd really find words like that scratched into the studs behind our walls. And another whole message that goes with it."

"I know. I'm dying to know what the rest of it says. In some ways, it's kind of like one of those Time Capsule things. You know, where they bury some kind of waterproof canister underground with a bunch of stuff in it from their time. Then people open it decades later and marvel at how much different things were then than they are now. I mean, whoever carved that message, he was probably young. Like a teenager. A mature person wouldn't do something like that."

"Assuming it was a prank," Rachel said. "What if it really was someone in trouble? We won't really know until we decipher the rest of the message."

"Well, I guess," Jack said. "But really, if someone was desperate and needed help, why would you scratch a message into the side of a stack of lumber? They had phones back then. Just call the cops. They might just as well have written a message in a bottle, tossed it into the sea."

"I still want to figure out the rest of it."

"Me, too," Jack said. "Just as soon as I finish this coffee and take in this view just a little longer."

About five minutes later, they both got up. Jack suggested they start by just simply trying to match the boards together, the correct top halves with the correct bottom halves, without trying to figure out what any of the words meant. Rachel agreed.

Ten minutes later, they had matched several of the studs together. But had about an equal number with no match. Which meant, the missing halves for those studs were probably still in place behind one of the remaining walls in the house. Jack didn't mention that.

He didn't have to. Rachel did. But neither took it any further. Instead, they decided to focus on the boards they had paired together, see if they could come up with any new words in this mystery message.

It only took a few minutes more to accomplish this. Once done, they stood back to read what the words said:

HELP
ME. I'M CHAINED UP
VERY DARK. HARD TO
IF I GO MISSING

Rachel spoke first. "Oh Jack, this is awful."

He didn't know what to say. It didn't seem like such a harmless thing anymore.

"What should we do?" she said.

Jack still hesitated. He really didn't want to say what he was thinking. Reading it again, he felt he had no choice. "Maybe we should call Joe."

10

W ell, this week hadn't gone the way Joe planned.

Like most every week, he'd figured there'd be no serious cases to work on, nothing the boys in blue couldn't handle anyway. He figured he and Hank would really get to make a dent organizing this new cold case squad into something that made at least a little bit of sense. Something to justify the new raises they'd both gotten, which weren't half bad.

Enough for him and Kate to eat at a swanky place like the River Bend restaurant twice a month, if they wanted. Of course, Kate would never want to spend the raise money on something like that.

But lo and behold, five days ago one of the officers who'd spent most days doling out speeding tickets accidentally uncovered a crooked pharmacist making some serious money on the side, selling fentanyl and oxycodone to street dealers.

The officer had the good sense not to overreact but to report it to Hank. Of course, to make sure they'd catch everyone involved in the net, Pendleton wanted Joe and Hank to take over things. They spent the next three days on the case, surveilling and getting search warrants ready before making the bust.

Joe made sure to have the officer who'd originally discovered the thing present to make the actual arrest. Now, all that was left to do was to get caught up on the paperwork. He and Hank had split that assignment up fifty-fifty. Since there was a good deal of overlap, Hank was working at a table in Joe's office. It was Saturday. They both agreed to put in a half-day, just to show the Captain they were earning their keep.

Joe heard Hank's chair squeak as he leaned back. That squeak always preceded Hank sharing something on his mind. Joe lifted his head from the keyboard, waited for it.

"I don't get it, Joe. What's a guy like this pharmacist doing, throwing his whole life away to make some extra cash? I get maybe some high school dropout doing something like this, or some guy whose business just went belly up. But why this guy? You know how many years those guys go to school? These pharmacists? It's like eight years of college. I looked it up...they actually have to get a Doctor of Pharmacology degree. And you know what they make? I looked that up, too. On average, these guys get paid $122,000 a year. Do you believe that? That works out to almost sixty-dollars an hour. Can you imagine getting sixty-dollars an hour? And then, at some point, feeling like, Hey, I don't make nearly enough money doing this. I know, I'll risk every-thing to make some easy money on the side, selling prescription drugs to dope dealers. Who cares how many kids die of overdoses because of me, or get strung out on drugs for the next ten years and ruin the lives of everyone around them?"

"Yeah," Joe said, "put that way it makes no sense at all." He turned around to face Hank. "But what I've usually found when you dig a little deeper into cases like these, the ones that make no sense, is that there really is some kind of method to the madness going on. In fact, that'll be part of what you and I gotta dig up on this guy. Why'd he do something so stupid? Is he up to his eyeballs in gambling debt? Is he unhappily married and maybe he has some expensive lady friend he's keeping on the side? This report says he's married. Maybe it's his third one, and the first two drained him dry. I don't know. But we've got to figure it out. It goes to motive."

Joe's cell phone rang. "Hold on a minute." He looked at the screen. It was Jack Turner calling. He hit the button. "Hey Jack, how are you doing, my friend? I don't usually hear from you in the middle of the day. Is it Rachel? You guys on the way to the hospital?"

Jack laughed. "No, nothing like that. We're still almost two months out."

"Then you calling to cancel our little metal detecting outing two weekends from now?"

"No, but now that you mention it, I guess I am going to have to reschedule that. But that's not why I called, either."

"So, what's up?"

There was a long pause.

"I'm not exactly sure how to get into this," Jack said.

Joe involuntarily stiffened a little.

"And before I do try to explain, I should mention... Rachel agreed I should call you about this."

"Geez Jack, why all the buildup? Just say it. I'm a big boy. I can handle it."

"I know. My hesitation has nothing to do with you. It's just...I can't believe I'm calling you to talk about something like this."

"Like what, Jack?"

"Okay, you know that property I have out by the lake?"

"Where we've been metal detecting?"

"Right. I don't know if I've mentioned I've been thinking of selling it."

"Don't think you have."

"Well, it happened pretty fast. A colleague made me an offer, and I decided to say yes. We really loved the property. It's just I've been so busy here at the University, I haven't even begun to design the new cabin. So, I accepted the offer and we decided to buy an already-built place. One that was big enough to accommodate the kids we're planning to have, beyond this one. Anyway, the place we picked out was perfect except for one thing."

Joe wondered if he should try and rush Jack along. He wouldn't normally if he was here by himself, but because of Hank... "So, what was that one thing?"

"It was built in the sixties. The bedrooms are great, but they used too many walls to divide up the living space. I found out they weren't load-bearing and decided to take them down myself. I've actually been out here all morning doing just that."

"Say Jack," Joe interrupted. "Any chance you and I can get

together for coffee a little later, so you could tell me all this then? I'm actually here at the office working on some paperwork with Hank."

"I'm sorry. I'm sharing way too much detail. But believe me, this isn't a social call. I'm calling because of something pretty crazy we found carved into the 2 x 4 studs, once I started pulling off the drywall."

"You're kidding."

"I wish I was."

"So, what did you find?"

"A message. It's kind of cryptic, because of the way it was originally etched into the wood. But we kept finding these boards with all these letters carved into them. It took some time to get them together, so that the words made any sense. But eventually we did. And what we read was pretty disturbing."

"Really? What did it say?"

"Maybe you should come out here and see for yourself."

"Okay, but first why don't you just tell me?"

"Okay, but you gotta understand, this is clearly only a part of the message. We're thinking there might be a lot more to it, etched on other boards we haven't uncovered yet."

"All right, give me what you got."

"It says:

HELP
ME. I'M CHAINED UP
VERY DARK. HARD TO
IF I GO MISSING

"Hmmm," Joe muttered. "And you say this house was built in the sixties?"

"Early sixties, yes."

Joe sighed. "Okay, text me the address, and I'll be there in twenty."

11

"Wait a minute, Joe," Hank said. "I just hear you say you'll be there in twenty? As in twenty minutes? What, you leaving me for some adventure, and I finish all this paperwork myself?"

"Well technically, Hank, even with this promotion, I still outrank you. You may be a sergeant now, but I'm a lieutenant. I could just order you to do all the paperwork, while I go out for some donuts. But since I'm not that kinda guy, the answer is, no. I ain't leaving you to do all the paperwork yourself. In fact, if you want, you can come with me. That was Jack Turner who called."

"I gathered as much," Hank said. "I didn't catch much else. So, what's he saying that's got you dropping everything and running off to see him? I thought we were only working half-a-day, since it's Saturday."

"Well, you coming or not?"

Hank looked down at his stack of paperwork. "I was

really hoping to knock this off before I left, but hey, guess it can wait." He closed his laptop and stood.

Joe opened his office door and stepped into the hallway, started walking. When he heard Hank's footsteps behind him, he said, "You're not gonna believe this, but he's calling about some crazy message he found carved into some 2 x 4 wall studs. They're in this old house he's apparently renovating out by the lake."

"Wait, I thought you told me Jack owned some property out by the lake, but there was nothing on it. You guys go metal detecting out there sometimes, right?"

They reached the front glass doors and walked out into the sunlight. The air was a little nippy, but Joe liked it that way. "Well, not anymore. He just told me he sold it. Bought another property with an old house on it, built in the early sixties. For some reason, he's tearing down some walls, and he finds these words on some wall studs. Can't remember exactly what the message was, but it was something like HELP ME, I'M TIED UP, or something. IT'S DARK IN HERE. And then something else about IF I GO MISSING."

They reached the car. "You're kidding? I mean, of course you're not kidding. But what is it with Jack and lakefront properties? It's like he's jinxed, or something. What do you figure it means?"

Joe got in, then Hank. As usual, Joe would drive. "Haven't a clue. But you know Jack. He wouldn't call unless he believed it might be something. And the way I figure it, the fact that this message got carved onto these 2 x 4's back in the early sixties, makes this potentially a job for Culpepper's new Cold Case Squad."

Hank smiled. "At the very least, a good excuse to take a break from this lousy paperwork."

IT TOOK Joe and Hank about twenty-five minutes to reach the address Jack had texted him. Turned out, this property was on the far side of Lake Sampson. Joe could tell driving around, all the dwellings out this way were much older than the ones he'd seen before. And more spread out. The woods seemed thicker, too.

But maybe Jack selling his old property wasn't such a bad thing. They'd pretty much finished metal detecting on most of it. Now they'd have a fresh shot at someplace new. Who knows? Maybe no one had ever used detectors in this area of the woods.

"Hey Joe," Hank said. "You see the turnoff on the GPS, right? It's just up there on the left."

Joe quickly glanced down at the screen, let his foot off the gas. "I see it."

"What were you thinking about?"

"Who says I was thinking about anything?"

"Nobody. You just had that look."

"There you go, Hank. Sounding like my wife again."

"What? I'm not asking you how you feel. I just wondered if you had any new thoughts on this thing Jack asked us to come out and see? I thought about it some. And I'm thinking, it's pretty weird to find words like that carved into some studs that were going to be covered up with drywall or plaster. Who would ever see them? Whoever did it had to know the message wouldn't be discovered until the walls were torn down decades later. I mean, could be even longer than that. Some of the lakefront cottages and houses out here were built way before the sixties. So, what's the point? I'm thinking maybe it was just some kind of prank. You know, two carpenters thinking up a fun practical joke to pull on some unsuspecting people way off in the future."

"It could very well be that, Hank. But Jack thinks there might be a lot more to the message behind some of the other studs. Ones he hasn't pulled the drywall off yet."

"So, what...are we going to help him tear down some walls?"

"No, I don't know. Let's just see what he's got to say."

After turning off the main road, they drove through some sharp S-turns then down a straight stretch of road that gave way to a clearing. They could see the house just to the left and beyond that the lake. And there was Jack's familiar blue BMW.

It was a nice place, Joe thought. Nothing fancy. Had a nice porch. Bigger than the last place Jack had rented. Looked more like a house than a cabin. Before Joe and Hank got out of the car, Jack came out of the front door and greeted them.

"Sorry to get you guys out here on a Saturday," Jack said.

"Not a problem," Hank said. "Saved us from a bunch of paperwork."

Jack shook both their hands. "Congratulations on the promotions. Something about starting a new Cold Case squad?"

"How'd you hear about that?" Joe said.

"Read it in the local online newspaper."

Joe couldn't believe Pendleton had already started generating publicity about this. "Yeah, something the Captain came up with to keep us busy. He actually used you and the cases we worked on together as part of his reasoning. Since two of them were based on old crimes."

"Really?" Jack said. "Well, glad I could be of help then. Who knows? Maybe I'm about to give you your first case."

The three men stepped up onto the porch. "Actually," Hank said, "the Captain has already got us working on some. Nothing specific yet. Just digging through a lot of boxes from a bunch of unsolved murders that took place in the eighties."

"The eighties?" Jack repeated. "I think this one—if this turns out to be a case—beats those. At least in terms of age. Whatever this cryptic message is referring to, had to happen before this house was built in the early sixties."

"That's what Joe said." Hank put his hand on the knob. "Okay if I go in?"

"Sure," Jack said. "Rachel and I had pretty much decided we were all done for the day. She's in there putting on some coffee."

"I like the sound of that," Joe said.

The men came in, greeted Rachel. She hugged Joe since they were good friends now, shook Hank's hand. Joe was surprised at the size of her belly. Jack said the baby was coming in less than two months. She looked kind of small for being so far along, at least as much as he remembered from when Kate had been expecting.

"I know how Joe takes his coffee, Hank," Rachel said. "How about you?"

"If it's good coffee, I'll take it black. If it's the cheap stuff, maybe a teaspoon of sugar."

"We only buy the good stuff," Jack said. "While she's

doing that, you guys want to take a look at the mystery message?"

"Sure." It wasn't hard to spot. Joe walked right over to it. They had a couple of stacks of 2 x 4's, next to a big pile of broken up drywall. But he could see, the smaller stack of studs were all evened up and placed just so.

"The message is on the other side," Jack said, "facing the window. And here, let me shine a flashlight on it from the side. It casts a little shadow, makes the letters stand out better."

Joe walked around one side, Hank the other. As soon as Jack clicked on the light, you could see the message pretty clearly:

HELP

ME. I'M CHAINED UP

VERY DARK. HARD TO

IF I GO MISSING

Both men stared at it, without saying anything a few moments. Hank broke the silence. "Whatta you think, Joe?"

Every instinct in Joe's gut told him...this was no prank.

12

"**Y**ou think there's something to this, don't you Joe?" Jack said. "I can tell by that look in your eyes."

Joe didn't realize he had a certain look. But then again, he and Jack had worked closely on several cases before. In some ways, Jack knew him better than Hank. "I know I wish there was more to this...message." He looked up at Jack, Rachel standing right beside him. "What do you think, Rachel? I know Jack eats this stuff up, and you're the more pragmatic one. You think there's something here?"

"I don't want there to be," she said. "This was just supposed to be a quickie project. Tear down a few walls, open up the living area. You know? No offense, but you weren't supposed to be a part of this day."

"No offense taken. But you didn't really answer my question. What's your women's intuition telling you about this?"

"At first, I was leaning heavily toward the prank idea. But the more words we put together, the less I'm thinking that.

Jack, explain to him and Hank your idea about this message being carved when the 2 x 4's were all stacked together...at the store."

Before Jack had finished explaining his idea, Joe had already imagined the same scenario in his head.

"But why would somebody carve a plea for help on the side of a stack of 2 x 4's?" Hank said. "I know it was the early sixties, but they had phones back then. Are you thinking some guy got locked after hours inside the store?"

"I was thinking along those same lines, too...at first" Jack said. "But like you said, they had phones. Even if the phone was locked behind some office door, throw a brick through a window if you have to. You don't carve a message into the side of a stack of lumber."

"You do if you're chained," Joe said. "Look at line two: I'M CHAINED UP. Whoever carved this couldn't get to a phone or a brick...or anything else."

"Exactly," Jack said.

"Which is why we called you," Rachel said. "It's pretty much that line. And the last one...IF I GO MISSING."

Joe looked at Hank. He was seeing it now. The prank idea didn't add up. Neither did the guy getting locked up in the building supply store after hours. To Joe, this thing was becoming officially sinister. He looked around at the other walls. "Are these the only ones you guys are tearing down? The ones you've already done?"

"That's the plan," Rachel said.

"It sure would be nice to get a peek at some of those other studs," Joe said. "There's a good chance that these were all coming from the same stack, and that the rest of the carved-up boards are in these walls."

"We were thinking the same thing," Jack said.

"Jack." Rachel sighed. "We can't go tearing down the rest of the walls in this house just to see if there might be a few more boards with letters carved into them."

"Well..." Jack said. "Maybe not the rest of the walls, but hear me out. What if we just started with the second bedroom? It's just some ugly paneling in there now. Wouldn't you want something nicer for the baby's room? Something more colorful and kid-like?"

"I guess," she said. "But aren't they load-bearing walls? You can't take down load-bearing walls."

"I won't take them down. I'll just rip off the paneling, expose the studs. Then I'll shine a light on the boards to see if any are carved up. I was thinking if I brought out a bright floor lamp from home, I could get enough light to take pictures of any carved words, right from the studs. Then we could do our little puzzle thing, except moving around the pictures on my laptop, instead of the studs themselves."

"What about the upstairs area?" Hank said. "I noticed the dormers on the roof out front. Have you checked the studs up there?"

"No, we didn't. But that's a great idea," Jack said. They'd all probably be coming from the same stack of lumber when they built the upstairs."

"Maybe you could even start up there," Rachel said. "And just maybe, we'd uncover enough of the message so we wouldn't have to tear out the bedroom paneling...just yet."

"Sure," Jack said. "I'll start up there then."

"Sounds like a plan is starting to come together." Joe bent down and studied the carved words more closely. "Maybe I'll head back to the office and do some digging. See if I can find exactly when this place was built, and by whom. Who knows? Maybe I can even figure out who was selling the building materials for the homes out here then. That might generate a few leads."

"That's what you'll be doing," Hank said. "What about me?"

"You'll be finishing up all that paperwork we left back on our desks..." Joe smiled. "...*Sergeant.*"

13

Rhodes Plantation
Just South of Culpepper, GA
July 1964

Mason Rhodes sat on his favorite rocker in the shade provided by a one-hundred-and-ten-year-old, weather-worn gazebo, which itself sat in the shade provided by a sprawling live oak tree at least twice that old. The rocker was his favorite, not because it was so comfortable but because of its location.

Out here he was far enough away from the Big House to have his own thoughts and freely discuss ideas and opinions prompted by those thoughts, without fear of consequence.

Considering who his father was, and his older brother Boone, for that matter, those consequences could be quite severe. Both men were hard-hearted, born-and-bred Southern racists who still refused to call the Civil War by its rightful name. Instead, it was the "War of Northern Aggression."

People from the North were, of course, Yanks and as such of a lesser caliber and stature than almost anyone born in the South; excepting blacks who, although declared legally free and fully human by Law, would never enjoy such status in the minds of his father or Boone, not for a single moment till the day they died.

Mason didn't think this way, and never had. How could he?

He was waiting there in the gazebo for his best friend Roy Lewis to show up. One hundred years ago, Roy would have been a slave working on the Rhodes Plantation, probably a field hand forbidden to even learn how to read or write. Today, Mason was waiting there to congratulate Roy for receiving a full scholarship to Shaw University, an all-colored school in Raleigh.

Roy didn't know that Mason had already heard the good news. His Mama let it slip when Mason had stopped by their tiny lap-board house earlier that morning, to see if Roy had come back into town yet.

Mason wasn't surprised. Roy had always been the book-smartest guy he'd known growing up. Got nothing but straight A's from grade 1 to high school. Of course, Boone would say whenever anyone mentioned how bright Roy was, that such grades didn't mean nothing, coming from a no-account school for colored kids.

Heck, even Mason was smarter than his brother Boone, and that wasn't saying much. Mason didn't recall Boone ever getting higher than a B on any report card. Daddy had always said getting high marks in school didn't count for much. What counted, was your genes and bloodlines.

Boone had been born a Rhodes. That's all that needed saying.

The Rhodes bloodline—as far as Daddy viewed it—had been the nearest thing to southern royalty ever since 1842, the year Jefferson Rhodes had bought and paid for the one thousand-acre-tract of land ten miles south of Culpepper that would—within eighteen months—become the Rhodes Plantation.

Judson Rhodes, Mason's father, was even dumber than Boone. More ignorant. Twice as hateful. Three times as hard-headed. Of course, Mason would never say such a thing. Not unless he was far enough away that such a thing could not be overheard.

Like...out here in the gazebo.

"Figured I'd find you out here."

Mason instantly recognized his friend's voice from behind and stood to greet him. Roy walked around the railing toward the front steps. Just before they hugged, Mason glanced quickly toward the house, to make sure no one saw him greet Roy this way. He'd get grief for a friendly handshake, let alone a brotherly embrace.

"How long's it been?" Roy said.

"Since last August. When I went off to start my freshman year at the University of Maryland, and you stayed here to finish your senior year of high school." Mason liked to remind Roy of their age difference, whenever he could.

Roy liked to point out that age was the only advantage Mason had over him. That and being born white. And being filthy rich. And getting to relieve himself in nice bathrooms. And never being called "boy" by ignorant rednecks.

"Wow," Roy said. "Think that's the longest time we haven't seen each other since we were kids. But hey, at least I was able to stay up on everything because of all your letters."

Mason sat back in his rocker, shook his head. "You know me, I'm no good with letters."

"I'm not *any* good with letters. You've gotta watch those southern slang expressions, Mason, you want those northern college fraternity brothers to take you seriously."

"Okay, I'm not any good with letters."

"I still can't believe your father let you attend a college in Maryland. Doesn't he consider that a Yankee state? How'd you ever pull that off?"

"I never told you?" Mason said.

Roy shook his head no. "But I'm dying to hear it. I checked into it. Though they say Negroes are allowed, hardly any attend. I guess, no surprise there. I'd always read Maryland was sympathetic to the South during the war."

"Most folks in Maryland were," Mason said. "In fact, that was one of the selling points I had to use with my dad to get him to let me go there. That, and what you just said, almost no Negroes are enrolled. This'll probably be hard for you to hear, but I played that part up pretty strong. I said, Dad, how can it be considered a Yankee college if black students aren't welcome there? Then to strengthen my argument even more, I pointed out how much folks in Baltimore hated Lincoln during the war. When he traveled through there by train, he had to wear a disguise so no Southern sympathizers would kill him."

"Is that true?" Roy said.

"What I read. He actually smiled after I said it. When we were kids, we took a trip up near Washington DC. I wanted to see all the usual things people want to see up there, including the Lincoln Memorial. Daddy wouldn't even drive by it. Boone suggested Daddy drive by and stop, just long enough for him to run up the stairs and toss a bucket of paint on it."

Roy laughed. "I could just see Boone saying that."

"Yeah, the highlight of the trip for both of them was going up to Arlington, to tour the home of Robert E Lee. Oh, and he was okay with us visiting Mount Vernon, Washington's place, and the Jefferson Memorial because, hey, like our family they both owned slaves."

"Well, it's true. They did," Roy said. "Of course it's also true, Washington put it in his will that all his slaves would be freed when he died. I don't suppose your daddy mentioned that. And some say the last great love in Thomas Jefferson's life was a black slave woman, with whom he fathered a whole bunch of kids. Probably not one of the tidbits your daddy shared on the tour."

Mason smiled, looked at Roy. "No, Daddy neglected to mention that."

"Well, enough about history. Tell me something you learned at that big northern university you've been attending this past year."

Mason looked around nervously. No one was even close, but what he had to tell his friend was something so serious, he had to make sure he could not be overheard. "Well, the biggest things I've learned, and the biggest things I've been doing this past year have nothing to do with classes or college lectures. They have to do with changing the way things are in this country into the way things are supposed to be. Especially here in the South." Mason didn't realize it, but he was talking just barely above a whisper.

"What are you talking about?"

Mason looked around again. "I'm talking about...have you ever heard of a group called the SNCC?"

"Sounds familiar, but I'm not sure. What's it stand for?"

"It stands for Student Non-violent Coordinating Committee. It's basically a Negro organization. Anyway, a bunch of their leaders are visiting universities all over the north looking for volunteers, including whites. People like me who hate the way blacks are treated down here. Anyway, some friends invited me to one of their meetings at U-of-M. So, I went. And we've been meeting together ever since. You can't believe it, Roy. We've got all kinds of big operations planned. Things that are going to really shake things up here in the South before we're through."

"Wait a minute, Mason. I have heard about this group. Black and white students working together to end racism in the South. It's a great cause, and I'm sure I agree with probably everything they're saying. But I've also been hearing some other things. Like, a lot of people are starting to get hurt. Are you aware of that?"

"Maybe a few people are. But nothing widespread," Mason said. "Nobody in our group anyway. Besides, they're training us, Roy. About how to handle situations so that things don't turn violent. That's the goal. It's even in the name, Non-Violent Coordinating Committee."

"Mason, the Non-Violent part is only talking about your

side—our side—of the equation. You can't expect all these angry white racists to take some pledge not to get violent. They hate what groups like SNCC stand for. And you better believe, they're going to do whatever they've gotta do to put a stop to it."

14

Both men looked at each other a few moments. Mason knew Roy was just concerned for him, so he didn't get upset. "If you'd been to any of the meetings I attended, you'd see what I'm talking about. They've really thought all this stuff through."

Still, Roy didn't reply. Mason could tell he was sitting on something. "Just say it, Roy. I won't bite your head off. What are you thinking about? I thought you'd be excited."

"I am excited. We've been talking about wanting to make a difference on this for years. I actually wondered if you'd drop it all together once you got free of this place. But look at you, you're even more on fire than ever."

Mason leaned forward. "So, what's the problem?"

Roy sighed. "I'm not sure where all this is going. I want to hope things can turn around. But think about it, Mason. White folks in the South went through a horrible, bloody Civil War to keep things from changing. Hundreds of thousands were killed. More than that were wounded and maimed for life. Whole towns left in ruins. Even after they lost the war and all these federal laws got changed...same white folks been fighting all those changes for the last hundred years. Almost every southern state has passed new laws to undermine everything Lincoln wanted to change. I just don't see them giving up now, because a bunch of well-meaning college kids come down and start protesting."

Mason stood, leaned next to Roy on the railing. "I agree, things won't change, not overnight. That's why we've got a whole series of events planned throughout the summer. It's already getting all kinds of publicity, and we've barely got started."

"Oh, I don't doubt...there's going to be all kinds of publicity once this thing starts happening. But I don't think it's going to be the kind y'all are hoping for."

"What do you mean?" Mason said.

Roy looked out across the fields toward the setting sun. "People are going to get hurt, Mason. Lots of people. Maybe even worse than hurt. If I'm reading this right, most of the publicity is going to center on stuff like that. And there'll be plenty to see. You and your friends are going to be driving into a whirlwind. And I'm not just talking about folks like the KKK coming out to fight this. All kinds of regular white folks—folks you wouldn't normally think could get that angry—will be joining in the fight, trying to stop this thing. Trying to keep things the way they've always been."

"I don't know," Mason said. "You may be right. There'll certainly be plenty of people who'll fight the changes. Folks like my Dad and Boone will be leading the pack. But I think there's a lot more like me, who are sick of seeing how your people have been treated all these years. You should see the enthusiasm at these meetings I've been attending. In most, there's more whites than blacks. And the meetings themselves are being run by young black leaders. Can you picture that, Roy? A room full of young white college students sitting happily alongside black students, as a black leader gives them instructions on how they want them to behave at these events?"

"That's certainly not something I'd expect to see every day," Roy said. "And I'm really glad to see how worked up you are about this, Mason. It does give me hope that maybe some things are changing. In some places. Like at a nice northern college filled with open-minded white kids, like yourself. But that's not what you're going to find down here. And I'm not so sure those student leaders you're talking about are preparing y'all for what y'all will be dealing with, once you actually come face-to-face with these hardline racists."

Mason just looked at him. Didn't really know what to say. He sure hoped Roy was just wrong about this. Roy had always said Mason was too much of an optimist. Mason always said Roy was too much the pessimist. Roy would come back with, "No, I'm just a realist."

"The truth is, Mason. I really wish you'd find a way to quietly back out of this group. Just focus on getting that degree of yours and let other folks work on changing the world."

"I can hardly believe my ears, Roy. You just want me to sit on the sidelines when we have a chance to turn this evil thing around?"

"This time, yes. That's exactly what I want. But I know you're gonna do whatever you think is right."

"Man, this conversation isn't going at all like I pictured. I figured you'd be all kinds of proud of me for doing this, then I'd be motivating you to get involved with this same group when they show up at Shaw. Heck, they probably already got a group going up there."

"Mason, you're not tracking with me on this. In some ways, I love you for it. You've never seen much of a difference between the two of us, all these years growing up side-by-side. But we aren't kids anymore, and these differences are real. And they're not going away. The SNCC may already be going on at Shaw. And I may very well become a part of it once I get there. But me getting involved in this, and you getting involved are not the same thing."

"I do get it. You're black, and I'm white. And people don't treat us the same."

"No Mason, you don't get it. Maybe if you were a white kid raised up north, I'd feel differently. But you're not. You're a white kid born and raised in the Deep South. And your family's not just a little racist. Mason, look at where we are. A hundred years ago your forebears probably sat in this very same gazebo, sipping tea, wearing their fancy clothes, looking out over that very field as dozens of my forebears broke their backs in the hot sun picking cotton. My folks were the slaves, and your folks the slave-owners. And as long as I've known your daddy and brother Boone, they talk about those times like they were the good old days. Like they wished they'd never ended. What do you think they'd do to you, they ever found out what you were doing this past year at school? Or if they caught a whiff-a-you being part of some black-and-white group down here protesting the evils of the very things they cherish and hold dear?"

"Well, they're not going to find out, so I don't gotta think about the answer to that question. For one thing, I've seen the plans for all the target cities we're going to this summer. Closest we'll get to Culpepper is three hours away. And the only one I'm telling about all this is you. So how would my dad and Boone know what I've been up to?"

Roy didn't reply.

"Look Roy, I know you're just trying to stop me because you're afraid something might happen to me. I don't think it will. We're taking every precaution we can. But even if something does happen, I don't care. I'm tired of living my whole life in silence, watching what's going on right under my very roof and never saying a word. For the first time, I feel like I'm making a difference. Doing something to fight this thing. I can't stop now. I'd hate myself if I did."

Again, Roy made no reply. But for a moment, Mason saw his eyes get a little watery. But he quickly blinked it away. They both heard a loud engine sound coming down the road and knew exactly what it was.

"There's your brother Boone," Roy said. "I better get out of here before he sees me." He straightened up, walked toward the gazebo steps.

"Too late," Mason said. "He's looking right this way."

Roy turned to see. "Well, give him a big hug for me. Tell him how much I've missed our thoughtful conversations."

Mason laughed, as Roy started walking away.

"You really don't have to leave. It's not like he doesn't know you. Your mom still works up at the house, and you been around this place as long as I can remember. He might razz you, some. But I don't think—"

"No, I really need to go. He's changed since you been

gone, Mason. I don't know if he's gone off and joined the Klan, or what. But he's worse than I've ever seen him. But let's make sure we get together again before you head back to school."

And with that, Roy hurried off just shy of a run in the direction of his place. Mason looked over at Boone, coming this way in his pickup truck. His face as mean as it gets.

Mason sighed. He couldn't wait to get out of here.

15

Mason decided to come down from the gazebo to face his brother. Didn't care to hear Boone's comments about him relaxing in the shade while he was off working. Mason noticed, as usual, the back of Boone's pickup was loaded with construction material and so dusty and dirty you could hardly tell it was painted blue.

"So, the little brother's come home," Boone yelled out his window as he swung the truck around and stopped just before hitting Mason. "Finally going to start earning your keep around here? At least through the summer?"

He didn't waste any time. "Not exactly, Boone. Daddy didn't tell you? Got signed up for summer school. Only home for a week, then I gotta head back."

His mean look was replaced by disgust. "No, he didn't tell me. I was working up a list of crap jobs to put you on. Now who am I going to get to do them?" He got out of his truck, walked around the gazebo. "That Roy I saw you talking to?

Looked like his face, but he looked bigger than when I saw him last. Maybe I can get him to do some honest work."

Boone was four years older than Mason, worked as a foreman in the family's construction business. "I don't think he's your answer. Just found out, Roy got a full scholarship to Shaw University, based on his grades in high school."

Boone turned around, looked back at Mason. "Shaw? That one of them colored schools, ain't it?"

"Yeah, but that doesn't mean it's not legit. It just means white-only schools don't let blacks in yet. If they did, Roy'd have gotten a scholarship at one of them, too."

"Listen to you," Boone said. "Still care more about them than your own kind? I was hoping you might've outgrown that. I told Daddy not to send you to no Yankee school."

Mason hated it when his brother talked this way. "Roy's my friend, so that makes him my kind. And I don't know why you can't accept the fact that he's smart. Smarter than either one of us. You watch if he doesn't become someone important after he graduates college."

"Just shut up, Mason. Makes me sick to hear you talk like that. He may be smarter than you, but Roy certainly ain't smarter than me. I'm running three separate construction projects for the company, on my own. I doubt someone like Roy would even know the difference between a hammer and a drill. For that matter, you probably don't know the difference, either."

"I do, too."

"Can't be too smart, you got stuck going to summer school after your first year of college."

You dumb hick. "I didn't get *stuck* in summer school, I signed up for it on purpose." Mason did it mainly to spend more time away from this place, but also to enable him to take part in all of SNCC's summer events.

"Why would you do something stupid like that...on purpose? Daddy know you did this?"

"Of course, he did. I had to get his permission before I could sign up."

Boone looked down to the ground, shook his head. "Now, why would he do something like that? He knew I was planning on having you work for me."

"He said yes because I explained to him if I went to school through each summer, I could graduate almost a whole year early."

Boone was still upset. "I don't know why he's even having you go to college. A waste of money and time. I never went. And he never went. Seems like it's just a good excuse for you skipping out on paying your dues, like I had to. Can't believe he's gonna let you sit on your butt the next four years. He had me working as a laborer the first two years out of high school, then two more years as a carpenter's apprentice. Which was just two more years of back-breaking work."

Should Mason say it? Daddy knew Boone would never make it through the first semester of college? Mason wasn't even sure he knew how to read, had never seen him open a book. Ever.

Instead, what he said was, "Daddy wants me to learn all there is to know about commercial construction. All we've been building are houses all these years. Commercial construction's totally different. A lot more complicated. All kinds of engineering and design stuff that never come in to play when building a house. All kinds of new codes and regulations to learn, too."

Boone walked back toward his truck. "I don't know why we're heading in that direction. Ain't like Culpepper's gonna start building skyscrapers. We got our hands full with all these new homes going up. Things are booming all over town. Even out by Lake Sampson. I just started bidding on a bunch of new projects out there. We don't need you sitting on your butt the next four years reading books. We need you here. Doing real work."

"With summer school, it's more like three-and-a-half years."

"You're missing the point."

"I get your point. Guess your beef is with Daddy then, not me. He's the one paying for me to go to school."

"Yeah, after you begged him and squealed like a little piglet this past year to let you go."

"That's not true."

Boone whipped around, came at Mason. "You calling me a liar?"

Mason wasn't stupid. "No," he muttered. "I'm...I'm just saying you're mistaken. You're right. I did want to go to college. I've wanted to go since I was in junior high. But you know Daddy. Can you make him do anything he doesn't want to do? If he didn't want me there, I'd be here, working with you."

Boone stayed there in his face several more seconds. Close enough to smell the Jack Daniel's on his breath. The only reason Mason didn't cower in fear was the knowledge their father had absolutely forbidden Boone from ever laying a hand on him. Of course, that boundary line had been crossed routinely by Daddy himself throughout Mason's childhood.

Really, he'd only stopped laying into Mason a couple of years ago. His preferred method was the back of his hand, swung with enough force to knock Mason off his feet.

Finally, Boone backed away, headed to his truck. He opened the door, got in. Then through the open window, said, "Guess I better get. Some of us have to work for a living. But a word of warning." He glanced in the direction where Roy had just left a few minutes ago. "It's high time you parted ways with that boy. The two of you ain't kids no more. You hearing me? I don't know if you're getting wind of the kind of things that are going on these days. But things are starting to boil up, and I don't think it'll be too much longer before they boil over. You don't want to be on the wrong side of this thing when it does. Believe me. People around here catch you two hanging out like that, they won't be as forgiving as me. It's time you started hanging out with your own kind."

He turned his pickup on, revved up the engine and peeled out, leaving a dust cloud in his wake.

16

THE PRESENT
Monday Morning - Culpepper, GA

Joe stopped by Dunkin' Donuts on the way in—just for the coffee, not the donuts. He began his workday down at the City Hall. A nice old gal down there named Gladys, who'd been there since the days she wore her hair in a beehive, was helping him out. He'd explained to her about his new job working on cold case files, which would likely mean he'd be down there a lot more often digging through old records. As he figured, Gladys was a fan of cold case murder mysteries, so she was eager to assist.

Took about an hour-and-a-half, but she was finally able to unearth exactly when the permits were pulled on Jack and Rachel's lakefront property.

Joe opened his office door to find Hank already there,

still working on the paperwork from Saturday. "How you coming with that?"

"Almost got it done. Maybe another hour."

"Here, brought you a coffee from Dunkin's. You still take it black, no sugar?"

"Yeah, thanks. Just about time for a coffee break anyway." He took the paper cup, leaned back in his chair. "What, no donuts?"

"Get thee behind me, Devil."

"I think the saying is, Get thee behind me, Satan."

"I know that. Didn't want to call my good friend Satan."

"But you're okay calling me the devil? Great. Don't see the difference, but thanks for the coffee."

"You're welcome."

"So, where you been again this morning?" Hank said. "I know you told me, but I forgot."

"City Hall. I've been thinking all weekend about that weird case Jack and Rachel told us about on Saturday. You know, the cryptic message carved in the 2 x 4's."

"Yeah, me too. My daydreams on that are way more interesting than this paperwork. What did you dig up down at City Hall?"

Joe sat in his chair, set his brief bag against the file cabinet. "Some good stuff, I think. A start anyway. The realtor was right, what he told Jack about the place. It was built in the sixties. The summer of 1964 to be exact. A whole bunch of houses out at that part of the lake were built around the same time apparently."

"You mean cabins, don't you?"

"No, houses. That's why it doesn't look like a cabin. That's why none of the houses around there look like cabins.

Gladys said it was some kind of development going on at the time. Its big selling point was that they were houses being offered for the same price as a lakefront cabin. Or something like that. Anyway, I've got a copy of the permit for the place."

"So, who was the builder?" Hank said.

"Some now-defunct company called Rhodes Construction. Gladys said it sounded familiar to her, from way back when. She thinks it was owned by the Rhodes family, but that it went belly up like a lot of construction companies did in one of the big economic crashes that took place decades ago."

"Rhodes," Hank repeated. "You mean as in Councilman Rhodes?"

"I guess," Joe said. "She said the Rhodes family goes back a whole bunch of generations in this area. And I guess they used to be involved in the house-building business."

"She's right about the first part," Hank said. "They've got some big plantation house on the outskirts of town, supposedly goes back to the slave days. I don't know if Councilman Rhodes had anything to do with the construction business bearing his name, but that's a good guess. I've never heard of a construction company called that, so they must've gone bust before my time. He's a lawyer now, I think. Been involved in city politics as long as I can remember."

"Well, it's a lead anyway," Joe said. "Gives me something to check out. But I don't think I'll start off by talking to him."

"Why not? The guy's gotta be in his seventies. He seems sharp enough. He might not have been involved in construction, but it might've been someone else in his family. In any case, he's old enough to probably remember some of what took place back then. Might generate some more leads, if you talk to him."

Joe took a sip of his coffee. "Oh, I plan on talking to him. I said I don't think I'll start off with him. Want to do a little more digging first. If I remember what the captain said, Councilman Rhodes was the one negative vote when the Council made the decision to create our new Cold Case squad here, and these nice raises we just got. Don't want my first conversation with him to be something that brings up some old sore spot in his family history."

"Yeah, I get that," Hank said. "Besides, the construction company that built the place is probably not where you want to start. That stack of 2 x 4's was probably delivered to the site by a building supply company, don't you think? Finding whoever that is, or was, that's probably where you want to start."

17

J oe pulled into the local Home Depot parking lot, found a space as close to the entrance as possible. Kate had suggested, just to get some exercise, whenever he parked at one of these big places he should park toward the back. Force himself to make the walk. Joe's answer? "You gotta be kidding me, right?" What if it starts to rain once you're inside? You get soaked getting out to your car. And what about the stuff you bought? You supposed to carry it all that way? If there's too much to carry, what, you supposed to leave the cart all the way at the end of the parking lot for some poor kid to fetch?

She gave up after that. But he did agree to take more walks with her around the neighborhood.

He stepped through the glass doors as they slid open before him. The AC felt good. There was a line at the customer service counter, but he figured they wouldn't know what he needed anyway. He walked all the way down to the other end, where there was no line, and talked to the service guy who worked with commercial builders. Joe smiled, glanced at the guy's name tag. "So Bob, I'm wondering if you could help me." He took out his ID.

"Sure, sir. Would be glad to. What you need?" He lifted Joe's badge and ID. "Okay, Sgt. Boyd. I'm guessing you're not here for lumber. Whatever it is, I promise, it wasn't me."

Joe feigned a laugh. Bob probably had no idea how many times people used that line with him. "It's actually Lieutenant now, haven't gotten the badge fixed. What I'm here for is probably a little unusual. I'm actually working on a cold case file for the department, something that goes way back to the early sixties."

"Definitely before my time. I was born in '84."

"Believe it or not, it was before my time, too. And I'm pretty certain it was before Home Depot's time also. Maybe the easiest thing would be to talk to the oldest guy you have working here. I don't just mean physical age, but also someone who's worked in the building supply business the longest. I'm wondering if maybe they might remember something helpful."

"Hmmm, let's see. Got three old-timers working here now, but two of them are fairly new to Home Depot. Just started working here in the last couple of years. But Sid, he's probably the guy you want to see. I think he might've even been on the first crew that opened up this place. Let me see if I can get him." Bob asked for Sid over the microphone, apparently he was selling appliances now.

A couple of minutes later, this pleasant older gentleman, looked to be late sixties, showed up. "Hey Bob, how can I help?"

Bob made the introductions. Another customer came in

behind Joe, so the two men moved off to the side so Bob could wait on him.

"This shouldn't take but a minute, Sid. As Bob said, I'm working on a case that happened in the early sixties."

"I don't know how old Bob thinks I am, but I was only a kid then. Don't know how much help I can be."

"You still might. The thing is, this case involves a house out by the lake that was built then by a certain builder. It would take too long to explain why, but we're interested in trying to figure out what company might have supplied the building materials for that house to the contractor. Do you follow? Sort of like, the equivalent of the Home Depot of Culpepper back then. Probably some Ma and Pa outfit would be my guess."

"I do follow you," Sid said. "And that would be my guess, too. Of course, an eight-year-old wouldn't be buying too much in the way of building supplies, but I do remember going to a hardware store with my father on Sycamore Street downtown. It's still there, if I recall. Do you know where that is?"

"I know where Sycamore Street is. I didn't know there was a hardware store there. But I can look it up. Any idea if they have some old-timers working down there? Older than you, I mean?"

"As a matter of fact, I do. Name's Mr. Hadley. I'm thinking he's gotta be near eighty. It's actually his store. Well, his son's now. But I know he still comes down there a couple days a week, just to piddle around is how he puts it. Real nice fella. I'll bet he can help you figure out what you're after."

"Well, I'm glad I came in here after all. You've been very

helpful, Sid. I'll take a drive over there right now. You have a good day."

"You, too. Glad I could help."

JOE DROVE through Culpepper's nice little downtown area. He always loved coming through here. Kate described it as "quaint." That seemed like a good word for it. Kinda reminded him a little bit of the downtown area in the first Back To The Future movie. Pretty much the polar opposite of the big city downtown area of Pittsburgh, where they were from. He turned left off Main Street and, after a few blocks, turned right on Sycamore.

Even that. Imagine a downtown street being called Sycamore.

Glancing down at his GPS screen, he figured out where Hadley's Hardware Store was, drove there and started looking for a parking spot. Of course, he found one. And—he still loved this part—there wasn't any parking meter. So far, this homicide investigation was unfolding very nicely. Even this task, talking to an old fella at a local hardware store. Joe had really been looking forward to this the whole drive here from Home Depot.

The reason resurfaced in his memory the moment he stepped through the front door. It was just like every hardware store he ever went to as a kid. He loved the look of it, the feelings it generated, even the smell of the place. His Dad would always take him with him whenever he went, and then use the time to teach Joe all kinds of manly things. Maybe it wasn't so much the life lessons he learned. Maybe it was just being with his Dad, having him all to himself for a little while.

Joe walked slowly through the center aisle taking it all in, finding himself drawn to a half-dozen things on the shelves. But he kept walking. He was on a mission. Soon, he arrived at the counter at the center of the store. The guy that looked maybe ten years older than Joe was ringing something up for a lady. Maybe this guy was the son, the younger Hadley.

He and the woman chatted a few moments. Then she walked past, nodded at Joe. He walked to the counter, took out his badge and ID, and introduced himself.

"Well, Sgt. Boyd," Hadley said, "I thought you looked familiar. You had your picture in the paper a couple times the last few years, haven't you? Solving some big murder mystery and doing some heroic things, if I recall."

"That's possible," Joe said. "Would you be the owner of this fine place?"

"I am. Actually, the son of the original owner. The name's John Hadley. My father's Jim. He's retired, supposedly. But he still comes in every now and then."

"That's what I was told by a fellow named Sid over at the Home Depot. He's the one who sent me here."

"Nice to hear our biggest competitor sending customers our way."

Joe laughed. "Actually, I'm not here to buy something. Although, I might walk out with a few unplanned purchases. I'm really here to discuss a cold case homicide I'm working on that dates back to the early sixties."

"Homicide," John repeated. "That sounds serious."

"Well, maybe I jumped the gun. It's not confirmed to be a homicide. Not yet anyway. But my question involves trying to nail down what company might have sent some building supplies out to a construction site, a house being built out by the lake."

"Well, my Dad's upstairs, doing some inventory or something. Let me buzz him, see if he can come down and chat with you."

"That would be great."

The younger Hadley did that then said, "He'll be right down. But you know, this is as big as our store ever got. I can pretty much guarantee we weren't involved with anything as big as building supplies."

"No, I figured that. But I'm hoping maybe your dad remembers what company in town might have been doing that sort of thing then."

Joe heard someone coming down some stairs. The door opened behind the counter and the elder Hadley appeared. A shorter, thinner version of the son with a trimmed white beard. John did his best to explain why Joe was there. Joe filled in a few details he'd missed.

"Well, Sergeant. You did say, Sergeant, didn't you?"

"It's actually, Lieutenant now, but I haven't got a new badge yet. And I don't really care about labels anyway. Do you think you can help me? Do you recall back in the early sixties when a bunch of new houses were being built out by the lake?"

"I do as a matter of fact. And there was just one building supply company in Culpepper back then. I know this because I happened to be in my early twenties and actually worked for them. Of course, I had my mind set on opening this hardware store, even then. But I remember that place very well...Dunn's Lumber and Supply. All the builders used them, pretty much for the whole county."

Good, Joe thought, now we're getting somewhere. "By any chance, do you know if any of the owners or managers of the store are still alive? I'm trying to solve a crime, well, a possible crime, that involves a stack of 2 x 4's probably shipped from the construction supply store out to a specific house being built on the lake."

The old man sighed. "Sorry, but pretty much everyone I worked for at Dunn's is long since dead and gone. And I doubt you can even find any records from those days. The company went out of business in the early eighties, during that spell in the Carter era when home interest rates went through the roof. But I do recall one detail from my time working there...Dunn Brothers didn't ship all the building supplies out to every construction site. They did for the smaller builders, but the bigger ones had their own trucks, usually came and got their own materials themselves."

Now Joe sighed. Maybe this was a dead-end, after all. "You remember a company called Rhodes Construction? Because I think they were the ones who pulled the permit for the house I have in mind."

"Rhodes Construction?" Hadley repeated. "Oh yeah, I remember them pretty well."

18

Rhodes Plantation
Just South of Culpepper, GA
July 1964

Judson Rhodes sat back down in his office chair. Not the fancy leather one at his desk in the construction office downtown, but the uglier more-comfortable one in his home office. That office occupied the space formerly known as the brandy-and-cigars parlor in the plantation days. He'd stood up to get a look out the back window, which had a nice view of the barn across the way.

He was relieved to find Leroy and Samuel, the two colored fellows who maintained the grounds, doing what they were supposed to be doing. Just the other day, he'd caught them both sitting on their butts smack dab in the middle of the afternoon. "I don't pay you boys to sit," he'd said. "You're paid to work."

"We's all done with the chores you gave us," Leroy had said in reply.

"Well, I pay you to work until five, and I expect you to keep working until five. You done with your assignments, you pick up a broom and start sweeping. Barn always needs sweeping every hour of the day."

Looked like Leroy and Samuel had gotten the message. Both men were pushing brooms in the barn. Well, hadn't really been a barn for at least two generations. Still looked like one on the outside, though. Inside, they'd set it up to function more like a small warehouse, concrete floor and tall metal racks, strong enough to hold wooden pallets of heavy building supplies.

It wasn't anything like the bigger warehouse next to the construction office in town. The barn version was more for miscellaneous tools and building materials they might need —last minute like—on construction projects out by Lake Sampson. Having certain things stored here saved them a forty minute round trip.

Judson was just about to get refocused on the paperwork when his thoughts were interrupted by a loud familiar noise. His son Boone's old pickup truck coming up the drive. Judson had told him to get that thing fixed only to find Boone already had it fixed. He'd actually paid someone to make it that noisy. Supposed to make it sound like a hot rod, or something.

Dang fool waste of money. One of the reasons Judson still had no confidence turning the family business over to his eldest son. Thankfully, he was still five to ten years away from facing that moment.

Boone's pickup came to a stop in front of the barn. He

heard the car door open and slam shut, Boone's loud voice yelling something. Judson stood again, looked out the window.

"Samuel, Leroy...stop what you're doing and get over here."

"But your daddy told us we needed to be sweeping this barn every day," Leroy said.

"Well, I'm telling you to get over here. Unload these supplies in the back of my truck. You know where they go, or you should. You can go back to sweeping after that."

"Yes sir, Mr. Boone," both men said.

Well, at least Boone had no trouble getting workers to work. Judson saw him head toward the back door of the house, sat back at his desk chair. In less than two minutes, Judson heard his loud work boots thumping down the hall. The office door flew open.

"Daddy, I need a word with you."

"How many times I gotta tell you to knock before you come in here? This is my office, boy. Would you ever barge into my office downtown like you just did? Without knocking first?"

"No, Daddy. I apologize. You want me to go back out come back in, knocking first?"

"No, damage is already done, I expect. What is so important that you've gotta rush in here like this?"

"It's Mason. I just bumped into him out by the gazebo, chatting with Roy Lewis."

"Okay," Judson said. "You came in here to tell me you caught your little brother having a chat with his boyhood friend out by the gazebo? What, were they kissing or something?"

"No, it was nothing like that. They were just talking. It's just —"

"So, Mason was just talking to Roy? You didn't like that they were talking at the gazebo? Boone, they haven't seen each other in a year. What's the big deal? I've got some serious work to do here."

"I don't care that they were talking," Boone said. "Well, I wish Mason would start making friends with his own kind. But that's not my point. It's what Mason said. He's only home for a week, then he's going back to college? For...summer school?"

"Well, that's the plan we discussed. Why?"

"Why? Daddy, you didn't even talk this over with me. I had the whole summer planned out. A whole list of things I was going to have Mason do out at those new houses we're building on Lake Sampson. You keep telling me you want me to take more initiative on these jobs I'm running, then you go and let Mason off the hook. Now I've got to hire another laborer for the whole summer. That's gonna throw my budget off."

"First off, Boone. I don't have to discuss my plans with you before I make decisions. Don't get too big for your britches, boy. I'm starting to raise you up in this company, but you ain't at that place yet, where I gotta start asking your permission before I do things. And secondly, in your grand plan, you were planning on paying your brother nothing? For the whole summer?"

"I never got paid nothing when I started off. Don't you remember? My whole first summer out of high school. Cause I sure do. You said I was on probation. You said I was paying my dues. The only extra you paid me was some gas money and a few extra dollars in my allowance for the weekend."

Judson did remember. Sometimes it was hard being a parent. Especially now that his wife, Nadine, wasn't here anymore. She always had a way of smoothing these kinds of things over. The problem was, Boone was the firstborn and by rights, he should be getting special privileges. But the fact was, he just wasn't that bright. And Mason had all kinds of smarts by comparison.

He looked up at Boone's face. What should he tell him? "Perhaps I was wrong not to pay you properly that first summer. I'm willing to admit that now. And I won't hold it against you if you're a little over budget on your projects, because you had to hire a laborer to replace your brother. But...you hire a colored boy as your laborer, it won't set you back that much. How does that sound?"

Boone sighed. His face lightened, just a little. "I guess that helps, some. But still, Daddy...and I know you don't answer to me none. But...I don't get this whole idea of sending him off to college like this. It's not so much the money. Although it's gotta be costing a fortune to send him there. But how's that going to help him learn a decent work ethic? Sitting on his butt the next four years, reading books and taking tests? And what's all this about him learning all about commercial construction? That's what he said he's going to college for."

Judson suppressed the urge to lay into Boone, like he might have done when he was younger. "Come over here, son. Sit down in the chair. This won't take long, but I don't want you towering over me while I speak."

Boone obeyed and sat down.

"I think I understand where you're coming from. But hard, manual labor isn't the only kind of work that builds character. Think about it. Look around you. We're sitting in what was once part of a majestic plantation house. You know, just before the War of Northern Aggression, Rhodes Plantation had over seventy-five slaves working here every day. Most of them out in those fields. Hard manual labor. Even the house slaves worked hard, with their hands, every day. You think they were the only ones on the plantation with a good work ethic?"

"No, I don't guess so," Boone said.

"There ain't no guessing about it. All the white folk were working just as hard in their own way. It takes hard work to make big things happen. To plan and organize. To make schedules and solve problems. To write up contracts and make sure all your laborers are doing what they're supposed to. All of that is work, too. Take what I'm doing here. This dang paperwork. Think I want to do this? I don't. But I got to. Because I'm in charge."

"Okay," Boone said. "I guess I see your point there. But why do you have Mason going to school to learn about commercial construction? We've got more houses to build than we've ever had before. Seems to me, like there's no end in sight."

"You're right," Judson said. "We've got lots to do right now. And I'm glad of it. But see, I need you to start thinking big with me. We're doing what, eight homes right now?"

"Eight with three more getting ready to start."

"And that's good. But I want more for Rhodes Construction. I want this company to be as big as this plantation was in its heyday. And building eight to ten houses at a time, to put it plainly, isn't going to get us there."

"And commercial construction is?" Boone said.

"Yes Boone, it is. Not stopping what we're doing with the houses but adding a brand-new commercial component to our business. I happen to know, on good authority, that the Regents of Culpepper University are planning to add several new wings to the school in the next few years, including a whole college of military history. What that means is, they're going to be awarding some construction company hundreds of thousands of dollars in commercial contracts. Maybe millions. Think about it, we can make ten times the profit on one commercial project like that, compared to all these little house contracts we're doing right now."

He stood up. "And that, my boy, is why I'm sending your brother Mason to college. I want in on that barrel of money."

19

M ason walked up to the front of the Big House, amazed that such a place still existed and that it had been the only place he'd ever called home. The thought mostly made him feel ashamed.

The house and the grounds, due to the growing fortunes of the Rhodes Construction business, had almost been restored to the grandeur and greatness it had known just before the Civil War. From that standpoint, he marveled at its beauty.

Like most plantation houses, it stood two stories tall. Large white pillars spread out every ten feet or so across the front, supporting a double-decker porch, which also spanned the entirety of the house. White painted railings stretched across both floors between the pillars, except for the opening by the steps and double-front doors.

As a child, he'd only ever been told the polished version of the plantation's history, that he'd inherited a legacy of southern nobility and unbridled prestige. The Rhodes family consisted of an unbroken line of fine country gentlemen and refined southern ladies, who had only and always ever treated their slaves, and later their hired help, with the measure of respect befitting their lesser status in life.

But this family story stood in stark contrast to the realities of life he'd witnessed with his own eyes in the little clapboard shanties where Roy, his family and the rest of "the help" lived. Even though they never had much, Roy's folks had always treated him with so much kindness. More times than he could count, Mason had been invited to share one of their meager meals. Of course, he'd never been allowed to return the favor. He wouldn't have even asked. Roy would've never expected him to. But Mason regularly saw Roy's family enjoying great fits of laughter around the dinner table with lots of generous smiles.

In contrast, in the Big House where he lived, with all its luxury and refinements, there was mostly tension and anger, jealousy and competition. He always had to walk around on eggshells doing his best not to offend, trying to dodge his brother's outbursts or his father's harsh punishments. When he'd thought about it then and again now, he never really doubted which family was the wealthier of the two.

"You going to stand out there all day?"

Mason looked over his shoulder, saw his father standing behind the screen door. "No, just taking a little stroll down memory lane."

"Easy to do, I guess, when you been gone a spell. But I'd like to get some kind of a report on how this grand experiment of ours is working."

"Experiment?"

"You going off to college. First Rhodes' man who ever did. And me, the one paying for it. Come off the porch and join me in the parlor, fill me in. Got Maisie to pour us both some iced tea." Maisie was the primary housekeeper and cook and also Roy's mother.

"I'll be right in."

His father backed away from the door, started walking toward the parlor. Mason just needed a moment to prepare himself for the grilling he was about to get. He had discussed this anticipated moment with his new and good friend, Whitney Wilkins, one of the SNCC leaders he'd met. Mason had never been good at lying, but it was a skill he knew he must master if he hoped to safely tread these waters between these two very different worlds. Whitney had actually coached Mason on how to lie effectively. He rehearsed some of Whitney's tips as he walked through the screen door.

As Mason came into the parlor, Maisie was bringing in the tray of iced tea. "Here, let me get that," he said, reaching for the tray.

"No, you won't get that," Daddy said. "Maisie's not an invalid. Let her do her work."

Mason knew he'd just said that to humiliate her, keep her in her proper place. Mattered more to him than even a trivial act of kindness. Mason sat in an upholstered chair across from his father, who was sitting where he always sat on the sofa. Mason thanked Maisie after she handed him the iced tea. She smiled. Of course, Daddy didn't even acknowledge her presence.

Daddy lifted the glass, took a sip, clearly enjoyed it. "So, my newly-college-educated boy, tell me how your freshman year at this Yankee university went? What kind of corrupt ideas did they plant in that brain of yours?"

"Daddy, it's not a Yankee university. We went over that before I even filled out the application. Most of Maryland was sympathetic to the cause, remember? They don't even let Negroes in my school. And I didn't hear a single college lecture that even talked about racial issues, let alone one that favored one side or the other. You want to know the kind of stuff I learned in my freshman year?"

"Why I asked?"

"I had an algebra class. Another class on biology, talking all about evolution and natural order and survival of the fittest. I had a class on humanities, still not sure what that was about. Could barely keep my eyes open through talks by the most boring professor I ever heard."

"You didn't have any classes on commercial construction? That's why I'm sending you up there."

Mason sipped his iced tea. Maisie really did make the best. "No, didn't have a single class on commercial construction. Guess you don't remember what I said when I explained the curriculum. This is a four-year degree program, Daddy. The first two years cover the basics. You only get a few electives, meaning classes where you can pick things you want to study. I don't even have any of those until this coming year. And for those, I will pick classes about construction. When I get past these first two years, almost all my classes will be about the reason you sent me there."

"I do remember you saying something about that. So tell me, there's no blacks at the school, right? None of those so-called civil rights activists running around stirring up trouble? I keep reading more about this kind of thing in the papers. Boone's been telling me about some disturbing things he keeps hearing at these meetings he's been going to."

Mason had to think fast. *You don't need to answer the question being asked. Answer with something similar you know to be true.* "Daddy, like I said, they don't have any black students at the University of Maryland. Not a single one, let alone any black professors. None of the teachers at the school are trying to subvert our southern values. They don't even get near topics like that."

"Well, glad to hear it. Don't want to be wasting my money, getting your head all polluted with crazy ideas. So, you making any new friends?"

"A few. But I've been pretty busy, so I don't have much of a social life."

"Well, I want you to be busy. But you ought to make a little time for socializing. Business is all about connecting with people. That's never really been your strength, but I'm hoping you're gonna shake that off while you're up there. I want you to really work on that, getting comfortable talking to all kinds of people. Of course, I mean the right kind of people. And by *right*, I mean the *white* kind of people. You follow me?"

"I hear what you're saying, and I am socializing quite a bit more, really trying to stretch myself in that area." He was just about to mention all the wonderful new people he'd met at the SNCC meetings, leaving off what kind of meetings they were and that half of them were black. But figured he better tread lightly. "And like I said, Daddy...all the students attending my school are the white kind of people."

He restrained a smile, but turned one loose on the inside,

as he thought about the friend he'd grown the closest to this past year. Whitney Wilkins, who like Roy, was also black.

20

1 Week Later
Near Howard University, Washington DC

Mason had survived his week-long visit home without getting into too many skirmishes with his father or Boone. Like his initial chat with Daddy, he kept his answers short and shallow. Whitney's tips came to his rescue more than once. Thankfully, his father rarely asked follow-up questions, which wasn't surprising. As a family, they weren't known for in-depth conversation even when his mother was still alive. But ever since her passing from a sudden heart attack last year, they were more like three strangers who shared the same last name and occasionally the same roof.

He'd arrived back at his dorm room at the University of Maryland in College Park last night. At the moment, he was looking for a parking place on a side street just off of Georgia Avenue, right across from Howard University.

He looked forward to reconnecting with Whitney and hearing any news or fresh updates about the group's planned protests into the South in a few weeks. Mason had missed two SNCC meetings while he'd been gone.

Just up ahead on the right, a car was pulling out from the curb. Mason waited till the spot was free and slipped in. That may be one of the only valuable things Boone had ever taught him...how to parallel park.

As he got out of the car, he realized one fairly significant change that had taken place inside him the past few months. He wasn't afraid of being around so many black people anymore. They were all over the place here, since Howard was an all-black school. He'd see an occasional white person here and there, but being the minority race for a change had definitely been a different experience for him.

He had met Whitney at his first SNCC meeting at a different college, and they'd become fast friends. When Whitney learned Mason went to U-of-M, only a half-hour drive from Howard, they agreed to meet for lunch the following week. Of course, neither of them entertained for a minute that Whitney would drive up to Mason's campus.

Whitney would not be welcome there, especially eating at the same table with a white friend. He wouldn't be attacked, which might very well happen in the South. But there'd be constant stares and maybe even a few comments. Not to mention the fact that many of the restaurants didn't serve coloreds, or else stuck them in a separate spot in the back.

But here in the streets around Howard, the blacks he encountered were usually very friendly. Especially since the civil rights movement was now in full swing, and so many white students were joining the fight to end segregation.

Another unique experience for Mason was seeing so many middle-class blacks. Take for example the young black man whose parking space Mason had taken. It was a pretty nice car. Nicer than the one Mason drove. He hardly ever saw a black person driving a nice car where he lived. Or a not-so-nice car, either, for that matter. And the clothes everyone wore around here...every bit as nice as white people wore. Again, didn't see that down South.

As he came around the corner, Mason smiled and nodded at the black folks he passed along the way, trying not to look nervous. He looked up the sidewalk, saw Whitney standing just outside the diner where they usually met. He waved and motioned that he'd go in and get them a seat. Mason nodded and picked up his pace.

From all his many suppers eaten with Roy and his mom, Mason was used to the kind of food served at this diner. He didn't care for some of it at all, like all the innards, for example. Fried okra almost made him gag. He didn't mind the collard greens if cooked with enough pork. But he really liked the fried chicken, fried catfish, skillet cornbread, red beans and rice, and black-eyed peas. But he especially loved the macaroni and cheese.

Once inside the diner, he spotted Whitney at a table along the wall. The fact that Mason was the only white person in the place only created a moment's hesitation, then everyone returned to their food and conversations.

"So how did you make out back home?" Whitney said. "And by the way, I ordered you the mac and cheese. It's what you always get. If you want—"

"Macaroni and cheese is what I'd have ordered myself," Mason said.

"Got us both Coca-Cola's, too."

"What's it gonna be for you today, Whit, fried chicken or catfish?"

"Chicken. Theirs is so much better here than what my mama makes. Don't ever tell her I said that."

"Yeah, Maisie makes some pretty delicious fried chicken back home. That was about the only thing I enjoyed my whole trip, her cooking. That and getting to see her son, Roy. He got that scholarship to Shaw, by the way."

"Did he? Well, good for him. So, did your father and brother give you a hard time about coming back up here for the summer?"

"Boone did, a real hard time. My dad was fine with it. Of course, neither one of them know the real reason I wanted to be here for the summer, or what our plans are."

"Good. So, your cover story's still intact?"

"Yep. And my guess is, it'll stay that way the rest of the summer. Unless I get arrested on one of these trips down south. Speaking of that, what did I miss at the meetings this past week? Have they nailed down any of the details?"

A waitress served the two glasses of Coke. Whitney took a sip and said, "Yeah, things have firmed up pretty well. They're already gathering the bus trips together, picked out all the first cities we'll be heading to. I figured you'd want to be on the same bus as me."

"Definitely. Where's it going?"

"Ashburn, Mississippi. In fact, that's where all the activity this summer is being planned."

"In Mississippi?"

"Yeah."

"That's good," Mason said. "I'm glad."

"You're glad it's Mississippi? Why?"

"Because it's a full day's drive from where I live in Culpepper, Georgia. No chance of anyone I know seeing me there."

"Well, I guess that matters," Whitney said. "I'm glad it's Ashburn for a different reason."

"What's that?"

"Less chance of us get beaten up there, or worse."

"Is that starting to happen? I didn't even know any of the buses had gone down there yet."

"None of the buses yet, but quite a few of the organizers have gone down, to get the lay of the land. Word has already spread about what we're trying to do. And white folks in Mississippi are none too happy about it. Several of them came back with black eyes and fat lips and pretty shook up about the whole thing."

Mason didn't like the sound of that. "Did the police arrest any of the folks who attacked our people?"

"Mason, the police not only didn't stop the attacks, they were some of the people doing the attacking. And they told our people that those buses had better not come down here, or else they'd be treated to a lot worse."

"Then why don't we just go somewhere else? Why do we have to go to Mississippi?"

"Yeah, I was thinking that, too. Plenty of places we could target in the South. But Mississippi has the worst voting situation of all of 'em. Less than seven percent of Negroes are registered to vote there. And in some towns, they make up almost fifty percent of the population. White folks have stacked the deck against them, intimidating them in all kinds of ways."

"Like how?"

"Like making ridiculously hard colored-only tests they have to pass to get registered. White landlords threaten to evict black tenants if they register. Employers threaten to fire them if they do. All kinds of things. Then you add to all that the threats of physical violence, which obviously, they are more than willing to carry out."

All this stuff was kind of hard for Mason to hear. "Whitney, let me ask you something. How come you don't hate white people? All of us? I think if I was you, and these kinds of things were happening to me, I don't think I'd be planning on doing peaceful protests. I think I'd be looking for payback."

"Oh, I can get angry about it, believe me. If I stopped and thought about it a while. But my Mama taught me to look at things different. She'd say if I treated them the same bad way they're treating me, that only makes me as bad as they are. And how is that any better? How does that improve things one bit? The fact is, none of us have any control over the timing or circumstances of our birth. That's God's territory. If I was born white, like you, I'd still be the same man on the inside. And look at you...you are white. And you are different on the inside from all these white racists we're trying to reach. Has nothing to do with the color of a man's skin. Has to do with his heart. Has to do with his mind, with the way he thinks. If I started hating all whites, I'd miss out on having this fine meal with you and all these great conversations we've had, wouldn't I?"

Mason smiled. "I suppose you would. Even still, I apologize for all the white people who are messed up on the inside. Sadly, that includes my own family." He took another bite of his macaroni and cheese. Finished chewing and said, "So, why will white people treat us better if we go to Ashburn? I don't recall you saying."

"We heard some local clergymen there been organizing folks, and even the mayor is getting involved, trying to calm the waters before we arrive."

"Which is when?" Mason asked.

"Better get ready, my friend. Our bus leaves next week."

21

4 Days Later
Back Room of Haley's Bar
Culpepper, GA

It was well after hours, had to be past midnight, but Boone got the word...everyone needed to be here tonight. At least it was a Friday. If need be, he could catch up on some sleep in the morning.

Looking around the room, the regulars were all here plus a few newcomers Boone didn't recognize. Rufus Stillwell, their fearless leader, was upfront chatting with one. He hoped whatever this meeting was about, it didn't include heading out somewhere tonight to render southern justice on someone or someplace. He was bone-tired from a long day spent mostly in the sun.

Someone yelled out behind him. "Hey Rufus, let's get this show on the road. Some of us gotta work in the morning."

Boone turned around. It was George Caldwell, a local chicken farmer.

"Hold your horses, George. I was just fixing to start her up. Okay gentlemen, if I could have your attention. Appreciate y'all coming out here tonight on such short notice. When you hear what I have to say, you'll understand the reason for the urgency, and why we're meeting here after hours."

"I don't get why we don't just join the Klan," someone else said. "Be a whole lot simpler." While everyone in the room was certainly a Klan sympathizer, Culpepper had never officially formed a Klavern.

"Josiah, we've been over this," Rufus said, "at least a half-dozen times. Things being the way they are in the country right now, it just don't make sense. All kinds of heat are on the Klan right now, especially after that bombing last September in Birmingham. The feds have a target on their backs. We can still get the job done in our...less official capacity. Now, can I continue?"

Josiah nodded. "I guess."

"If it helps any, all the intel I'm sharing tonight has come directly from Klan headquarters in Mississippi, which is where a bunch of us will be headed shortly if I can get enough of you fired up enough to join me."

"When we leaving?" someone in the back yelled out. "Can't be soon enough for me. It's high time we got in this fight, instead of just talking about it. You hear what's going on over there? Things are boiling over."

"They ain't boiled over just yet," Rufus said. "But they're about to. Now quit interrupting me, so I can get this out. As I was saying, groups like ours all over are being recruited to jump into this thing. Apparently, a whole bunch of buses filled with college kids from the north will be headed to Mississippi on the fifteenth, just a few days from now. Colored kids from those all-black schools mingled together with white Yankee kids, all coming to Mississippi to stir up trouble. There's way more of them coming down than they got Klan members to stop 'em. So, they're asking for our help."

"I heard they're trying to stir up a big uprising," Josiah said, "like they tried in the slave days. Some of them towns in Mississippi got more blacks than whites."

"That's not what we're being told," Rufus said. "It's trouble of a different kind. They're trying to get things changed there so black folks can vote. But you are right about some towns having more coloreds than whites. And that's the problem. They all start voting, they can take over them towns all legal like. Can you imagine? Black folks suddenly being mayors, being in charge of whites? Telling them what they can and cannot do? It's gotta be stopped! And that's why we're having this meeting. Groups like ours are being sent to cities all over the state to help. We been asked to get a group of us together to drive to Ashburn, Mississippi so that we're there to meet these buses that arrive on the fifteenth. Who's with me?"

Boone sat through all this just listening. He agreed, something had to be done. But he didn't see how he could be a part of it. He raised his hand.

"Boone?" Rufus said. "See that folks? Boone Rhodes' hand just shot right up."

"No, I'm not volunteering to go. I got a question."

"Okay, let's have it."

."Best I recall," Boone said, "Ashburn is a full day's drive from here. One way. So you figure, driving there, driving back, spending at least a day fighting with these college kids, maybe two. That's three or four lost days of lost wages. These Mississippi folks gonna help us out any to make up for the money we'll be losing?"

"No Boone," Rufus said. "There's no funds available for something like that. But you gotta see it another way. This is a call to arms, like the Revolutionary War days. Every man to the fight. They dropped their pitchforks back then, their plows and their hammers...every one of them, and rushed into battle. That's what's going on here. We're fighting to preserve our very way of life."

"Sounds like we're being asked to preserve the way of life for folks in Mississippi," George said. "I'm with Boone. I got a farm to run. It's a sad state of affairs, I agree. But it's their fight, not ours."

"George, it's all of our fight. Them and us. What, you don't think these college kids won't come here next? If they win in Mississippi, you don't think they'll try the same thing here?"

"I don't know," George replied. "If they do, I'll throw down my plow and pick up my rifle. But I do it for this? Three or four days, me being gone? There's no one there to tend to things but me."

"Okay George," Rufus said. "I get what you're saying. You've got a unique situation there. But how about the rest of you men? Surely, you can see the urgency of the hour. I've got a business to run myself, but I'm gonna close up shop for a few days. Maybe I lose a few dollars. But can you think of a better cause than this?"

Rufus was looking right at Boone as he said this last part. Boone could certainly feel the tug and the heat being applied.

"How about a show of hands? Who's gonna drive with me to Ashburn, Mississippi?"

About half the hands went up. Boone wanted to raise his, but he couldn't see his dad being okay with that, even if he totally agreed with the cause, which he did. But there was no way Boone was going to commit himself to shut down all the work he had going on for four days.

Not without Daddy's say so.

22

The following morning, Boone allowed himself to get up an hour later, seeing it was Saturday. Technically, he had the weekends off and none of the union contractors showed up to the job sites. But that made Saturday mornings perfect for inspecting their work without anyone giving him any hassle.

Presently, he was drinking his coffee out on the front porch as Maisie cooked up a big breakfast. He picked up the morning paper laying there on the wicker table from under a stone paperweight. Left there, as usual, by his dad who probably got up at the crack of dawn.

Before he'd even started reading the headlines, he heard the screen door open and close behind him.

"So how that big meeting go last night at Haley's Bar? What was all the fuss about?" It was Judson Rhodes, Boone's father.

"It was fine, I guess." Boone laid the newspaper back down. "Rufus was trying to talk everyone into heading over to Mississippi to help the Klan chase off some college kids coming down from up north. Apparently, a whole slew of them are invading on the fifteenth, driving down here in buses. Lots of them. Coming into cities all over the state. Sounds like there's gonna be way more of them than the Klan can handle, so they're putting out the word. To hear Rufus tell it, you'd think he saw himself as Paul Revere last night."

Daddy came around and sat in his usual rocker. Had all the signs of a first-rate lecture heading his way. "I just got off the phone with Rufus," he said. "Not to put too fine a point on it, but he was a little concerned about your disposition at the meeting. Enough so that he took the time to call me."

Boone sighed. "So, what'd he say?"

"Well, he felt you weren't being very supportive, said you weren't trying to grasp the importance of what he was trying to say."

"Well Daddy, guess I'm guilty as charged then. At least with the first part. I wasn't being supportive...on purpose. I can't be takin' three or four days off in the middle of the week to go chasing around some college kids in Mississippi. To hear him go on, you'd think it was like some D-Day invasion underway."

"I caught a little bit of that in our phone chat just now," Judson said. "But son, there's some things you're not picking up on here. Rufus might be ringing the bell a little too loud, but to look at your reaction, you'd think everything was hunky-dory. And it's definitely not. To be honest, I'm a little surprised at how casually you're taking this whole thing. I think it's a pretty serious situation myself."

"I think it's serious, too, Daddy. I'm picking up on that.

We got a bunch of misguided Yankee white kids mingling with a bunch of angry colored kids driving down to Mississippi to try to change things. But you and me both know, ain't nothing going to change the way things are in Mississippi. Or anywhere else here in the South. Things been the way they been for a hundred years. Now, I'm not saying if those buses were coming here to Culpepper, I wouldn't drop everything and try and stop 'em. Cause I would. But Daddy they ain't coming here. And we got a ton of work going on right now with these house projects. You know as well as me, I take off for three or four days and those union boys will cut back their workload by way more than half. And then the budget will get all off-track. And then what'll we—"

"Boone, Boone, take a breath, son." Judson leaned forward in his rocker. "I know all about the workload and all about what'll happen if you take off all them days. But son, there's a bigger picture going on here than you're seeing. In fact, seems like I'm always beating that drum with you, trying to get you to see the bigger picture. You're forgetting who you are, and who this family is in this town. We're Rhodes, boy. The Rhodes Plantation. People look up to us, and they have been for over a hundred years. Why do you think Rufus called me? Why he was so concerned about your attitude at the meeting? It's because he knows when a Rhodes' man says something or does something, other people are paying attention. Other people follow your example. Rufus told me better than half the men who said before the meeting they were going, changed their minds after what you said."

Boone could hardly believe what he was hearing. "You serious?"

"Of course, I'm serious. And see, I've known that going on decades now. What I say or do in this town carries weight with lots of people. Puts a little bit of pressure on me, to be sure, but it also opens up a whole lot of doors. A lot of doors with a whole lot of important and wealthy people, not just the small fries who show up at your meetings. That's the kind of thing I've been trying to get you to see for some time now. It's not just you focusing on what matters to you, and no one else. You've got standing in this community, son. And it's time you started believing that."

Boone took a sip of his coffee, set the cup back down. Maybe his father had been trying to get him to see this thing for quite a while. If so, he didn't remember it. But he was hearing it now. "So, you want me to go on this trip? That what you're saying?"

"Yeah, I want you to go. Mainly to keep growing the family name in this town, but I also believe in the cause our brothers in Mississippi are fighting for. And I know you do, too. Remember what Governor Wallace said in that speech he gave in Alabama last year? *'Segregation now, segregation tomorr-ah...'*"

"—*Segregation forever*," Boone said. "Yeah, I know."

"That's what we fighting to protect, Boone. I know you believe in that as strongly as I do."

"I do, Daddy."

"You just been too focused on the business matters at hand. And I appreciate that. They matter, too. But right now? This thing matters a tad more. You followin' me?"

"Yeah Daddy, I think I am."

"Good. Glad I came out here then."

"But what are we going to do about all the work that won't get done if I go?"

"Well, I tell you what...you make a list of things I need to do, people I need to keep an eye on, and I'll look after things on the house projects out by Lake Sampson while you're gone."

"You will?"

"I will. Besides that, you heading out that way will let me check something important off my list. Something I been needing to do ever since your mother died but never got the chance."

"What's that?" Boone said.

"Stopping off in Tupelo to see your Aunt Betsy. There's something I need you to give her for me. Well, actually for your mother."

"For mother? What is it?"

"Just a box of personal things. Not even sure what's in it. Your mother knew she was dying, so she divided up her personal things to give away to folks she cared about. I delivered most of them a month or so after she passed, but I never had an occasion to make the all-day drive to Mississippi, where Aunt Betsy lives. You can make a quick stop in Tupelo on your way to Ashburn."

Boone stood.

"Where you going?" Judson said.

"Guess I'm going inside. Eat breakfast and call old Rufus, tell him I'll be going to Mississippi after all."

23

THE PRESENT
Monday Evening - Culpepper, GA

Jack decided it was time to call it a day. Thankfully, he didn't have to teach any classes today or have any critical appointments with important people. That was good, because he'd been distracted pretty much the whole day. He knew why. It was the mysterious, cryptic message he and Rachel had discovered etched into the studs of their new lake house. The fact that both Joe and his partner, Hank, agreed that it was probably real and probably meant something sinister had happened back in 1964, didn't help.

Having worked with Joe on several investigations, Jack knew a bit about how Joe thought and the kind of things that piqued his curiosity. This would definitely be one of those kinds of things. And now that Joe had been put in charge of this new cold case squad, he was certain Joe probably already had rearranged his schedule and put this new mystery at the top of his list. He'd probably already spent a good part of this day looking into it and digging up new leads.

Jack was dying to call him and find out what he might have uncovered. But it wouldn't be appropriate. He wasn't a detective; he was a history professor. More than that, he was in charge of the entire military history department. He had a Ph.D. He was an academic with real and significant responsibilities, for which he got paid very well.

But he'd give anything to work with Joe on this, to be right there every day uncovering new leads, putting the puzzle pieces of this case together until the entire mystery was solved. How was he ever supposed to work the rest of this week doing business as usual, biding his time until Saturday comes, when he could get back out there to the lake house, start looking for more 2 x 4's with letters carved into them? There had to be more. They were sitting out there right now, upstairs in the attic or hiding behind that ugly paneling in the bedroom, just waiting for someone to uncover them.

JACK PULLED INTO THE DRIVEWAY, thinking through several different ways to approach the subject with Rachel at dinner. Most of them had merit, but they all suffered from the same malady: they all pointed to the fact that Jack was becoming obsessed with this thing. Because he was. And that wasn't good. Rachel was interested in these kinds of things to a point, but these days she was mostly concerned with building the nest. Creating a nice, normal, stable environment in which to raise a family.

Jack was interested in that, too. She was glad Jack had chosen this profession, that he didn't go off to work every day dealing with potentially dangerous people like Joe's job. Joe was good at it. He'd been doing it most of his adult life. She said she prayed for him every day that he'd return safely home to Kate and the kids. But at the same time, she was immensely grateful she didn't have to pray similar things about Jack.

He got out of the car and headed for the front door. He looked back at the car in the driveway and looked around at the neighborhood he got to come home to every day. This really was a nice life. He thanked God afresh for it, remembering a Bible passage he'd read a few mornings ago. One of the Psalms. David was saying something about how God had *"set the boundary lines for him in pleasant places."*

That was Jack's life now. It wasn't boring. He wasn't some kind of adrenaline junkie in need of a fix. He had a beautiful wife, a great job, their first baby on the way. Went to a good church. Nice pastor who clearly still loved his wife. No scandals. No weirdness. Not too many hypocrites, as far as he could tell. He even had a fun hobby, metal detecting for Civil War relics with his good buddy Joe.

But as he turned the doorknob and walked inside, he thought, *Man, I really wish I could work on that case.* He was greeted by amazing smells. Something baking. Some kind of bread maybe.

Rachel came out from the kitchen, walked toward him, greatly with child but looking gorgeous, as usual. "What is that smell?"

"Baked chicken breasts with cream cheese and chives, wrapped in filo dough. You know, like a puff pastry."

"You haven't made that since we were first married."

She reached up and gave him a kiss. "I know. I was in the mood. So, I picked up the stuff on the way home. You do like it, right?"

"Are you kidding? I love it. You could make it twice a week, if you want."

She turned and headed back toward the kitchen. "Maybe not that often, but I can stick it on the menu so it shows up more than once every few years. It's almost ready, so go and get comfortable. But not in your PJs. It's really nice outside, thought maybe we could get out of the house for a bit."

He'd just started heading up the stairs but stopped. "Really? What do you have in mind?"

She peeked her head out from the kitchen. "I can tell you over dinner."

"Why the mystery? Don't keep me in suspense, tell me now."

She stepped into the hallway. "You'll think it's silly. And we don't have to do it, if you don't want. I mean, if you're tired. We don't even have to go out. I just thought—"

"Rach, just tell me. I'm open to whatever it is. I'm really not that tired."

"It's just, well, I don't know why exactly, but I can't get this 2 x 4 thing out of my head. I've been thinking about it all day. I guess especially after seeing Hank and Joe's reaction, it just hit me. There's really something to this. Nobody would take the time to carve all those letters into the wood like that, especially with that kind of message, unless there was something pretty serious going on. And it makes sense to me that those boards probably all came from the same stack. Which also makes sense that the stack of boards was delivered to our lake house when it was being built. Which means, the rest of that message is probably on the other boards in our house, the ones we didn't rip off the drywall and paneling. So, I was thinking...maybe after dinner we could take a drive out to the lake and you could work on that a little. It doesn't get dark until around 8:30. That's probably only enough time to do the baby's room, not the whole attic. But, if you're too tired..."

"Rachel, I can't believe you're saying this. I can't believe you're wanting to do this. I can't believe I get to come home to someone like you, who looks like you, and cooks a fancy baked chicken puff pastry for me, for dinner, then wants to go out after to our lakefront house and have me yank off paneling in our new baby's room, looking for a mystery message carved into the studs."

She looked confused. "So, is that a yes or no?"

"It's a definite yes."

Was this a great life, or what?

24

A s expected, the dinner was delicious. Jack and Rachel had agreed, the dishes could wait till they got home. Or later. They didn't want to waste the remaining light left in this day doing dishes. Most of his tools were still in the car trunk, so there was no delay getting them together. In no time at all, they were in the car, driving the now familiar route out to their lakefront house.

On the way, they'd talked about the different possible explanations for this mystery message in the wood. Jack was sure that wherever this trail led, they would find a murder at its end. Rachel hoped he was wrong. "I agree," she'd said, "whoever carved that message was afraid for their life. But I'm hoping it didn't come to that. Maybe we're going to find that he escaped from wherever he was chained up before the bad guys got him."

Jack told her he was afraid endings like that only happened in the movies. But this conversation had given him an idea. He'd been thinking about the possibilities for the last few minutes, as they turned off the main road onto the dirt road leading to their lakefront place. "You know something we didn't think of, Rach? I can't believe it hasn't come up yet. I wonder if Joe's thought of it, though. He probably has already."

"Jack, what are you talking about? You realize, you haven't told me what the idea is yet?"

"I'm sorry. I was just thinking, we should check the library for newspaper clippings around the time the house was built. Joe was looking into who pulled the permit on the project and when. Once we have that, it would narrow down the search range at the library. In a town as small as this, I'm sure somebody going missing would be pretty big news. Even if they never found him, there would've been articles written about it in the newspapers."

"That's a great idea," she said. "And if they found his body at some point, we can see if the case was ever solved. If it hasn't been, this message carved into our walls might be just the lead they need to help them solve it."

They reached the house. Jack pulled his car up close to the front porch and got out. "Why don't you go ahead and get it open? I'll get the tools out of the trunk. Won't need all of them. We're just yanking paneling off the studs. Shouldn't be too hard. Well, I'll be yanking the paneling off. I want you just to sit there and keep me company."

"I can help once the 2 x 4's are exposed, right? I mean, you said you weren't knocking down any walls tonight."

"Yeah, you can help then. Literally, you can hold the flashlight for me."

"Literally? Is there any other way to hold a flashlight?"

"Guess you haven't heard that saying, *All I did was hold the flashlight*. My Dad used to say it whenever he talked about making a really small contribution to a project."

"But I thought we needed the flashlight," she said, "to help us see the letters carved into the wood. It would be pretty hard for you to hold the flashlight by yourself and take pics of the letters with your tablet."

"We do need the flashlight. I don't mean you're making a really small contribution. That's why I said, you can hold the flashlight, literally."

She unlocked the front door. "So, you weren't insulting me."

"Not at all. Guess I thought everyone knew that saying. Maybe it was something my Dad made up, and I just thought it was something everybody said."

"There is an old saying about holding a torch for someone," she said. "But that's about someone still loving an old flame years later after the relationship ended. Don't think your holding-the-flashlight thing is real. Though it's kinda cute. And it does work...the way your Dad used it, I mean."

He approached her on the porch, holding the toolbox. "Well, you can hold the flashlight for me anytime, my love. And tonight? It's a seriously important contribution to the success of this endeavor."

"Oh, stop."

He leaned forward and kissed her, and they headed into the living room.

"There's plenty of lighting here right now," Jack said. "I'm thinking it's only gonna take me twenty or thirty minutes to yank this paneling down. It's way easier than doing wallboard. Why don't you relax out on the front porch, take in the beautiful view? I'll come get you when all the studs are exposed."

"You sure you don't need my help?"

"I will...when it's flashlight time."

She laughed. "Okay, but don't go crazy in there."

Jack went at the assignment with abandon. All he really needed was a hammer and the prybar. Fortunately, whoever put this up didn't use any glue. Judging by how ugly the paneling looked, they figured it was installed in the mid-70s. It really needed to come down anyway. They had already discussed some ideas for what to do with the walls once the secret messages had been uncovered, and it could go back to being just the baby's room.

Thirty minutes later, he had all the paneling off and stacked in a pile behind the house. He had a guy he could call to come haul it away. Before getting Rachel, he decided to sweep the floor then join her on the porch for a bit to let the dust settle down.

"So, are you going to call Joe when we get home?" Rachel asked. "Tell him about the library idea, you know, looking for the newspaper articles on somebody going missing in the early 60s?"

"I was kinda hoping to do that one myself. He might think of it, too, without me. But thought I might take a run down there during my lunch break tomorrow. I am going to call him though, see if he nailed down the date the permits were pulled. It'll make the search a lot easier if I know."

"How do they have the newspapers stored?" she asked. "I'm guessing they're not actually the original newspapers."

"No, but it's pretty cool what they've got, for old-school technology. I've used it a bunch of times when doing research for my books. Basically, they got these cabinets full of drawers, broken down by year, then month. Inside are little containers holding rolls of microfilm. You load it into this viewer and turn the knob. The entire newspaper, page by page, shows up on this big screen. You just zip past until you find the date you're looking for, then you slow it down. You can just read it then, page by page, like you're reading an old newspaper until you find a headline or a picture that seems relevant. Of course, the hardest thing for me, since I love history so much, is staying focused on the reason I'm there. I could easily get lost just reading all the articles of the time. Seeing how they covered news stories fairly, for example, the way journalists used to do. Seeing what they thought about things and how radically different people viewed things from the way they do today. Even just freaking out about how little things cost."

"That actually does seem kind of fun," she said. "Think you'll turn up anything connected to this?"

"Hope so. I mean, just one article about someone going missing around the time this house was built? That would be huge. Might give us a name and open this whole thing up." Jack stood. "Well, think it should be okay to head in there now. Ready with your flashlight?"

"Isn't it in the toolbox?"

"Yeah, sorry. Let me get it, and I'll meet you in there."

Jack got the flashlight and his tablet then he and Rachel began going through the room, from left to right, one stud at a time, top to bottom, scanning each one for any signs of carved letters. The first five were duds. On the sixth one, they hit pay dirt. As with the others, the letters began and ended at around the same height on the board. Which made sense, if they were all stacked together neatly on a pallet.

Two more boards with nothing. Then the next one, more carved letters. This continued for the next twenty-five minutes, with Rachel holding the flashlight and Jack taking pictures on his tablet. When they were done, they had found five 2 x 4's that were part of the carved message.

"That looks like it," Jack said. Holding his tablet, he said, "We can take this out to the dining room where there's more light. Start maneuvering the pics around till we figure out what the letters are saying."

So, that's what they did. The first task was to rotate the photos, so that the letters were facing horizontally and right-side-up. As with the other studs, some contained whole letters and words. Some just the top or bottom half. Once that was done, it was kind of like working with a jigsaw puzzle or a game of Scrabble. Before long, they had the pictures assembled into a handful of words they could comprehend.

It appeared that two distinct new lines of the message had been revealed.

Rachel grabbed Jack's hand, as she read the words aloud. Both could instantly see, what they contributed was very significant. Jack was certain Joe and Hank would agree.

The lines read:

SEE. MY NAME IS

And:

I AM PROBABLY DEAD

"Wait a minute," Jack said. "Let's put them together with the other lines we've already uncovered. See what we've got.

HELP
ME. I'M CHAINED UP
VERY DARK. HARD TO
SEE. MY NAME IS

IF I GO MISSING
I AM PROBABLY DEAD

"My gosh, Jack."

"I know," he said. "I better call Joe."

25

June 15th, 1964
On a Bus just north of Ashburn, MS

The singing in the back half of the bus had finally died down. Mason joined in a little, but he really just mouthed the words, as he'd been taught to do by the choir director at his church way back in sixth grade. Apparently, his singing was that awful. Besides, he had been trying to impress a blonde coed named Amy Hampton for several weeks now. Why ruin it by letting her hear just how bad he was?

He glanced over at her several times during the singing and, on at least one occasion, was certain he'd caught her looking his way. He sat back in his seat closer to the front.

A moment later, Whitney joined him. "I'm surprised you came back up here. Cause we both know you weren't back there because you love to sing."

"What are you talking about?" Mason whispered loudly. "And keep your voice down. That's supposed to be a secret, that I sing like a crow."

Whitney leaned forward. "Got it. Won't tell a soul. Especially a pretty blonde one."

Mason looked back over his shoulder, caught a glance of Amy chatting with a friend about six rows back. He resisted the urge to just sit there and stare at her for several seconds.

"I paid attention," Whitney said, "like you asked me to. I did see her checking you out on several occasions. So, I think it's safe to say, it's not all in your imagination. I'm not saying she's clearly nuts over you, but there is some interest there. I think you could make some progress on this trip in that direction, if you play your cards right."

"That's just it," Mason said, "I'm terrible at cards. You got all that charm and gift of gab going for you. I know of at least three or four gals on this bus alone would jump at the chance to go out with you, if you asked."

"What can I say? It's a curse."

"What you can say is, tell me how to make some progress with Amy on this trip. That sign we just passed said we're only five miles away from Ashburn. Which means, we're all going to be pretty distracted in just a few minutes. I don't see how I can get anywhere with her until this trip is over."

"Maybe you can't," Whitney said. "But if you lower your expectations a little, I think there's still hope. For example, look for ways to be closer to her. But be subtle. Do it enough so she can tell it's on purpose. Like during the march, pay attention to where she walks and walk nearby. It won't be a good time to strike up a conversation, since we're there to protest against racism. You focus too much on her instead of the real reason you're there, she'll smell what you're up to and get turned off. Again, be subtle."

"I can do that."

"Then tomorrow, when we start organizing to go out in teams and start canvassing black neighborhoods, you know, trying to get them registered to vote...there's your next opportunity. Wait to find out which team she gets on then make your move. Get on the same team. Matter of fact, most of the time we're down here we'll be on those same teams doing the same thing. Seems like a guaranteed way to make some progress."

"That's a great idea," Mason said.

"But remember...the key is...subtlety. You're trying to reel her in slowly. Creating opportunities for her to get to know you a little better. That's all. I guarantee you, that's all it will take. She gets to know you better, finds out what a decent guy you are, the stage'll be all set."

"All set for what?"

"For you asking her out on the bus ride home."

Mason liked the sound of that. Wasn't sure he shared all of Whitney's optimism, but he hoped that's how things worked out. His infatuation with Amy inadvertently served another purpose. Kept him from worrying too much about what they were going to face today, and over the next few days, here in Mississippi.

It was funny in a way; his two best friends were both black and both very intelligent, but that was about all they had in common. As optimistic as Whitney tended to be, Roy was as equally pessimistic. Mason thought about the phone conversation he and Roy had last night.

Couldn't talk long, because it was long-distance. Mason had called all excited wanting to fill Roy in on everything that was happening on the eve of this historic bus ride today. Before he had even finished saying all he planned to say, Roy had interrupted him.

"Mason, Mason," he'd said, "promise me you're not getting on that bus tomorrow. Find some kind of reason to get out of it."

"Roy, what are you talking about?" Mason said. "I don't want to get out of it. We've been preparing for this for weeks now. Everything is all set."

"I guarantee you," Roy said, "they haven't prepared y'all for what you're really gonna face on that trip."

"Roy, please don't do this. Don't try to talk me out of it. That's not why I called. And I only have another minute or two before I gotta hang up."

"I'm sorry, Mason. I don't want to be so negative. But the kind of stuff I'm hearing? I can't be any other way. I know these buses are coming in all over Mississippi. But I've been hearing the Klan is getting all riled up to try and put a stop to it. Our whole church has started praying real hard. Pastor asked everyone to storm heaven on this, to protect y'all from any harm. But I'm sorry, when I pray it just fills me with fear. I'm fearing for your life, Mason. You and everyone on that bus."

"Well, I appreciate you praying," was all Mason could say. "I'm sure we're going to need it." And then his time ran out, and he had to hang up the phone.

Of course, he didn't mention a word of this to Whitney afterward. Wasn't like it would do any good. The plans were all set. Everything was in motion. And here they were, just two or three minutes away from Ashburn.

Which of his two black friends had a better bead on the outcome of the events about to unfold today?

He hoped it was Whitney.

26

B arely fifteen minutes after the bus had pulled into downtown Ashburn, Mason had his answer.

Roy, sadly, had it right.

Even as they exited the bus, white people were gathering in small groups on the sidewalks and around the intersection. Pointing, shaking their heads, expressions of disgust on their faces. At first, they were just talking amongst themselves. Then different ones began to yell out from the crowd, in every direction.

"Nobody wants you here!"

"Go back where you came from!"

"Why can't you leave things alone?"

"This is our town, go home!"

"You white Yankee kids are traitors to your race!"

Different ones started throwing in more colorful language, including racial slurs and profanity. Although Mason had heard worse things before, some from the mouths of his own family members, he had never seen so many people so angry, and all in such a small space.

And it wasn't just the men, women were joining in with just as much passion and volume. Some wearing their bright summer dresses, holding their shiny purses, wearing their white pearls, faces all twisted in rage.

"Remember your training everyone," said Dennis, one of the SNCC leaders. "Remember what the N in our name stands for!" Reminding them they were a Non-violent organization. "Everyone cross your arms and hold hands to form a chain, and don't yell anything back."

So they did, whites and blacks, girls and guys mingling together.

"Why don't we sing that last song we sang on the bus?" one of the girls said.

> *"We shall not, we shall not be moved.*
> *We shall not, we shall not be moved*
> *Like a tree, that's standing by the water.*
> *We shall not be moved."*

They sang just the chorus, several times in a row. Out there, maybe fueled by the passion of the moment, the group sang even louder than they did on the bus. And to Mason, they didn't sound half-bad.

People continued to yell out things, but after a while, the screamers quieted down a little. Some actually seemed to be listening. Many just started walking away.

At one point, Dennis came forward holding a slip of paper in his hand. He turned to the group and whispered,

"Keep singing, but..." then motioned with his hands for them to lower the volume.

"Citizens of Ashburn, we come to your town in peace," Dennis yelled out. "We mean you no harm, and we will cause you no trouble."

"You already have," someone shouted.

Dennis ignored it, kept talking. "We just believe that it is time for certain things to change. Not everything, just some things. I'm holding here in my hand the words to the speech by our late president, John F. Kennedy. Maybe some of you saw this on TV. He said these things almost one year ago, just five months before he was shot down in Dallas."

Mason noticed, for a few moments at least, everyone seemed to be listening.

Dennis held the paper up. "I won't read it all, just a few parts."

'This Nation was founded by men of many nations and backgrounds. It was founded on the principle that all men are created equal, and that the rights of every man are diminished when the rights of one man are threatened...It ought to be possible for American consumers of any color to receive equal service in places of public accommodation, such as hotels and restaurants and theaters and retail stores, without being forced to resort to demonstrations in the street, and it ought to be possible for American citizens of any color to register to vote in a free election without interference or fear of reprisal. It ought to be possible, in short, for every American to enjoy the privileges of being American without regard to his race or his color. In short, every American ought to have the right to be treated as

he would wish to be treated, as one would wish his children to
be treated.'

"Ladies and gentlemen of Ashburn. Our president died before he got to see this vision come to pass. That's all we're here for. That's all we're here to do. To take a stand for these very things the President talked about. We're just asking y'all to treat us as you would wish to be treated, as you would wish your children would be treated. That's all."

"He weren't my president!" someone yelled.

"I didn't vote for him," someone else said. "And I been a Democrat all my life."

"Good riddance, you ask me!"

Others yelled out similar things. But Mason noticed only a handful were yelling now compared to before. And many of their faces had softened, if just a little.

Dennis stepped back and turned to a few of the ladies standing near the back of the bus. "Okay, start passing out the signs. Just like we planned, we're gonna walk slowly down the center of the street toward the AME church a few blocks away. People are still going to yell and say hateful things, but don't you yell back. Just keep looking forward, eyes on the prize."

Mason tried to calm himself, remembering what Whitney had said on the bus ride down. They were supposedly getting light-duty coming to a town like Ashburn, compared to the way things were in places like Jackson, the state capitol and even some smaller towns where the Klan presence was the heaviest. Apparently, the sheriff in Ashburn had said publicly he wouldn't stand for any violence in his town, from the protestors or against them.

"Of course, there won't be any violence coming from us," Whitney had said. "So, we should be in the clear."

Then again, Mason thought, Whitney was always the optimist.

27

Boone glanced down at his watch as he drove along the rural highway that connected Tupelo with Ashburn, Mississippi. It was just a few minutes after eleven in the morning. He was sure the gang from Culpepper had already been in Ashburn for the better part of two hours, and equally sure they'd be wondering if he was ever going to show up.

A decision had been made to leave Culpepper last night around 1AM, which would put them in Ashburn at about breakfast time. That way they'd be all set to confront the Yankee college kids being bussed in that morning. Working through the Klan, Rufus had been able to secure guest houses for them to sleep in, since most of the men couldn't afford a several-night's stay at a motel.

The idea was, they'd spend the morning harassing the protesters. Then those who needed to could catch a nap in the afternoon. By then, Rufus would meet with the locals and find out what other kinds of activities they could do to help the cause.

Of course, Boone didn't have money troubles, so there was no way he was staying at no guest house. And though he'd driven all night with the caravan of cars from Culpepper, he had to drive alone in his pickup so he could split off from the pack when they made the turn south toward Ashburn.

That was on account of the obligation he had to fulfill for his father, dropping off that box of personal things his late mama wanted to give his Aunt Betsy. When he'd called her last evening to inform her of his plans, of course she was thrilled.

She had insisted Boone stay for a big breakfast at the farmhouse before getting back on the road. How could he say no to that? She was considered to be the best cook on his mother's entire side of the family.

And she'd certainly proved worthy of that honor this morning. Boone couldn't recall eating a breakfast so fine going back at least several years. It was mainly all that good eating and all that catching up on family gossip that was the reason he was racing down the road toward Ashburn now, and probably going to catch it from the guys when he arrived.

TWENTY-FIVE MINUTES LATER, he pulled into town. The first few streets he drove through seemed deserted. Finally found a fellow sticking some envelopes in his mailbox. Boone pulled his car off to the side, rolled the window down. "Excuse me, sir, this is the town of Ashburn, isn't it?"

"Sure is."

"Where is everybody?" Boone said. "You're the first person I've seen since I came off the highway."

"Oh, you keep on driving down this road. About three-quarter of a mile or so, you'll find the rest of the town. Never seen such a ruckus before. Apparently, a bunch of Yankee college kids arrived in a bus this morning. Everyone rushed off to go see 'em, mad as hornets. Guess they're here trying to straighten us out, or something."

"Why didn't you go on down there, too?"

"Did for a spell. But I figure ain't none of my business, either way. Besides, why would I want to pass up on all this peace and quiet 'round here?"

"Well, I better get down there," Boone said. "Thanks for the help." The man nodded and headed back toward his house. Boone headed down the road toward the center of town.

Sure enough, a few blocks later the houses gave way to small businesses and stores. A few blocks after that, Boone saw the crowd up ahead clogging up the street. He pulled his pickup into the first open parking place he found.

He got out of his truck and hurried toward the scene but was surprised to find things relatively quiet. He expected all kinds of shouts and angry chanting, coming from the locals as well as volunteers like him who'd been pressed into service by the Klan. Instead, it almost seemed like folks were standing around in groups waiting for a parade to start.

It took him a few moments but he spotted some familiar faces across the street. He saw Rufus, Josiah and even George Caldwell, the chicken farmer who, after hearing Boone had agreed to go, decided to make the trip. He told Boone his wife insisted he make the time for it, promising to look after things while he was gone. "This thing is too important to ignore," she'd said.

As Boone made his way across the street, he noticed everyone was looking the same way down toward the opposite end. He looked and realized what they were staring at. About four blocks up, a group of college kids was standing in the middle of the road, all of them holding picket signs with various slogans. He was too far away to read any of the words clearly, but it wasn't hard to guess the kind of crap messages they proclaimed.

As he approached, Rufus noticed him. "There you are, Boone. You finally made it."

"Glad you could join us," Josiah said sarcastically.

"I told you I had an errand to run in Tupelo," Boone said.

"Well, you're here now," Rufus said. "That's all that matters."

"What did I miss?"

"Not too much," Rufus said. "We came out of a diner up the road a ways just in time as their bus pulled in. The whole town came out to see. So many in fact, we could hardly see through the crowd. The college kids started singing some old Negro church song and folks started yelling things trying to drown them out. So, of course, we joined in on that. Then one of their leaders got up, gave a little speech. Couldn't hear most of what he said, but apparently, they're getting ready to march down the road here right through the center of town. So, we're going to do our civic duty, along with the rest of these good folks, and tell them where they can shove their Yankee ideas and ideals."

"Feel free to jump right in," Josiah said. Then he leaned

forward and whispered, "I got a bunch of rocks in my overall pocket. You can have some if you want."

Just then, Boone felt someone tugging on his sleeve. He turned and saw it was George Caldwell, a serious look of concern on his face.

"Hey Boone, come here a sec. Something I need to tell ya."

Boone followed George down a walkway behind a store, till they were almost in the next block. "What is it, George?"

"Now, you know how good my vision is, right? Don't quite recall what the numbers are, but I can see a squirrel on a branch from a hundred yards away, shoot the nut right out of his hands."

What in the world was George going on about? "I think I remember you saying something about that. So, what's that have to do with what you need to tell me?"

George looked around, made sure there was no one close enough to hear. "Now, I'm sure no one else saw this but me. And we was far enough away from that bus, and there was enough people in front of us to where I could have gotten this wrong. But I don't think I did."

"George, what are you trying to say? Just say it."

He looked around some more. "Boone, I don't know how to quite say it. And maybe I saw it wrong, but it looked like to me that your little brother Mason was among those college kids coming out of that bus."

"Mason?"

George nodded. "I can't be a hunnerd-percent sure it was him. Maybe it was just someone who looked a whole lot like him from this distance. But I thought I should tell you. You know, before those kids start marching down the street in front of everyone. Especially all the guys that came up here with us from Culpepper. If'n it was Mason, and I'm not saying a hunnerd-percent it was him, maybe more like ninety-five, but if'n it was him, I thought you'd like to get up there and see for yourself. You know, so you'd have time to fix things. You know?"

Boone suddenly felt like he'd swallowed a stone or someone punched him in the gut. "Thanks, George. I'm sure it ain't Mason. But I tell you what. Just to be sure, I'll go up and check, like you said."

"I think that's smart, Boone. If you want, you could head up this street here. I checked. Runs the same direction as the one they'll be marching down in a few minutes."

"Alright, George."

"I'll think up something to tell Rufus and the guys," George said.

"Appreciate it, George. Really. I'll make it up to you somehow."

Boone shook his hand and ran like the dickens up the road, hoping against hope he wouldn't find Mason when he got to the other end.

28

M ason was still nervous, despite all the encouragement from Whitney, Dennis and others. He envied the boldness of some in the group who talked openly about their willingness not only to be beaten but even to die for the cause.

He did care. Just not that much.

But of course, he kept such thoughts to himself. He especially didn't want Amy to see anything but confidence on his face.

He looked down the street. Curious onlookers still glared at them from the sidewalks, talking loudly among themselves about how wrong it was for these young northern intruders to come down here and disrupt their peaceful lives. But they seemed harmless enough, compared to the larger and angrier-looking crowd gathered at the end of the street. What were they doing down there? Were they waiting to ambush them when they finished the march?

The group hadn't started marching because they were waiting for some local clergymen to arrive. Two preachers had agreed to walk up front arm in arm with Dennis and the other leaders of their group. Mason had used the delay to work his way back in line next to Amy. She'd smiled at him warmly as he took his place by her side.

Then he remembered something Whitney had suggested. "Say Amy, how about we switch places? I think it would be better for a guy to be on the outside, closest to the sidewalk. Just in case any of these locals give us any trouble."

"Oh, okay Mason," she said. "Maybe that would be best. Thank you. Now that we're here, I'm actually feeling a little scared."

"You'll be all right. I won't let anything happen to you." He rested his hands on her shoulders as they changed spots. An unnecessary gesture, but it gave him a legitimate reason to touch her, so it was worth it. Whitney, in the line just ahead, heard the exchange, turned around and gave Mason an approving wink.

A few minutes later, Mason saw the local clergymen had arrived and got in place, standing on either side of Dennis. Dennis gave the signal and the group started marching slowly down the street.

Mason held up his sign, which read: "Give Everyone the Right to Vote!" Amy's sign said: "All Men are Created Equal!" Most of the signs said similar things. As they marched, Mason kept his gaze forward, so he wouldn't be intimidated by the hateful stares from the folks on the sidewalks.

They were just coming up to a small alleyway in between two buildings, when Mason caught a blur of activity in his peripheral vision on the right. Suddenly, someone grabbed his arm and shirt by the shoulder, then yanked him off his feet toward the sidewalk.

Amy screamed.

Whitney turned around, looked down at Mason now being dragged into the alley. "Leave him alone," he yelled. "He's not hurting anyone. This is a free country."

"Shut up boy and mind your own business."

Mason instantly recognized the voice.

BOONE COULDN'T BELIEVE IT. It was him. Marching right down the street with all these troublemakers for all to see. His stupid, useless kid brother.

Fortunately, Boone had gotten there in time.

"Boone, Boone, what are you doing? Let me go!"

"Shut up, Mason. Getting you out of here. What's it look like I'm doing?"

"Let me up."

Boone grabbed him by the shirt and, in one motion, lifted him up and slammed him against a wooden clapboard wall. "I can't believe you'd do something so stupid."

"It's not stupid. Now, let me down."

Boone lowered him to where his feet rested on the ground but still kept him pinned to the wall. "Do you have any idea the kind of trouble you're in. I can't believe it, marching in broad daylight with these...these..."

"These what?" Mason said. "These people are my friends."

"Your friends," Boone shouted. "Your friends?"

"Let go of me."

"Hey man, let him go."

Boone and Mason turned toward the voice. It was that same colored kid who'd mouthed off to Boone a moment ago in the street. Boone let go of Mason and walked toward him, pointed his finger in his face. "You best just turn around, boy. Get back there with your friends on that march, or I'll put you down right now where you stand."

The kid looked afraid but kept his stand. "I'll go, when you let go of my friend here, so he can join us."

Boone took a step closer to the kid. If he wanted some, he'd give him some.

"Whitney, stop. It's okay. This...he's my brother."

"What?"

"My brother. This guy's my brother, Boone."

"Your brother? But I thought you said no one in your family knew—"

"I thought no one in my family did know about this. Boone, what are you doing here?"

"What am I doing here? Apparently, saving your hide and keeping you from ruining our family's good name."

"What are you talking about?" Mason said. "Nobody knows I'm here from back home. How do you even know?"

"I'll tell you when this little colored boy goes back and joins the others. I ain't telling you our family business in front of him."

"You can go on, Whitney. I'll join you in a few minutes."

"Like heck you will," Boone said. "You're leaving with me...now. Before anyone else finds out what you've done."

"How is anyone else gonna find out?"

"Because Mason, you see that crowd down the end of the street? Well, there's about fifteen to twenty more folks from Culpepper mixed in there with them. The Klan put out a call asking folks from all over to come help stop all these Yankee college kids coming down here. Who would've guessed my own brother would be with them? Mr. Caldwell spotted you a few minutes ago, told me I better get up here in a hurry, before anyone else saw you."

"So Mason, you're really okay?" Whitney said.

"He's fine," Boone shouted.

"Yeah, I'm fine. But Boone, I can't go back with you now."

"Why not? You know what Daddy's gonna say the moment he hears about this. Your days at that Yankee college are over. For good."

MASON SIGHED. He knew Boone was right. "Even so, Boone, I can't just leave and go home with you now. All my stuff is back at the college. Even my car's back there. I came down here on a bus."

"Well Mason, I can't just leave you here like this. You have to go...now. Nobody else from town can see you here. Don't you get that?" He turned toward Whitney. "Would you just leave us, please? Nothing else we say here concerns you."

Whitney held up his hands in a gesture of concession. "I just needed to make sure your brother was okay."

"As you can see, he's fine."

Mason looked at his friend. "I don't know what I'm going to do, Whitney. But obviously, I won't be able to participate in the march anymore, or any of the other things you guys are gonna do down here. I'll get word to you somehow and let you know my plans."

"I'll tell you what your plans are, little brother. You are sneaking out of here and hitching a ride to the nearest town with a Greyhound bus station. You're going to go back to that Yankee school, gather up your things, get your car and get your tail back home where you belong."

29

After insisting Mason swear on their dead mother's grave that he would by no means rejoin the marchers, and that he would leave today and head back to his school, Boone hurried back and joined the rest of the Culpepper group. Before anyone started getting too curious about what he was up to.

He found them all, mostly together, shouting out appropriate comments and remarks to the marchers, who were now just a few blocks up the road. George Caldwell was the first to see him. He separated from the others before Boone got too close. "So, was it him? Was it your brother?"

"Thank God, but no, it wasn't. I can see why you thought it was. Found a kid up there who looked very similar. I even thought it was him till I got closer. But thanks for warning me anyway. That would've been mighty embarrassing if it had been him."

"Well, glad to hear it then," George said. "We better get back to the group."

"What did you tell them, about why I left so quick?"

"Told them you remembered your Pa asked you to call him as soon as you got into Ashburn. Seemed to work okay."

"Thanks again, George. Now let's go give these Yankee kids what for."

WITH EACH STEP, Mason sunk into a deeper depression. He couldn't believe what just happened. Of all the things he feared might happen, he never imagined something like this. He'd have rather been spit on or beaten up by the angry mob.

How in the world, of all places, could he have picked the one town in Mississippi where his brother would come? Boone almost never left Culpepper. And when he did, at the most he'd travel one or two counties away to pick up some building supplies.

Never two states away.

But he did come. And this did happen. And now Mason's life, and all his future plans, had just been destroyed. Boone was right. Daddy would never let him stay at the University of Maryland, not for a single day more. If he even let Mason keep going to college, he'd make sure it would be a proper southern school with proper and traditional Southern values.

Which meant, of course, a college where every professor was a true believer in the southern cause, in the inherent superiority of the white race and the inherent inferiority of Negroes. Where everyone believed in segregation as a God-given mandate. Mason would never have another enlightened conversation with young people his own age who believed what he believed. Instead, he'd have to sit there in class, in whatever school he ended up in, and listen to utter nonsense being spewed from the mouths of teachers and students alike.

How could he do it? It would be unbearable. But he knew what the alternative would be if he didn't cooperate. He'd be instantly cut off from the family finances.

He reached the block where the bus had been parked. All this time, he had been walking down the same street where the confrontation with Boone occurred, one block in from the alley. So, he would avoid any possibility of running into anyone from Culpepper.

He saw the bus up ahead, headed for it. Still unsure of what to do once he got there. When he got to the bus, the driver was sitting there reading a book. He was startled by Mason's sudden appearance. Mason motioned for him to let him enter, and he opened the door.

"They asked me to wait here to keep an eye on things," the driver said. He was actually a part of their group.

"I'm just here to get my things."

"Leaving us so soon? Hey, that's okay. It's pretty scary being down here. And from what I hear, this is one of the better towns in Mississippi."

Mason stepped up into the bus. "No, it's not that. Well, I agree. It is pretty scary being around all this hate. But that's not why I'm leaving." Well, in a way, Mason thought, he was leaving because of hate. "I just got word about a family emergency, guess you could say. I'm needed back home right away."

"You want me to tell Dennis for you? You know he wants to keep close tabs on everyone while we're down here."

"Yeah, would you? Whitney knows about it too. But it can't hurt to have you let him know, in case Whitney forgets."

"Will do."

Mason headed back to his seat, gathered up his things, then headed back toward the front. As he did, he saw Whitney coming up on the side of the bus toward the front door. They waved. Mason pointed to the door, saying he would meet him there.

When he got off, Whitney said, "Had a feeling you'd be leaving pretty quick after that scene back there with your brother."

"Is the march over?"

"Not quite, but I just ducked out of there. I was worried about you, man. You told me a little about your family situation. But seeing it up close, made me realize what you've been dealing with. I'm really sorry."

"Yeah, well me too. But there's nothing can be done about it. It is what it is."

"So, are you really leaving? I don't just mean Mississippi and what we're doing this week. I'm talking about leaving school and heading back home to Georgia."

"I don't really have a choice. So, yeah. That's the plan."

Whitney looked down, shook his head. "That really stinks, man. I mean, after all the talks we've had. I know you're seeing things clearly now. The way things really are, the things that need to change. You believe in this, Mason. In all of it. I know you do."

"Of course I do. I'm hating what's happening here. I can't believe I have to go back to all that. But I've got no choice. I just finished my freshman year. The grand plan was to save up as much money as I could during school, get a great job after I graduate, and then make a clean break with the family. But I can't afford to do that now. It's too soon."

"Well maybe," Whitney said. "Maybe not."

"What do you mean?"

"I don't have it all figured out yet, but I'm already thinking about an alternative. Just do me a favor, I know you got to leave here now, but don't leave Maryland and head back home till I get back up there."

"Whitney, I can't wait that long. You guys are going to be down here at least a week. Boone is going to tell my dad what's happened the first chance he gets. They're going to expect me back home in—"

"Two days," Whitney said. "That's all I'm asking. Two days. Dennis knows I can't be here the whole week. I was heading back in two days anyway. Just don't leave till I get back, and we can talk."

"Okay, I guess I can wait till then."

30

The Next Day – Late Evening
Culpepper, GA

Boone pulled into the long driveway leading to the Big House. It had been a long day, spent driving back from Ashburn. Of course, Rufus was upset with him for cutting out early. The rest of the Culpepper men were still there doing their level best to harass, heckle and cause all manner of trouble for the troublemaking Yankee college kids. Truth be told, Boone would have much rather stayed with them.

But this thing with Mason was too hot a potato to hold on to any longer, and it wasn't the kind of thing he could tell Daddy about over the phone. He had called to let him know that he had taken care of the errand he'd been given with Aunt Betsy and had met up with the guys in Ashburn. But that something pretty serious had come up, and he was cutting his trip short. He'd be heading for home first thing this morning.

Daddy, of course, wanted to hear more detail. "I'll tell you when I see you. Has to do with Mason," was all Boone had said.

He pulled his pickup as close to the front porch as he dared, shut it down and got out. Daddy must've heard him coming. The front door opened before Boone had cleared the steps.

"Thought it was you," Daddy said. The screen door slapped behind him.

"You can have a seat out here, if you want to talk right away," Boone said. "I'll be back out directly. I've had to use the john for the last sixty miles."

"Well, don't keep me waiting out here long."

"I won't."

Boone did what he had to, grabbed himself a cold glass of tea from the icebox and joined Daddy on the porch.

"You bring me one?" Daddy was pointing at Boone's iced tea.

"Here." Boone handed him his, hurried back to fetch another. Changed his mind when he opened the icebox and grabbed a cold beer instead.

Back on the porch, Daddy started off before Boone had even taken his seat. "Now, what's all this about Mason? And why would he have anything to do with you cutting your trip short in Mississippi?"

Boone took a nice strong pull from the beer. "Well, as it turns out, he had everything to do with my trip getting cut short. You're not going to believe what happened when I tell you. I can still hardly believe it myself. I know you like to always say how smart Mason is, and how he's the one with the superior intellect, and I'm the one with all the ambition and drive." Which to Boone was just his father's way of implying Boone was the stupid one.

"But after you hear what I'm about to tell you, Daddy I think you're gonna have to revise your very high opinion of Mason and your much lower opinion of me."

"Boone, whatever are you talking about, son? Would you just stop with the riddles and tell me what happened?"

"Okay, I'll get right to it then. Guess who I found in Ashburn when I got there? Well, actually it was George Caldwell who found him first. Good thing it was George instead of Rufus or Josiah, or one of the others. Else we might have a whole 'nother firestorm to be dealing with."

Daddy sat up straight in his chair, set his iced tea down on a table. "You're telling me Mason was there—our Mason —in Ashburn?"

Boone nodded. "That's exactly what I'm telling you. And that ain't the worst of it. He weren't there just playing hooky from summer school. He was actually there marching with all the other white Yankee kids who came down on that bus. Marching arm in arm with all the colored college kids, too. All of them holding signs saying how wrong we all are here in the South, and how we need to end segregation and give these poor Negroes the right to vote."

The look on Daddy's face made the long hard road trip worth it all. His jaw dropped, his mouth hung open, and his eyes were bugging out. Boone might just as well have hit him upside the head with a broomstick. "Finally," he said, "I can't believe it. My God, I just can't believe it."

"Believe it, Daddy. Saw it for myself. And like I said, if it weren't for good ole George, this situation would have been ten times worse."

Daddy sighed. "What did George do?"

"He saved our hides, is what he done. As you know, I arrived late to the party, on account of that errand with Aunt Betsy. The college kids were all gathered at one end of the main street, and all us Culpepper men were down the other, mingled in with local folks. George has got that eagle vision going on and he spots Mason way up the street with these kids. So, when I get there he pulls me aside, tells me what he saw. I hurry up there just as the marching starts. And sure enough, there's Mason right in there with them."

"My God. Lord help us," Daddy said.

"That's right, God help us. And I guess he did, because I was able to yank him off that street down some alley before anyone else saw him."

Daddy let out some more sighs and groans.

"It took all my strength," Boone said, "not to beat him senseless. But I did give him a proper whupping with my words."

"What did he say?" Daddy asked. "No, I don't want to know what he said. Doesn't matter what he said. Just him being there with that bunch tells me everything I need to know." He banged the armrest with his fist. "I knew I shouldn't have sent him to that Yankee school in Maryland. I knew it."

You knew no such thing, Boone thought. I must've warned you a dozen times about doing that, and each and every time you blew me off.

"Well, I figured you'd want him to leave that school right away. So, that's what I told him."

"Dang right, I want him out of that school. I don't want him there another day, and I'm not paying them another dollar of my hard-earned money."

"At first, I told him he had to come home with me right then, but he pointed out that he'd gotten there on a bus and all his things were up at that school, including his car. So, I told him he needed to leave Mississippi right away before anyone else saw him, and get back up there, get his things and get back home ASAP."

No one said anything else for a few moments. Really, what else was there to say? Boone took another few sips of his beer, looked at Daddy, trying to figure out what was clicking in that head of his. All he knew was, his own net worth in the family situation had ticked up considerably, while Mason's had rightly plummeted. Finally, a terrible injustice had been corrected. A wrong situation had finally been made right.

Daddy looked up, held out his hand. "You done good, son. Real good."

Boone shook his father's hand. "Thank you, Daddy."

"Oh, what about George Caldwell? How did you handle him? You say he saw Mason with all them kids getting ready to march."

"George's a good guy. A decent man. He understands the value of family. I thanked him right off, went up to see about Mason for myself. When I came back, I said it wasn't him, just some kid who looked a lot like him from a distance."

"Think he believed you?"

"I don't think so, though he acted like he did. But that'll be the end of it with George. He won't tell a soul."

"I think you're right," Daddy said. "But still, a deed like

that needs repaying. You think of a nice way to say thank you proper."

"I will, Daddy."

"While I think of a way to deal a good dose of retribution to your little brother."

31

THE PRESENT
8PM Monday Evening - Culpepper, GA

Joe had just gotten comfy in his recliner, remote in one hand, Diet Pepsi in the other, when his phone rang.

"Don't get it, Joe," Kate said from her favorite side of the sofa. "You gave them enough hours today. The movie is all set to watch."

Joe's heart was with Kate, but his head turned and his eyes looked down at the screen. "It's not work. It's Jack."

"Jack? Well, I guess you guys never talk that long. But don't get distracted. I'm sitting here with the screen on pause."

"I'll be quick." Joe picked up the phone and answered it as he got out of the chair. "Hey Jack, how's it going?" He started moving into the dining room where he could hear a little better.

"Hi, Joe. Going pretty good. I guess."

"You guess? Everything okay with Rachel?"

"She's fine. She's right here, in fact. We're not home. We're out at the lake house."

"Now? I thought you weren't getting back there till the weekend."

"That was the idea. But this mystery-message thing started getting to both of us, so we thought we'd come out here after dinner, while it was still light out."

Joe glanced out the window. "Pretty dark out there now."

"Right. Same here."

"Well, it would be Jack. Seeing as you guys are only about twenty minutes from here."

Jack laughed. "Right, I wasn't thinking."

"You calling me now can only mean one thing. What did you find?"

He heard Jack sigh. "You remember my next task was to check the studs up in the attic? Well, Rachel thought we should go ahead and do the downstairs bedroom, since the paneling was so ugly. So, that's what we came out here to do. After I got it all off, she held the flashlight while I took pictures of the boards that had letters carved on them."

"So, you found some more then? How many?"

"Five. We sat down with the pics on my tablet. Moved them all around till they made sense."

"Let me guess...you got some more words for the message?" Whatever they were, Joe thought, they were serious enough for Jack to call Joe at home.

"Yeah. It's like that saying, *the plot thickens*. We added two more lines of words. Don't think this is the complete message yet. But putting the new lines together with the ones we already found...Joe, it's looking pretty bad now. Like something pretty serious went down here."

"Why don't you read them to me?"

"Okay. I'm going to read them as one continuous string. There's clearly some missing lines in between. But you'll get the idea right off the bat. The message now reads:

HELP

ME. I'M CHAINED UP

VERY DARK. HARD TO

SEE. MY NAME IS

IF I GO MISSING

I AM PROBABLY DEAD"

"Yeah," Joe said. "That turns up the heat a few degrees for sure. And that was from just doing the one bedroom?"

"Yep. Kinda makes you wonder, doesn't it?"

"About the rest of the house?"

"Yeah," Jack said. "That."

"What are you and Rachel thinking? About that, I mean."

"We haven't talked about it yet. But it turns out, I'm not the only one revved up about this case. I wouldn't be out here on a Monday night if she weren't just as curious."

"Well, clearly, there's more to the message. What was that one line...*My Name Is*?"

"Yeah. Means his name—the name of the guy chained up —is likely scratched onto one of these other 2 x 4's we haven't gotten to yet."

"Jack, you do realize how critical that piece of information is to solving this riddle?"

"Yeah, I do. I think we both do." Jack didn't say anything for a moment.

"You okay with this? You need some time to talk things over with Rachel?"

"I might. Wait a minute, she's nodding her head."

Joe heard them talking.

"She's figured out where this conversation is going, but she reminded me we don't have to start tearing perfectly good wallboard off the other walls."

"Why's that?"

"We still haven't done the attic. And it's unfinished. All the studs up there are already exposed. She's saying I should start with that. Maybe I'll uncover enough of the message doing that, that we could skip doing the rest of the downstairs."

"She's got a point, Jack."

"And I just thought of something else."

"What's that?"

"I was planning on going over to the library tomorrow on my lunch hour, do a little snooping through the old newspaper microfilms they've got. But now I'm thinking that checking out the attic studs should be the priority."

"I agree," Joe said. "Even though, I have no idea what you're going to do with the old newspapers. But if we can uncover this guy's name, that would be—"

"Yeah, that's what I'll do. Do you think maybe you could do the newspaper idea?"

"I'm sure I can, if you tell me what you're thinking. I was going to do some snooping of my own tomorrow. Already found out when the date permits were pulled on your place, and by who. It was in May 1964 by a construction company that's since gone out of business, Rhodes Construction. But having that date, I can go through our files and find out if we had any missing persons reported between then and a few months after. Figuring it takes a few months to build a house from scratch."

"I guess we were thinking along the same lines," Jack said. "My idea for the newspaper thing was to first get the date from you, then go down and look at all the local newspapers in and around that time. See if there were any news stories about someone going missing from this area. If so, we'd have the guy's name."

"That's good thinking, Jack. Maybe I'll do both things, your idea and mine. See what turns up. You think you could call me tomorrow and explain how to work that microfilm thing at the library? Never had a reason to do that before. But it might come in handy, not just in this case but in others, now that I'm working on these cold case files."

"I could explain it to you right now," Jack said. "It's not that complicated."

"Yeah, but see, I got Kate sitting in the other room waiting on me, so we can start this movie."

Jack laughed. "Okay, I get that. Don't want to be the cause of a domestic abuse situation."

Now Joe laughed.

"Anything else you want me to do?" Jack said.

"Yeah, if you don't mind...could you take a few minutes while things are fresh and jot down everything you've been telling me about this case? What's already been uncovered and how. Any of the details you can think of. With this new information you guys found tonight, I'm officially making this the first official homicide investigation of the Culpepper Cold Case Squad. I'll need all this information for the file. Hank will want to see it, too."

"Sure thing, Joe."

32

June 16th, 1964
University of Maryland

This had been the second day since Mason's nightmare began in Mississippi. He was in no hurry to face his dad. He'd done as Boone demanded; went to the nearest Greyhound station and took a bus back up here to the University of Maryland. That took up most of the first day. Since then, he'd pretty much just stayed in his dorm room. There really wasn't anyone to talk to. Summer school classes hadn't begun yet, and all his school friends had been on that bus and were still down in Mississippi. Except for a smattering of students stuck at the school like him, the campus felt pretty empty.

He'd been expecting Whitney to arrive anytime now. He'd called the dorm office a few hours ago, left a message that said: "Making good time on the road. Left pretty early. Should get there by six."

It was almost six now.

The only other communication he'd had were two messages from his father, both asking him to call home right away. Mason ignored them. If he'd called home, he already knew what he'd be told. *You better do what your brother said and get home right away.* It's not like he could ask permission to wait until he had time to hear what Whitney had to say. And he'd already told Whitney he'd wait till he got back.

So, he ignored the calls. What more could they do to him than what they'd already done? His future was over. All his plans destroyed. His one chance to break free from the stranglehold of the Rhodes' legacy was gone.

A knock on his door. "Hey Mason, it's Ralph. That colored friend of yours is in a car parked on the curb by the front door. He asked me to tell you he was here. Said you'd want to know."

"Thanks, Ralph," Mason yelled through the door. "I'll be right down."

Mason got up. Took a deep breath, tried to get himself together. He had no idea what Whitney wanted to say. Couldn't imagine he'd have come up with anything that would improve the situation at all. He opened the door and headed down the hall for the stairs.

He found Whitney right where Ralph said, sitting in the front seat of his blue, '55 Chevy. He waved. Whitney motioned for him to get in the car. "You just get into town?" Mason said, as he slid into the passenger seat and closed the car door.

"Just this very minute. I'm starving. Mind if we eat at the diner we always go to, across the street from my school?"

"Fine with me."

Whitney put the car in drive and headed down the road. "You really missed the show, leaving when you did."

"What do you mean? Things get pretty rough down there?"

"I guess you could say they did, relatively speaking. But sounds like we got off easy compared to some, listening to the war stories Dennis shared with us last night. We only got yelled at, cursed at and spat on. Some of our folks in other places got dogs turned on them, fire hoses sprayed on them, beat up with sticks and bats."

"You're kidding? No, of course you're not kidding. Didn't the police intervene?"

Whitney made a face. "Mason, I've told you, the police were leading the charge. Whatever good they might do elsewhere, they are not part of the solution in Mississippi, or in most of the South. To them, Jim Crow is the law of the land, and they're just upholding it."

Mason immediately recalled his friend Roy's warnings back in Culpepper.

"Some of what happened might even have made the nightly news. Dennis said there were journalists down there from the major networks filming some of it."

"I wouldn't have seen it. We don't have a TV in our dorm room, and I haven't been watching the news. So, how are our guys doing there in Ashburn? People getting kind of scared?"

"You mean, more scared? I'd say the answer is a definite yes. We are certainly striking a sour note with those folks down there. But hopefully, things will get a little less intense as we shift from the public protest marching to getting with the local colored folks in the neighborhoods. I'm guessing not too many of these white folks hang out where the Negroes live."

Mason found it interesting to hear how Whitney referred to his own people, sometimes as "colored," other times as Negroes. Colored was the slang term most often used by non-racist whites and even many blacks, but Dennis said he and the other civil rights leaders were trying to get the term *Negroes* to replace colored.

"Tell you one thing that kind of surprised me," Whitney said. "I didn't much see your brother after that morning when he grabbed you. Is he still there?"

"I doubt it. I'm pretty sure after he found out about me, he headed home quick as a jackrabbit. I can't see him talking about something like that on long distance. He'd have wanted to be there to tell my father the details, face to face. And I know my father knows all about it. He's already sending me threatening messages. I'm doomed, Whitney. I'm telling you, my life is over."

Whitney didn't offer his expected quick encouraging comeback.

"So, you agree then?"

"In a way, I guess I do. But not in the way you mean."

"What are you talking about? What way are you seeing it?"

"Like I told you before you left, I wanted some time to think about all this. And that's what I did, for most of the car ride back up here. The way I see it, Mason, your life is over. But I'm talking about your old life, the one you've always known till two days ago. The one where you are, basically, living a lie, pretending to be someone you're not. Or at least, not anymore. Your last name is Rhodes. And you do come from a long line of, well, white southern racists. But somehow, in the midst of all that, you managed to break free. At least on the inside, where it counts. I knew you were different from the first time we met. You see it. You get it. And now that you've had all this time with all these other people who see things the same way, your eyes are open even more than they were before. You can't go back there, Mason. Not to that old life you been living. It would eat you up inside, tear you apart, little by little. Can't you see that?"

He did see it. Everything Whitney was saying. But thinking about it didn't fill him with boldness. It filled him with fear. "I have to go back, Whitney. I don't want to. I have to. Even though I agree with everything you're saying. I don't have any choice. I've saved up maybe a few thousand dollars so far. I'm going to need a lot more than that to start a new life that doesn't depend on my family. You're used to..."

"What...being poor? Yeah, you're right. We never had a lot of money. In fact, I'm only attending college because of a scholarship. Without that, I'm working in a factory somewhere, not studying medicine."

"See?" Mason said. "Even there, without my family's money, I can't even finish college. I don't have good enough grades for a scholarship."

"Maybe so, Mason. But there's lots of options to consider. You could work your way through school. You couldn't go to an expensive college like Maryland, but there's plenty of decent colleges that cost thousands less per year. That's what lots of my friends are doing, the ones going to school. They don't have scholarships. They work full time, go to school part-time. Might take a little longer, but it can be done. If you're willing to work hard enough. See, that's the thing I'm trying to get you to see. You have to work at this. You've got to want to make it work. But if you're willing, you have lots of friends who'll help. Starting with me. I'll help you any way I can."

Mason wanted to believe this, to latch on to what Whitney was saying and keep holding on till he believed it deep down inside. "Seriously Whitney, what can you do for me besides being a good friend?"

"Well, how's this? For starters, I drive down with you to Culpepper. You sneak in there, get your money and anything else you care about, and sneak back out. We drive back up here together, and I help you start to put things together for that great big new life waiting for you just down the road."

"Really? You'd do that?"

Whitney nodded.

"But we'd have to leave tomorrow," Mason said.

"Then we'll leave tomorrow."

33

"Confound it, that's the third day in a row your little brother hasn't returned my calls." Judson Rhodes slammed the receiver back on the telephone. "What do you think he's up to? He wouldn't run away, or nothing, would he?"

Boone lit a cigarette. "Mason? There's no chance he'd do that. Where would he go? He's got no money. And he's never been the adventurous type anyway."

"Then why ain't he returning my calls? And put that cigarette out, or else take it outside. You know I can't stand the smell of those things."

Boone did as he was told, stuffed the cigarette out in an ashtray. "Ain't it obvious, Daddy? He ain't called, because he knows he's in serious trouble this time. It's as simple as that. He'll either be calling soon or show up down the driveway anytime now. You watch."

"Well, he better be. The more time goes on, the madder I get."

.   .   .

Mason and Whitney had been on the road, riding in Mason's car, for two hours so far, traveling as often as they could on sections of the new interstate highway, called I-95. Whitney had picked up a map that showed all the latest completed sections. Someday, it would run in one continuous, unbroken string from Maine to Florida. Now, you had to drive on it in bits and pieces: four miles here, seventeen miles there. Then you'd have to take a ramp off and follow the signs through the state and county roads until the next section of the interstate picked up again.

But to Mason, it was worth the hassle. For two reasons. He got to drive much faster on the new highway without stopping for red lights. And second, on the highway he didn't feel near as self-conscious sitting in a car next to a Negro. Of course, he wouldn't have minded driving with Whitney all over creation. It was the other people on the road who had a problem with it. And he knew it would only get worse the further south they drove.

"Looks like we're going to have to get off again about a mile up ahead," Whitney said, looking at the map. "And not too far down the road after that, we'll cross into North Carolina. We're making good time."

North Carolina, Mason thought. He'd been seriously thinking of an idea, pretty much since he'd noticed certain people staring at their car when they passed. Now was as good a time as any to bring it up. "Say Whitney, have you been noticing...the way people are staring at us on the road? Because I have."

"I have, but I mostly try not to let it get to me. Maybe

they're just curious. You know, this whole Freedom Summer thing we've been working on's been making the TV news. Maybe they see us and wonder if we're part of it."

"Maybe. Whatever it is, I don't have a problem with it, the stares I mean. Not on a personal level anyway. I could care less what these bigots think about me. You know that. But there's another level to consider, and I've been thinking about it pretty often for the last hour or so." Really, every new fresh set of stares reminded him.

"What's that?"

"The personal safety level, I guess you could call it. On the interstate—when we do get to drive on it—I don't feel it so much. But you see the map...this thing stays broken up all the way into Georgia, where I live. Folks there and in the Carolinas, for that matter, can be almost as bad as folks in Mississippi. You know, on the segregation thing. We get on some of these lonely country roads, you know, after driving through some small, redneck town...after some good ole boys spy you and me sitting together in the same car, they could come after us. And it could get pretty ugly. For both of us."

Whitney set the map down on his lap. "The ramp is just up ahead. See the turnoff sign? Anyway, I can see your point. Not being from the South I guess I don't tend to think of things like that. But after what I saw just those two days in Mississippi...yeah, I can see that very thing happening. So, what do you suggest?"

"Well, I do have an idea, but I don't think you're going to like it. But I really think it's for our own good, so we make it all way down to Culpepper in one piece."

"Okay, I'm listening."

"I think...and we only have to do this idea when we're driving through populated areas. We can do like we're doing now whenever we're on the interstate, or we know we have miles in between the next town on a country road."

"Just say it, Mason. Whatever it is. Although, I think I can probably guess."

"I think you ought to hide in the back seat. And we cover you with a blanket. Just through these redneck towns."

"That's better than what I was thinking. I thought you were going to say I need to get in the trunk."

"No, I don't think that's necessary. I'll be driving the speed limit the entire time. I'm not worried about anybody stopping us to search the car. It's just, as we drive by, you know, through these redneck places, it would be better if when white people looked our way they just saw me, making my way through town. No stares. No fuss. Just a white college kid on a road trip back home. Then when the coast is clear, I'll give you the signal, and you hop back into the front seat. You okay with that?"

"Yeah, guess I have to be. It's a shame we even have to think of such a thing, but I know it makes sense. So yeah, let's do it."

Mason veered to the right, took the off-ramp toward the county road listed on the sign. And there's one other thing I've been thinking about, pretty much all morning."

"What's that?"

"When we stop for gas in this next town, I'm thinking I need to call home, let them know I'm coming."

"What, Mason? No, don't do that."

"Wait a sec, hear me out. I'm not changing the plan. Not completely. But I've been thinking, it just wouldn't make sense for me not to return my father's phone calls. Not for three days. I wouldn't put it past him to even file a missing persons' report on me."

"So, what's your new plan?"

They reached the bottom of the ramp. Good. No cars in sight in either direction. "The new plan is just to give them a quick call, apologize for the delay, then tell them I'm still coming but it will be a few more days, because my car broke down, and they had to order the part. That way, it will deflect some of the heat. And they won't be waiting around for me to arrive later this evening, but in a few days. Should make it even easier to get in there tonight without being detected."

Whitney didn't immediately reply.

"So, what do you think?"

"I think you're getting pretty good at this stuff."

"Good, glad you agree. Now hop in the backseat and get under a blanket. We'll be driving through a small town two miles up ahead."

34

They'd been driving all day. Both young men were pretty tired. The heat played a good part of it; it was always stifling in the South in mid-June. But the tension they'd felt from the danger they were in played a greater role. It intensified ever since that moment several hours ago, after they'd gotten off a section of I-95 in South Carolina and had to ride through one of those small, redneck towns. Whitney had hopped into the back seat and covered himself up with the blanket, but as they came to the town's one traffic light, Mason glanced over his shoulder and noticed Whitney's shoes were showing.

To make things worse, they'd stopped beside a red pickup truck full of white farm boys. Some of the guys in the back started heckling Mason, poking fun at him apparently for the way he was dressed. Saying things like: "Ain't you dressed real purty?" and "You must be one of them college boys," and "bet he never did an honest day's work in his life."

Mason just stared straight ahead and couldn't wait for the light to turn green.

Fortunately, his car easily pulled well ahead of the truck and none of them seemed to notice Whitney's shoes sticking out from under the blanket. He was so relieved when he saw the truck of rednecks turn left in his rearview mirror. But it really drove home the point that they had better watch their step for the rest of the long drive to Culpepper.

They finally reached the Culpepper city limits at about 8:30 PM. It still wasn't fully dark out then, but the sun had gone down quite a while ago, cooling things off. And now that they were in town, Mason told Whitney he could hop back in the front seat.

"You sure?" Whitney said. "I'd be thinking you'd want me to stay back here, so none of the folks who know you would see us together."

"I don't want the white folks who know me to see us together, or even see me, for that matter. I'm supposed to be sneaking back into town, remember? But see, I know this town like the back of my hand and I came in through the colored section of town. That's where we are now, so the coast is clear. They're not going to care about seeing you and me together."

Whitney sat up, set the blanket aside and hopped into the front seat. "How far are we from your place?"

"Couple of miles maybe. But we're not going there right off. Well, you're not going there at all. I'm going to go myself, but first, we got a stop to make."

"I'm not going there at all? Then where am I going?"

"That's why we're making a stop. The last hour or so I've been thinking this through. You know, how to make this thing work. And I was thinking, you'd be the safest and draw the least amount of attention if you stayed in the colored section of Culpepper the whole time we're here."

"That's a pretty smart idea," Whitney said. "But how are you going to sneak back to your house after you drop me off? Aren't folks around there gonna recognize you and your car? And where you going to drop me off exactly? This looks like a pretty small town. I'm guessing even amongst the Negroes everybody knows everybody. Won't they be trying to figure out what I'm doing here walking around their neighborhood at night?"

"They would, if that's what you were doing. But I'm going to drop you off at my friend Roy's house. I'm not sure he's even there now, but his mother Maisie will be. She's worked at our house my whole life. One of the finest ladies I know. She'll take good care of you till I'm back from my little adventure. And as far as folks recognizing my car when I get close to my house? We've got several hundred acres around our plantation house, and all kinds of back roads I can drive on between here and there. And, it's gonna be plenty dark out in no time at all, so I'll be just fine." He turned at a stop sign. "This is their street."

As Mason drove down the poorly-kept road, he was freshly reminded of the shocking disparity between the white and colored sections of town, especially here in the neighborhoods. He had been here more times than he could count, but seeing it again, for some reason, made him feel ashamed. Tiny dilapidated shanties, all in need of fresh paint and significant repairs. But who in this neighborhood had the money for such things? Where would they ever get it? When would they ever get it?

The system, as is, had been created to keep them "in their place." What place was that? This place, which was anything but "separate but equal." That's why he was coming back here for the last time. That's why he was going to go through with this. Things had to change, and they'd never change if people like him lacked the courage to oppose it.

"Here it is," Mason said. "And there's Maisie rocking on the porch." He eased his car into the two ruts which passed for their driveway.

Maisie stood, noticed Mason getting out of the car and was startled to see him.

"It's really me, Maisie. And this here is Whitney, my friend from up north. Could we chat just a minute inside? I'll explain why we're here."

"That'd be fine, Mason." She opened the screen door. "I was just out here trying to catch more this nighttime breeze. You know, Roy ain't here at the moment. He's out with some friends. Probably be gone a few hours or so."

"I kind of figured I'd miss him coming here now. But that's okay. I'm really here to see you."

"Me? Okay then."

All three of them stepped inside. Mason noticed Whitney looking around at the sparse interior, obviously not used to seeing poverty of this kind up close.

"You boys have a seat. Can I get you something to drink?"

"No thanks, Maisie. I'm going to be leaving in a few minutes. But Whitney here might like something."

"I'm fine, thanks."

"Okay then. So, what's this all about?" She sat in her usual chair.

"I have a favor to ask. I don't have time to explain all the details. But I will call Roy at some point in the next few days and explain everything to him. The bottom line is...I'm leaving Maisie. I can't stay living in the Big House anymore. That's all I can say for now. My plan is, to sneak back to the house right now, get some things I need together. Then I'll come back to fetch Whitney. At most, I should be gone an hour. Probably less. Would it be okay if he stays here till I return?"

"He can stay as long as he likes," she said. "You said you're going to be sneaking back to the house? I was in another room today when you called your Daddy. Figured from what he said to Boone you wouldn't be coming home for a couple more days. He was mighty upset with you. Madder than I seen him in quite a spell. That why you're sneaking in?"

"Something to do with that," Mason said. "I'd really like to tell you more, but I should get going. Like I said, I will tell Roy everything that's going on and I'll make sure to tell him to share with you the whole scoop. It's really a good thing, even though I'm being sneaky. You'll see what I mean when you hear the whole story. If you want, feel free to ask Whitney anything you like. He knows most of the story." He gave her a hug and, as she hugged back, he found himself suddenly overcome with emotion. She'd been like a second mother to him, and now he wasn't sure when he would see her again after tonight.

"You okay, Mason?" she asked, as they let go of each other.

"I'll be fine, Maisie. After tonight, better than fine." He turned to Whitney. "I'll be back to get you soon. Like I said, probably take less than an hour."

35

THE PRESENT
Lunchtime, Tuesday - Culpepper, GA

One of the privileges of being Dean of the military history department was that Jack didn't actually have any classes to teach anymore. Well, on a regular basis. So, he was able to maneuver some things around that morning and buy himself a two-hour lunch break. He'd gotten up a little earlier, so he could hammer out that report Joe had asked him to do last night; the one laying out his and Rachel's part in the investigation. So far, an easy-to-read timeline of events.

Jack sent it off to Joe and Hank before kissing Rachel goodbye and heading off to work. They were both disappointed that Rachel couldn't join him on his little lunch break excursion. She had already agreed to have lunch with her mom, to talk and plan out baby things. They didn't get enough time together, as it is, and neither Jack nor Rachel felt this task was worthy of postponing the visit. It was easier if Rachel held the flashlight, but Jack could manage on his own.

The drive to the lake house was five minutes shorter from the school. Jack pulled up near the front porch, grabbed a backpack containing a change of clothes and headed inside. He'd already eaten lunch, grabbed a Chick-fil-A sandwich on the way out of town. He changed into a T-shirt and jeans in what would soon be the master bedroom, grabbed the backpack again and headed upstairs.

Since Rachel wouldn't be there to hold the light, Jack brought this super-bright halogen lantern he'd picked up on the internet. It was this nifty little thing made of some fancy alloy. It didn't look like a lantern, more like a small, shiny metal cube. You pulled the top half from the bottom half and the tubular bulbs inside instantly lit up. He figured when he found boards with carved letters, he could set the lantern on a box close to the same position when Rachel held the flash-light and still be able to see the letters on the studs.

Once upstairs, Jack realized that while the three dormers did provide a good bit of sunlight in the attic, it was about half the amount that came in downstairs. But as soon as he got that new high-tech lantern going, all his lighting concerns quickly faded. The first ten studs were blank, just ordinary 2 x 4's. He was beginning to wonder if the attic had been built with a different stack of lumber. Then he came to board number eleven.

Pay dirt.

Before he set up the box and lantern and got out his tablet to take the pic, he examined the carving more closely. Good, another one where he could see both the top and bottom of the letters. As he studied it more, he could make out three distinct groups of letters. Probably three words. It wasn't nearly as complicated as interpreting ancient hiero-glyphics, but the rough way they had been carved and the fact that they were carved sideways on the boards, made it difficult to read the words easily.

After about five or ten minutes, Jack was pretty sure of what it said:

MY KILLER WILL

"Wow," he said aloud, "that really ups the ante." There could be no doubt now, not that there really was after what he and Rachel had found last night. This person was completely convinced they were about to die. He or she carved a message, not so much thinking it might save them, but that it might help the police catch their killer.

It was kind of sad, as he thought more about it. Here they were, some fifty-plus years later, and the victim's efforts so far had been in vain. The police didn't see it. Apparently, no one had. Not until now. Was his killer even still alive? Had they gotten away with it?

"My Killer Will..." Jack repeated. What did it mean? Where did it fit in the sequence of words they had uncovered so far? My killer will...do what? What was he saying his killer would do? Maybe he wasn't saying he'd do anything. Maybe the next line in the message would be something like: Turn Out To Be.

Jack was tempted to stop going through the rest of the boards, pull up the page on his tablet that contained the rest of the message, and start trying to decipher where these three new words should fit. But he resisted. He was the boss, but he couldn't take the whole afternoon off. He really needed to get back on track, take the pictures and start looking for more 2 x 4's with carved letters.

Once again, he methodically began to examine each stud, picking up where he had left off. And once again, with one board after another, he came up empty. Thirty minutes later, he had come to the studs used to frame the third and final dormer. He was actually about to skip it, certain there were no more relevant boards here in the attic. Then he noticed a rough patch as he gently slid his fingers across the side. Checking it further confirmed...more letters.

But this time the stud didn't run from floor-to-ceiling. It was cut at the halfway point by the window frame. Jack felt the stud, decided, nothing there. Then he felt the third stud. More carved letters. He was relieved. He stood and sized things up. Boards one and three were probably part of one board originally. Bringing the lantern closer, he began piecing together what all the letters said.

Finally, he felt sure they spelled out:

IN THIS BARN

That's interesting. All along, they had assumed the victim was chained up in some kind of building supply warehouse. But he wasn't. He was in a barn. But this revelation might have just complicated things a bit. Culpepper wasn't a farming town. It was a college town. Surrounded by lots of hills and forests. You go farther out, and there were some flatter areas. But what if they had been thinking this all wrong? What if the lumber used to build the lake house had come from some other less-hilly place in Georgia? Maybe even some other state? Wouldn't that put the crime well out of Joe's jurisdiction?

Well, those kinds of details needed to be sorted through another time. Right now, the main thing was getting this information to Joe. Jack looked at his watch. He had just enough time to take pictures of these two new studs and head back to the office. He decided to call Joe while he drove.

Once in the car, after setting his phone up for hands-free use, he thought about calling Rachel first but then reconsidered. He'd be interrupting her time with her mom, who would then be curious about the crazy things Jack and Rachel seemed to be talking about as she listened to a one-sided conversation. No, he'd just tell Rachel that night at dinner.

He touched the screen on Joe's pic. The phone started dialing. Rats, he'd gotten Joe's voicemail. After the beep, Jack said, "Hey Joe, Jack here. On my way back to work after taking a long lunch break up at the lake house. Did that thing you asked me to, checked all the exposed studs in the attic. Found two more boards with letters. So, two more lines to add to the mystery message. Definitely sheds some new light on things but still leaves some unanswered questions. Call me when you get a chance, and I'll fill you in."

He hung up. Then he wondered if he shouldn't have mentioned in the voicemail the line that talks specifically about the killer.

36

J oe and Hank were heading down the hall to
Captain Pendleton's office for a meeting that had
just been scheduled that morning. Joe's plan was to
get right on the lake house investigation first thing;
check the records downstairs for any missing persons'
reports from 1964 then head over to the library and search
for the same kind of thing through the old newspapers, like
Jack had suggested.

That was the plan. Now he wondered if he'd have to drop
the whole thing.

Ten minutes after he'd arrived at work, he bumped into
the captain coming out of the men's room. Pendleton asked
him how things were going with the cold case murder
investigation, and which case from the mid-80s Joe had
picked. That's when he realized, he hadn't briefed the
captain on his change of plans, nor ever mentioned the lake
house thing. Judging by Pendleton's reaction, Joe could
instantly tell...he probably should have. Pendleton came

close to blowing his top but restrained himself and simply said: "I gotta be somewhere. You and Hank, meeting with me right after lunch. Convince me why you're not doing what I asked you to. Until then, don't pursue this case any further."

As they turned the corner to Pendleton's section of the hallway, Hank asked, "You think you're going to be able to fix this thing? Or are we going to be dropping this case with Jack's lake house a few minutes from now?"

"Guess we'll see," Joe said. "I was all set to follow some new leads this morning, but the captain said to hit the pause button. So, I spent the morning making the case for why we should stay on this one."

"And why am I in this meeting? I've barely done anything with it yet."

"What, you want to bail? Afraid to take some heat?"

"No, I can take some heat...for something I believe in. This case's got some interesting angles, but I don't see anything all that compelling about it. Not yet anyway."

Joe realized, he hadn't briefed Hank on the latest findings. "Well, wait till you hear my spiel to the captain. You can decide after that if you want to help me persuade him, or bail."

They were there. Joe opened the door.

The secretary said, "You guys can go in. The Captain is expecting you."

Hank whispered, "Are we late?"

Joe glanced at his watch, shook his head no.

As they walked in, Pendleton hung up the phone and faced them. "Okay gentlemen, have a seat then let's hear why you decided to override the directions I gave you, and started working on a totally different case than the unsolved murders in the 1980s?"

Hank and Joe sat. Joe knew the question was really directed at him. "Well, for starters Captain, that's some pretty strong language you're using, compared to the tone of our conversation when we set this up. You led me to believe which case we worked on was up to my discretion. I wasn't under the impression you gave me some kind of direct order to work on the cases from the mid-80s. If you had, then I would have bitten down on that box of files like a bulldog and ignored everything else."

The captain's face instantly changed. He hadn't expected Joe to come back so strong. "Well, I guess I did give you the impression that the case you picked—"

"Gave me the impression, Captain? You said it plainly, sir. I would never ignore a direct order from a superior. Never."

"Okay Joe, I get your point. But I gotta say, I've been thinking all along you guys were working on one of those cases. That's why I asked you about it this morning. I've been trying to figure out which one you picked. See if it was the case I'd have picked if I were in your shoes. One of the Councilmen asked me about it at a meeting last night. I told him, in fact, I wasn't sure which one, but that it would definitely be one of those cases from the mid-80s."

"A Councilman asked you about which cases we're working on?" Joe said. "I had no idea they were that interested. If I had, sir, I would have briefed you on this change. I'd never do anything to embarrass you. Not on purpose, anyway."

"I appreciate that, Joe. Yeah, it didn't come up during the meeting. But one of them asked me about it after. Councilman Rhodes, who it turns out if you recall, was the one No-vote when I pitched this idea of setting up the Cold Case Squad in the first place."

Rhodes, Joe thought. Interesting. "So, how'd he seem after you told him what you thought we were working on?"

"He seemed pleased. Maybe he's starting to warm up to the idea."

Pleased, Joe thought. Hmmm. "Well, let me tell you why I made the shift to this other case. And if I don't convince you, I'll put it on the back burner and get right on one of those cases from the mid-80s."

Joe took about ten minutes to bring Pendleton up to date. As he talked, he could tell the captain was getting totally sucked in by the story. The last few items were things Hank hadn't even heard about yet. Then he said to both of them, "Today, I was going to start digging into our files from 1964, from the mid-summer onward, see if we had any missing persons reported. Figure a town like Culpepper, especially in 1964, wouldn't have very many. Might give us the name of our vic, the guy chained up in the warehouse by the stack of 2 x 4's. If I found any names, I'd head over to the library, check out the old newspapers from that time. Might fill in some more details."

Joe looked at his watch. "Even as we speak, Jack Turner is using his lunch break to examine all the exposed studs in his attic at the lake house. The theory is, that whole stack was delivered to Jack's house in '64. The whole message is probably spread throughout the house. It's like finding a note from a dead guy telling us all about the crime. It's a gold mine, sir, for solving a cold case. And didn't you say you wanted me to pick one that wouldn't take forever to solve?

Something we could get some instant publicity on? You know, to help justify the expense of creating the squad."

The look on the captain's face. That last part did the trick.

Pendleton didn't say anything for a few moments. Joe looked over at Hank, who nodded and made a face that said, "I think you got this."

Pendleton leaned back in his chair. "Okay, Joe. You made your case. I'm on board. How far away do you think you are from solving this murder? If it even turns out to be one?"

"My gut tells me there was a murder here, Captain. This isn't some kind of prank. I think we'll know, maybe in a couple of days, who the victim was and maybe even what happened to him. Hard to know if the perp is even still alive. Happened over fifty years ago. But we'll get this thing solved. I'm sure of it."

"Good. Well, keep me in the loop. So, I don't go on saying something else to somebody else that I gotta take back."

"Say, about that, sir. Could you do me a favor and not get back with Councilman Rhodes on this change we've made? At least not for a few days."

"Sure, I guess I can do that. No fire to put out. But why?"

"Probably nothing," Joe said, "But I may have to ask him a few questions, about the case I mean. Turns out, the construction company that built Jack's house out by the lake was owned by Councilman Rhodes' family. Doesn't mean there's a direct connection, since the message was probably carved on the lumber back at the supply warehouse. But still, I may need to talk to him. Would be great to get straight answers from him, whatever they turn out to be. You give him a heads up, he'll have all kinds of time to make up something."

Pendleton smiled. "Are you saying politicians don't always tell the truth?"

"Is the Pope Catholic, sir?"

37

June 16th, Evening, 1964
Culpepper, GA

Mason took the familiar backroads leading from Roy's house to the rear entrance of the planta-tion property, a route he'd taken hundreds of times growing up. Of course, in the early years he'd have ridden back-and-forth on his bike. There were no street-lights along the way so, unless the moon was cooperating, the ride home could get pretty scary.

Tonight he felt another kind of fear, made even more intense because the stakes were so high. He tried to block out the bundles of anxious thoughts trying to break through, but it was a constant struggle the whole way there. Normally, he'd play the radio nice and loud and that would do the trick. But he had to make this ride as quiet as possible, so that was out of the question. He was tempted to drive with the headlights off, but the moon wasn't cooperating tonight, so he'd just have to take his chances.

He reached a spot where a dirt road veered off to the left, leading to a nice swimming hole he and Roy had enjoyed through the years. Mason turned there, remembering it to be a five-minute walk to the Big House. A well-worn path through the woods joined the two places together. Two minutes later, Mason saw the pond up ahead and pulled his car off in a grassy area. Took just a few moments to get his bearings. Once he did, he found that path and started making his way to his primary destination.

It had been some years since he'd been to the old swimming hole. The path was overgrown with bushes and branches that got in his way, but it was still clear enough to make it through. The continual buzz of crickets and locusts filled the air with a steady and oddly comforting noise. He preferred it to silence and what his imagination might do with that. The mosquitoes came at him on several occasions, but he moved too fast for them to have their way.

Finally, Mason started seeing lights in the distance through the trees. The path ended where the woods gave way to a wide pasture area, formerly a cotton field. Mason knew this particular pasture had been blocked off from the horses, so it could be re-seeded for new growth. And he also knew the help would be clocked out by now, so it was a pretty straight shot from here to the house. Still, he ran crouched the whole way.

He reached the back of the house and was glad no one had turned on the switch in the kitchen that lit up this area. The lights in the kitchen were off also. They would be at this hour.

He paused to listen and only entered through the door when he was sure the coast was clear. It was a huge place but, for the most part, only occupied in the evening by his father and Boone. Being an old wooden structure it had its fair share of creaking floorboards and steps. Thanks to countless escapades in his junior and high school years, Mason knew the location of each and every one. It was still a good idea to slip out of his shoes and make the rest of the journey in his socks.

Sidestepping past each problem spot, Mason snuck past the large pantry, down a short hallway, then up the servants' back stairway, bypassing the most likely places Boone and his father would be at this hour. He opened the door slowly into a darkened hallway that led past what used to be the servants' rooms. So far, so good. He now came to a large open area that led to the main bedrooms. Again, everything was dark except for a dim light on a table beside the doorway to the bathroom.

Just to be safe he paused before going further. Maybe they weren't even home. What else could explain how quiet it was?

A loud bang.

Mason froze, but then realized it came from outside in the direction of the barn. It was followed by a high-pitched hydraulic sound, which Mason instantly recognized as a forklift. That must be where they were, out by the barn loading or unloading some building supplies from Boone's truck. Then he heard voices, Boone and his father talking about something, but he was too far away to hear. But it didn't matter, whatever they were saying.

After tonight, none of it would concern him.

Now knowing where they were, he walked a little more

confidently across the open hall to his bedroom. He left the light off. He knew where everything was and could locate them blindfolded, if needed. Sliding a duffel bag out from under his bed, he set it on top and began filling it with items from the checklist he'd created in his head on the drive over. Another large bang stopped him in his tracks. But there was that wheezing hydraulic sound of the forklift. Out of curiosity, he stepped over to the window and peeked out from behind the curtain. He could just make out the right side of the barn from his window.

Boone was lifting a pallet of 2 x 4's off the flatbed trailer attached to his pickup. Daddy was standing on the other side directing traffic. He knew how much Boone hated it when Daddy did that, tell him what to do or not do, as if Boone was still a ten-year-old. That was another thing Mason wouldn't miss after tonight, his father's constantly over-managing the lives of everyone around him.

Although his window was cracked several inches, he still couldn't make out what they were saying. Probably talking about whatever had gone wrong with some construction project, forcing Boone to have to make this after-hours run to the building supply store. Whatever it was, Mason was grateful for it. It put them away from the house far enough and long enough to do what he came here to do.

Really, there was just one last thing. He stood on his tiptoes and reached to the backside of his closet shelf until his fingers nabbed the edges of a cigar box. Straining just a little more, he was able to snag it and slide it forward. It wasn't heavy, but he still handled it with care. Laying it on the bed, he opened the lid and gazed at the almost three-thousand dollars it contained.

All the money he had in the world. Supposed to be the beginnings of a much larger fund he hoped to have when he launched into the adventure he'd been forced to start tonight. He shoved it into the duffel bag and zipped it shut before any more anxious thoughts began to take hold.

All that was left now was to retrace his steps back through the house, going the other way. Everything went smooth as silk right up until he reached the kitchen door. He opened it and gasped.

"What in the world? Mason, what are you doing here?"

It was Daddy. Standing behind him, Boone.

38

"Daddy, I uh...I'm...uh..."

His father glanced down at the duffel bag. "You uh...was what? Need a few minutes to come up with a good lie for me? That it?"

Behind him, Boone shook his head in disgust.

"I was just...just gonna..."

Daddy took a step back. "Looks like you was just gonna take your leave of us. That what it look like to you, Boone?"

"It does, Daddy. Like the boy was fixing to run away."

"No, no," Mason said. "It's not that."

"You never was good at lying," Daddy said. "Even growing up. I'm not sure you ever got away with anything, you were so bad at it."

"And here we thought you were stuck back at your school with a broken-down car," Boone said. "Ain't that what he told us?" He looked around quickly. "I don't see your car anywhere. How'd you get all the way down here without a car?"

"Maybe you flew down here, like Superman," Daddy said. "Why not try that one on me, see if I believe it?"

Mason dropped his duffel bag. Nothing he could say would improve this situation.

"Tell you what I'm gonna do," Daddy said. "Till I figure out the right way to punish you. Course, to do that, I need to know the full extent of all your wrongdoings against this family. But until then, I'm going to do what we used to do when you did something this bad, when you was ten years old." With lightning speed, he rushed through the doorway, grabbed Mason by the hair and started dragging him outside.

Mason yelled out. "Daddy, you're hurting me."

"Course I am. That's the whole point." He hurried across the grass then across the paved area in front of the barn, holding onto Mason's hair all the while.

Mason bent over, did his best to keep up and not trip.

"What you want me to do with his duffel bag?" Boone yelled.

"Bring it along for now."

Mason knew where they were going and what came next. He couldn't believe this was happening. A few moments later, they reached the opening to the barn. Daddy kept dragging him toward one of the main support pillars in the center. Right beside it was a stack of 2 x 4's. One of the pallets Mason had heard him offloading with the forklift a short while ago. "Daddy, you don't have to do this."

"Fraid I do, boy."

"Can't we just talk?"

"Oh, they'll be some talkin' all right, but it won't be you

doin' it. 'Cause I just learned the hard way I can't believe a word you say anymore."

They reached the pillar and Daddy threw Mason down beside it. His back smacked into the stack of 2 x 4's.

Boone followed close behind. "Where you want this duffel bag?"

"Just throw it down anywhere and get me some rope. There's some hanging on a hook over there."

Mason started to stand up. "Daddy, this is ridiculous. I'm not a—"

Daddy slapped him hard across the face, knocked him back against the stack of lumber. "I tell you you could get up yet, boy? That what you're gonna tell me, that you ain't a kid anymore? I beg to differ. Your behavior these past couple of days...really, much longer than that, tells me otherwise. You gonna act like a child, I'm going to treat you like one."

Boone handed Daddy the rope. Daddy gave it back to him. "I ain't gonna bend over. You tie him up." He looked down at Mason again. "You put your arms behind your back and up against that pillar, just like we did when you were a kid. And I'm sure you remember what happens if you pull your hands away when we're trying to tie the knot."

Mason did as he was told. Boone bent down, yanked his hands anyway and pulled, slamming Mason's back and head against the pillar. He'd have gotten whupped had he tried that when they were younger. But not tonight.

"I told you back in Ashburn, you were in a world of trouble," Boone muttered as he finished tightening the knot.

"Make sure he can't wiggle out of it," Daddy said.

"Oh, he can't. Believe me. He's not getting up from this until we come back and turn him loose."

"Whenever that is," Daddy said. "Have half a mind to leave you here for the next week, after the stunt you pulled." He started slowly walking back and forth.

Next came the lecture.

"I can't believe you'd do something like this to me, after all I've done for you. And of all the things you could've done to hurt me, you pick this. You do the very thing you knew would be like shoving a dagger in my heart. You link up with a bunch of Yankee white boys and turn against your own."

"Probably a bunch of Jews and papists in there with them," Boone added.

"And you get all buddy-buddy with a bunch of college-age colored boys, who think they can come down here and turn our world upside down, make it just like the mess they got going on up north. And there you are, my own flesh and blood, sneaking off to summer school just so you can join up with these troublemakers."

"They all rode down here in a bus, Daddy," Boone said. "Together. The boys said before I got there they were all up there by that bus, singing Negro slave songs, about how bad life is or some other such crap. And there Mason was, arm in arm, right up there singing with them."

Daddy shook his head. The more Boone talked, the redder his face got.

"And if it weren't for George Caldwell," Boone continued, "wouldn't just be the three of us knew about this disgrace. All of Culpepper would know about it by now."

"I can't believe it," Daddy said. "Just can't believe it. How could you do something so stupid? How could you care so little about your family's good name in this town? After all the work I've done, and your brother has done, to bring our family name back to that high and lofty place it once held. We were almost there. Just a little while longer, and we would be...right up there where we belong. Besides the loss of our good name, your utter foolishness could have cost us a veritable fortune in business. Do you think the Regents of Culpepper University would give those millions in construction contracts to a family-owned business with a tarnished reputation? They're doing everything they can to fight off these flaming liberals and high-minded integrationists from getting a foothold in that school. You think they'd give any work to Rhodes Construction if it came out that you were one of them yourself?" He stomped his foot on the ground. "My God, how could you be so stupid? And so disloyal to your own family?"

Mason's head dropped low. He'd never thought about any of these things.

"We'd be ruined," Boone said. "Is that what you want? Was that your goal?"

"No," Mason said, still not looking up. "I never meant to hurt you, either one of you." Well, that wasn't entirely true. He did hope his running away would cause them a little pain, but he'd never considered all these things would be a part of it.

"Never meant to hurt us, eh?" Daddy said. "That right? Well, you would have hurt us plenty if we hadn't bumped into each other back at the kitchen door a few moments ago. But it looks like fate stepped in and lent us a hand, stopped you cold in your tracks from pulling off your scheme. So, you're going to stay down here, tied up like a bad dog, just like when you were ten. I can't take away your dinner like I did back then, since you probably already ate. But you can stay in here, in the dark, for the next several hours. Till Boone and I figure out what to do with you. Come on, Boone. Close the doors and turn the light out behind you."

Daddy turned and headed out the barn door.

39

It was totally dark out now. Whitney came in off the little porch that fronted Maisie's shack, held his watch under a dim lamp parked on an end table. "It's been over an hour, Miss Maisie," he said.

"Almost an hour and a half," she said.

"Mason said he'd probably be gone less than an hour."

"That's right."

"Can you think of any reason why he'd be gone this long, considering what he went there to do?"

"I wish I could."

"So, you think something must've gone wrong, too?"

"I know I could get there and back in about twenty minutes," she said, "and that's walking."

Whitney was afraid of that. This just wasn't right. "I know we've gotta add some extra time, given that he's having to sneak around."

"I suppose so," Maisie said. "But I don't think that much

extra time is called for. I'm afraid somebody must've seen him."

"You mean like one of the workers?"

"Ain't no workers there at this hour. I mean like his Daddy or brother Boone."

Whitney sighed. "That would be terrible, if they did."

"Don't know what else it could be," she said. "You're welcome to wait as long as you please."

Whitney walked back onto the porch, stared off in the direction where he'd last seen Mason's car. "Maybe I will wait just a little while longer. Okay if I sit on one of these rockers a few more minutes?"

"Like I said, you're welcome to wait as long as you please."

Whitney rocked on that porch for what felt like another twenty minutes, then got up.

Maisie met him at the front door, talked through the screen. "Still no sign of him?"

Whitney looked down, shook his head no.

"Then I'm afraid poor Mason ain't coming back this way tonight. Which means, he's probably in a whole heap of trouble. But nothing much you can do about that. You came here in Mason's car, didn't you?"

"Yeah."

"So you got no way of getting back home from here. You're welcome to spend the night here on the couch. I'd let you use Roy's room, but he'll be coming back later on tonight."

"I can't do that."

"Do what?"

"Just leave Mason like that. I drove all this way to help

him get free from his family, from the bondage they've been keeping him in. I can't just abandon him now. Not if he needs my help."

"But son, you don't know these people. I've been working for 'em most of my adult life. They not like Mason. Truth is, they ain't in the Klan, but they might just as well be. You go in there, you asking for a world of trouble."

"But you said yourself, there aren't any other workers up there at this hour, right?"

"Yes, that's true. But—"

"But nothing. I'm sorry, Ma'am. I mean no disrespect, but if there's just the two of them, and they have Mason now, they wouldn't be expecting anyone else, right? And there's just a sliver of moon out tonight, so it'll be pretty dark. I think I can at least get in there, see what the situation is, see if there's anything I can do to get him out. He's desperate to get free of them. We've talked about it for hours. He knows they'll never change, and after what happened a couple of days ago in Mississippi, they'll be holding so tight onto him, they won't ever let go. It's pretty much now or never."

"What happened in Mississippi?"

Whitney took a few minutes to explain things. "Oh my, Lord," was all she said at the end.

"So you can see, I can't just leave. Not till I know I've done everything I can to help him break free."

"Well, you got quite a bit more courage than most young men I know, I'll hand you that."

"So, you'll help me?"

"How can I help?"

"Can you draw me a map of the place? First, how to get from here to there the best way? Then once there, maybe a sketch of how the house is laid out? Not too much detail. Mainly, where Mason's room is, and where you think his father and brother might be this time of night."

"I suppose I can do that. Let me go get some paper and a pencil." She walked back into the kitchen, started rummaging through a drawer. A moment later she brought them over to the dinette table and sat in a chair.

Whitney came over and stood behind her, watched her sketch out the map.

When she finished, she explained everything to him, made sure he knew what everything meant. "Got any questions?"

"Just one, what's this big rectangle over here?"

"That's the barn. Well, it still looks like a barn, but they use it as more of a warehouse. You'd be smart to come in from behind it and head around this way," she drew an imaginary line with her finger. "That way you'll be sure to avoid the front porch, in case either Boone or Mason's Daddy are sitting out there."

"How is it around the house and barn, in terms of trees and bushes? In case I need places to hide behind?"

"Not too many trees, not around the house or the barn. But plenty of bushes. You should be fine if you move real slow, keep your ears and eyes open. The thing is, I don't know what they might have done to poor Mason if they caught him sneaking into the house. Or where they might've put him. Especially after what you told me about Mississippi. They'd both be as mad as hornets. First place I'd check is his room. You see a light on in there, that's probably where he is, since that room would normally be dark right now."

Whitney continued looking at the map to make sure he

didn't have any more questions then lifted it off the table and began to fold it.

"Uh, wait just a minute," Maisie said. "What you doing with that map?"

"Just folding it up, so it fits in my pocket."

"No, sir." She held out her hand. "Give it here. You can't take that with you. You get caught with that map in your pocket, they'll know it came from me, and I'll be out of a job. Or worse. I can't take that chance."

Whitney couldn't believe it. But he understood. He sat down at the table and spread it out. "Then I better study it, make sure I have everything committed to memory before I go."

40

Maybe it was just exhaustion but, at some point, tied there to the pole in the barn, Mason had fallen asleep. It was anything but restful. He was suddenly awakened by a sound outside. It took a few moments to remember where he was, what was happening. How much time had passed? How long had he been tied up here?

There was that sound again. Branches scraping against a side window on his right. What could it be? An animal maybe. No. A moment later he saw the silhouette of a person moving slowly past. He realized it had to be Whitney. Who else would be sneaking around the barn? He had to get Whitney's attention somehow. The only thing he could think of was to bang his head against the stack of lumber.

It worked.

The silhouette of the person returned and looked inside the window. Now he could see Whitney's face, the look of shock as it appeared when he recognized Mason and saw his predicament. Mason silently mouthed the words: *Help Me.*

Whitney looked toward the main house then back through the window and gestured with his hands. He wanted to know the way in. With his head, Mason motioned in the direction of the rear door. He knew it would be unlocked. Whitney disappeared. A few moments later, the doorknob turned behind him. A brief ray of dim light shone on the floor as the door opened and closed. Quiet footsteps coming.

A moment later, Whitney squatted down beside him. "My Lord, Mason," he whispered, "they tied you up?" He started reaching for something in his pocket.

"What are you doing?"

"Getting my penknife. Always carry one. I'll have these ropes cut off in a few seconds, then we can get out of here. I passed your car back there about five minutes ago. We can—"

"No Whitney, stop."

"What do you mean? Stop what?"

"You can't cut me loose. And I'm not going anywhere. But you need to leave...now. Before anyone sees you."

"What are you talking about, Mason? I'm not going anywhere without you. I already checked out the house. Your dad and brother are sitting at the dining room table. No one else is in the house, and I didn't see anyone else on my way in. Maisie said to check your room, told me which window was yours. When I didn't see the light on, I figured maybe you were here in the barn. But I never expected to find you tied up to a pole like this."

"I appreciate you coming to my rescue. I really do. But it's no use. I can't go back with you. It's a nice idea, but it would never work."

"Of course it would work. Just the way we talked. It ain't gonna be easy, starting over with almost nothing. But you can do this, Mason. I know you can. Besides, you can't stay here with them. Who would treat their own kin like this? Tying you up like some kind of barnyard animal? And look at your eye. I just noticed, it's red and swelling up." He pulled out his penknife. "Come on now, let me cut you loose."

Mason sighed. "Put your knife away. I'm sorry that I dragged you down here with me. I don't know what I was thinking. But I can't just abandon my life here, and my family. Not like this. Maybe later, in a few years. Do as I'm told for now. I'll graduate from some other college here in the South. Then I can leave, start over the right way. But hearing what my father said as he chewed me out, made me realize, leaving this way would ruin them completely." He took another deep, slow breath, exhaled. "They are bigots and racists, and I despise everything they stand for. But they are still my family, and I don't want to be the reason our family business goes belly up, and they wind up losing everything. I can't have that on my conscience. It's just not right."

Whitney stood. "Are you sure, Mason? This is really what you want? This isn't just you coming under their iron claw again, reacting to their abuse? I don't understand how you leaving them would somehow destroy them financially. Sounds like a bunch of—"

"It would take too long to explain. But I think it would. But I am grateful for you. Not just driving down here with me. Or coming here tonight, trying to rescue me. You're a great friend. And I'll find some kind of way to stay in touch with you until the time comes when I really can leave. But for now, you need to go. While you still can. I'd offer you my car, but I'm afraid you'd get arrested for stealing it somewhere between here and your school. But there is something I can do for you. Not just for you, but for the cause."

"What's that?"

"See that the duffel bag over there? Go on over, open it up. You'll find a cigar box toward the bottom. Go ahead and get it out."

Whitney did as Mason said. Brought the cigar box back over, stood near him.

"Go ahead," Mason said. "Open it up."

Whitney did. "My gosh, Mason." He started leafing through the money. "There's gotta be hundreds of dollars in here."

"More like three-thousand."

Whitney repeated the sum. "I can't take your money, Mason. It's all you've got."

"Believe me, I can get more. Especially after I start behaving a while, doing what they want me to. I'll get that much and more. But I want you to take it. Use what you need to get safely back home, keep however much you want, then give the rest to the SNCC. I'm sure they could use the help."

"Mason, I—"

Suddenly, the barn doors flew open. The overhead lights turned on. Mason looked up, saw his father standing there holding a shotgun. Boone holding his Winchester rifle, standing by the light switch.

"Now, lookee at what we have here," Daddy said. "Boone, you see what I see?"

"I see a colored boy breaking into our barn. And what's that he's got in his hands?" Boone got closer, looked down at the box. "You see what's in there, Daddy? That cigar box is full of cash."

41

"Daddy, Whitney wasn't stealing that. It's my—"

"Shut up, Mason." He turned back to Whitney. "You think you can break into our barn, boy?" He leveled the shotgun at him. "Steal our hard-earned cash?"

"I wasn't stealing your—"

"Daddy, he wasn't—"

"I said shut up, Mason," Daddy said. "I ain't talking to you. I got eyes, don't I? Did I invite this boy onto our property?"

"No," Mason said.

"Did you invite him here?" Boone said.

"Well, no, not exactly. But—"

"Then he's trespassing," Daddy said. "So we got trespassing, breaking and entering, and stealing. That should be enough to lock him up a good long while, don't you think, Boone?"

"Around these parts, I'd say it's good enough for ten

years, maybe more. So, what we going to do with him, Daddy?"

"I'm not exactly sure yet. For starters, grab that box of cash."

Boone did. Whitney held it out without protest.

Still holding the shotgun on Whitney, Daddy said, "Now, cut your brother loose." Boone did that, too.

Mason stood, unsure of what was coming next.

"Mason, you march right up to your bedroom and close your door. I'll deal with you later."

Mason turned to Whitney. "I'm so sorry—"

"Not a word out of you, son. Hear me? Not a word."

Mason looked at Whitney, trying to communicate his grief with his eyes, then started walking, slowly. As he did, he looked back over his shoulder and listened.

"Now tie up this colored boy where your brother was sitting," Daddy said. "The same pole."

Boone dragged Whitney over to the spot. "I can't tie him up. I cut the rope. Now it ain't long enough."

"Well, use that chain hanging over there on that hook by the forklift. The key should be sticking out of the lock."

When Mason had gone far enough to where they couldn't see him anymore, he quietly doubled back to the barn. Close enough to hear what they were saying.

"Come over here, boy," Boone said. "You give me any trouble, and I will put your lights out for good. You hear me?"

Mason heard what sounded like a struggle. But given the size of Boone and the level of anger, he didn't imagine Whitney was fighting very much.

"Sit down, boy."

Mason heard a thump, could just imagine Boone tossing him to the ground.

"You can't do this," Whitney yelled. "You can't chain me up like some kind of dog. I know my rights. This is false imprisonment. I could have you arrested for this."

"Oh, could you now?" Daddy said.

"Not around here you won't," Boone added. "The law around here will be on our side. You'll be the one going to jail. Not us. Now shut your mouth."

Mason heard a slap, then Whitney yelling out in pain.

"I'm not talking about the law around here," Whitney said. "I know they'd side with you. But at some point, even they will have to grant me a telephone call. I've got connections to powerful people. I'll call them, and they'll have the FBI down here in no time at all. This is kidnapping what you're doing. I didn't come in here to steal anything. If you'd have let your son talk for two minutes, he'd have explained that we're friends. We drove down here together. He came back just to get his stuff and leave. Leave the two of you, for good. I was waiting for him not far from here. When he didn't come back, I figured something had gone wrong. I came back to rescue him, not steal his money. You talk to him. He was trying to give me that money, and I was trying to tell him to keep it. To use it to help him start a new life, away from here. Talk to him. He'll tell you. I'm not a thief. I'm studying to be a doctor, for crying out loud."

Then Mason heard a thump and another cry of pain. He waited a few moments, but Whitney said nothing more.

"Now, why'd you go and hit him like that?" Daddy said.

"I had to shut him up," Boone said. "You hear all that crap he was saying? He was threatening to call the FBI on us."

"I think he's out cold," Daddy said. "Hope you didn't crack his skull with that rifle butt."

"I hope I did," Boone said. "I truly do."

Mason couldn't believe what he was hearing. But then again, he could. Boone was certainly capable of hurting people. And he knew Daddy wouldn't do a thing to stop him.

"Now we need to make sure Mason stays in his room," Daddy said. "I'll go make sure he's there. He's gonna stay locked up in there all night."

They were walking this way. Mason hurried away from the barn toward the Big House before they could see him.

WHITNEY CAME TO, found his head throbbing. His instinct was to rub it then he remembered his hands were chained to a pole behind his back. It all came back to him: where he was, why he was chained up, and who had done it. How long has he been unconscious? He looked around. Everything seemed pretty much the same as before. The lights were still on in the barn, although the front doors were closed. Looking out the window, it was still dark. The only thing missing were Mason's father and brother.

Then he remembered the brother hitting him with the butt of his rifle. That's why his head was throbbing. How could he be so stupid? He shouldn't have said all that. You can't reason with unreasonable people. But he had to try something. They had chained him up and were going to call the local sheriff or police chief. Likely another white, racist redneck. And he'd be thrown in jail for who knows how long?

"We can't do that, Boone. Are you crazy?"

Whitney heard voices coming from the outside window, which he saw was open. Sounded like Mason's father.

"We got no choice, Daddy. You heard what he said. We can't call Chief Baker to come arrest him. What good would that do now? Sure, he'd come put him in jail on our say-so, but how long will that last? The kid is right. At some point, he'd have to give him his one phone call. And you heard him say who he'd call. Now, I don't think he's bluffing. He wasn't lying about being Mason's friend. He was the kid Mason was standing next to on that march when I found him. Which means, he's one of those college-educated colored folk. You heard him...he's studying to be a doctor. He's got the kind of smarts to deliver on those threats. He'd call the FBI down on us. They'd do one of their investigations. And no Chief Baker nor any of our other local friends could do a thing to stop it. They'd arrest us, charge us with kidnapping, probably try to make some kind of example out of us, and we'd go away to federal prison for good."

The father didn't reply. Whitney didn't like the sound of where this conversation was going. He missed the first part, but he could tell what Boone was implying. A moment later, Whitney didn't need to speculate anymore.

"I get what you're saying, Boone. But do you realize the consequences if we get caught?"

"Course I do. But we won't get caught. We got hundreds of acres around here, Daddy. A thousand different hiding places. I go hunting with this rifle all the time. People wouldn't even think twice when they heard the sound. I'll take care of this myself and won't even tell you any of the details. I'll just do what needs doing, and let you know when I'm done."

"I don't know, Boone. I just—"

"Daddy, you've got to trust me this time. Like all the times I've had to trust you. It's got to be done. We let him go, he calls the FBI on us, and we lose everything. Those are the consequences if I don't do this. You know what I'm saying is true."

"I guess you're right. But... but...it's just so, so final. Once it's done, there's no going back."

"I know that," Boone said. "That's the whole idea."

"Well, you're probably right. But you got him chained up real good. He'll keep through the night. You can take care of it in the morning, before the sun comes up. You can't do it now anyway. People hear gunshots in the woods at this time of night, they won't be thinking you're hunting. No, you wait and do it then. And like you said, I don't want to hear the details."

"I'll take care of it, Daddy. Just let you know when the deed is done."

Whitney heard their footsteps moving away. He couldn't believe what he'd just overheard. There could be no doubt. They were planning on shooting him, executing him in a few hours from now. For several minutes, he did everything he could to break free of his chains. But there was no use. He was able, though, to loosen how tight they were, especially around his right hand. He managed to pull his pocket knife out from his back pocket. Not that it would do any good against these chains, but it gave him an idea. If he twisted his body just so, he could reach several of the boards behind him.

If this was going to be his last night on earth, at least he could use the time to let someone know what happened here, and who was to blame. Considering how quickly Mason had collapsed under their intimidation, he held little hope that he'd come to Whitney's rescue any time soon.

Whitney said a quick prayer, then began carving a message into the stack of wood behind him.

42

THE PRESENT
1:30pm, Tuesday - Culpepper, GA

Hank and Joe had just come back from the meeting with Pendleton and were chatting in Joe's office. "Well, I thought that went pretty good. How about you?" Joe said.

"Yeah. Not like I made a contribution. But I was taking notes."

"I didn't see you writing anything down."

"Mental notes, Joe. You know me, mind like a steel trap."

"Oh yeah? So, what did you learn?"

"How to bully your superior into seeing things your way. I figure it'll come in handy down the road."

"What are you talking about? You think I bullied Pendleton back there? I think I was just trying to be...persuasive."

"I meant bully in a good way. Persuasive? Yeah, you could

say that if you want. Forcefully persuasive. It's not a dig, Joe. I agree with everything you said. I'm just glad Pendleton came your way. I'd really like to work on this case with you. Got my paperwork done from the drug bust. What do you say?"

"I'd say great. For starters, I'm going to call Jack back, see what he turned up at the lakefront place. Just listened to a message he left on my voicemail. Apparently, he did use his lunch break to check out all those studs in the attic. Turned up a couple more lines for our mystery message. I'll put the call back on speaker phone." Joe hit the call-back button. Jack's phone began to ring.

"Hey, Joe. Glad you called."

"Got a minute, Jack? Heard your message. Guess you turned up some new info during lunch? A couple more lines?"

"I can talk for a few," Jack said. "But yeah, examined quite a few boards up there. Wound up with two that appear to be part of our 2 x 4 stack. I'll write up a brief report for your file, email it to you. But for now, the essential info is these two lines, MY KILLER WILL and IN THIS BARN."

Joe repeated the two phrases out loud, looked over at Hank, who arched his eyebrows. "Wow Jack, they both sound pretty significant to me. Hank is here. He's nodding his head, too."

"I thought so, too," Jack said. "That first one pretty much leaves no doubt about whether this is a murder, or not."

"Well, at least, that our vic believed he was about to be killed," Hank said.

"Right," Jack said. "Guess I'm jumping the gun, a little. What do you think it'll take to confirm this guy—this vic—as you call him, was actually murdered? Do we need to find a body?"

"A body would certainly help," Joe said. "But no, it's not absolutely necessary we have one. But we're too early on to say this was definitely a homicide. My gut tells me it is. But we've got to keep pulling on the rest of the threads, see what they unravel. It's totally clear the guy thinks he's about to be killed, and that's why he's carving out this message, so the killer doesn't get away with it."

"It's a shame," Hank said. "Looks like he probably did."

"I thought that, too," Jack said. "What do you make of the second line? Where he talks about being in a barn?"

"Yeah, that one's a little puzzling," Joe said.

"Not like Culpepper is known as a farming community," Hank added.

"No, it's not," Jack said. "Made me wonder if the actual crime might've been committed in a totally different place, like maybe southern Georgia where you've got a lot of farms. Lots of farms in the Carolinas, too."

"Alabama and Mississippi, too," Hank said.

"Then," Jack said, "the stack of lumber gets shipped here to the job site by the lake."

Joe wasn't convinced. "Could be. We definitely need to be open to that. But there are a few farms around here. I've seen 'em driving around the outskirts of town. I'm sure they got barns. It's also possible the barn in our message was here fifty years ago, but ain't here no more. If it is local, that would be a great lead, the new line about the barn. That would narrow down the possible locations where this crime happened from a ton to just a handful. And you know something else? This new bit about the barn tells us the crime didn't happen at a supply warehouse. Or he would've carved that into the wood. The stack of lumber had already been delivered from the warehouse to some barn. That's a great new lead, you ask me. Great work, Jack."

"Thanks, I can see the fog lifting a little. But it's a real shame I didn't find any more studs than these two. I was really hoping I'd find one with a name on it, either the vic's or the killer's."

"Yeah, that would've been nice," Hank said. "But it does sound like the message is incomplete. Maybe he said more on a few of the other studs you haven't uncovered yet."

Joe remembered what Rachel had said about not wanting to tear the whole house up looking for more boards.

"I'm with you, Hank," Jack said. "I've been thinking about that ever since lunchtime. I'll have to talk to my wife, first. See if I can get her on board with something like that."

"Well, why don't you hold off having that chat for a little while?" Joe said. "We have two other leads to follow that might give us the vic's name. Hank and I can work on those this afternoon. One of them actually came from you, Jack. You remember, looking through the old newspapers?"

"I remember. So, you'll be doing that today? Good."

"Actually, I'm giving that one to Hank. I'm heading down to the basement as soon as I got off the phone. Start digging through missing person reports from May through the summer of '64."

JOE AND HANK parted ways after rehearsing Jack's instructions on how to find and then read the microfilm collection of old newspapers at the library. Joe wasn't too worried about

Hank figuring this thing out. He was quite the techie and usually the one who helped Joe solve his bouts with high-tech confusion. Joe headed down to the basement to the records room for an unquestionably low-tech assignment.

Because of all the work he and Hank had done reorganizing this area, it didn't take Joe long to locate the boxes from the summer of 1964. Since this wouldn't have been reported as a murder, Joe didn't expect to find much of a file on it. Really, he was probably looking for a page or two, at best. Whoever worked the system back then did things even more simply than whoever took care of the files in the mid-80s. Things were simply stuck in a box labeled by the month, like June 64, July 64, August 64, etc.

Joe spent about forty minutes thumbing through the June box but didn't find anything resembling a Missing Person's report. He was almost twenty minutes into the July box when he hit on something promising. He'd almost slipped past it, because it was labeled "Incident Report." Then he noticed someone had handwritten "Missing Person" in red beside it.

Pulling it out, he brought it over to an empty section of the table and sat down with it. "Okay, what's going on here?" Fortunately, it was an original, not a copy, so it hadn't faded very much. Secondly, it was partially typed, partially handwritten. But the handwritten parts were legible. He spent about five minutes reading over the data and learned that the race of both the missing person and the woman raising the concern were listed as "colored." The woman, an Ethel Wilkins, was apparently the missing person's mother.

Reading further, it said her son named Whitney Wilkins, had been missing since the middle of June. He was a student at Howard University. A hand-written note explained the reason for the delay in reporting her son missing was due to the fact that she was from the Raleigh area, didn't have much money, and couldn't get off work to look for him till now. When asked why she suspected he might be in Culpepper when he went to school near Washington DC, the woman said, she wasn't sure he'd been here. But some of his school friends said during the last conversation they had with him that he said he'd be coming down here "to help out a friend." No one seemed to have seen or heard from Whitney after that.

At the bottom of the report, another hand-written note said: *Told her we'd keep an eye out for her son and call if anything turned up. Won't waste much time on this. Got better things to do than track down some runaway colored boy.*

Joe reread the note. Obviously, taking down this information was the sum-total effort the Culpepper PD put into their search for Whitney Wilkins. But Joe's gut said there was something to this. The fact that he'd gone missing in mid-June was also relevant, because that coincided with the time-frame the permits were pulled on the lakefront house. He picked up his phone and called Hank.

"Yeah Joe, what's up?"

"How are you making out with the old newspapers?"

"This is actually a pretty fun assignment," Hank said. "Crazy what you could buy back then, for next to nothing."

"Anything a little more in line with the situation we're dealing with?"

"Nothing yet. Just finished going over all the papers in June. No stories about anybody going missing. Just getting ready to start reading through the first week of July."

"Well, I might've found something that matters. Do me a favor, go back to mid-June and reread the front-page stories. See if you can find anything significant about things happening in the South. If I recall, that was around the time things were really starting to heat up with the civil rights protests. Our missing kid is probably black. Maybe this is some kind of racial thing. I'm not sure. But let me know anything you find on stuff like that."

"Okay, Joe."

Joe spent the next two hours trying to find out whether Ethel Wilkins, the mother of the missing guy, might still be alive. It was a long shot. A quick sketch of the math told Joe, if she was, she'd be in her nineties. But these days, lots of people lived that long. The other thing would be whether she still lived in Raleigh, North Carolina like she did back in '64.

He found about twenty-five people with that last name who lived in the area, but none with the first name Ethel. That didn't mean it was a dead-end. Could be. But being that old, Ethel might live with one of her kids, who'd also be pretty old at this point. Nothing left to do but start calling folks the old-fashioned way, which was not a fun job these days. With all the telephone salespeople, lots of folks didn't even answer their phone if they didn't recognize the caller.

Joe made his way through the list, left a voicemail more than half the time. When people actually picked up the phone, he led with, "Hi, this is Lieutenant Joe Boyd with the Culpepper PD in Georgia. I'm conducting a homicide investigation." That usually kept them from hanging up right off the bat. He'd figured out a few other opening lines to say to quickly rule out whether or not the person had any connection to Ethel Wilkins.

On call number sixteen, he hit the jackpot.

"Why yes, Lieutenant, I know an Ethel Wilkins. She happens to be my mother."

Happens to be, not *was* my mother. "So, she's still alive?"

The woman on the other end laughed. "Hold on." A pause. "Yes sir, she's still alive."

"Who's that you're talking to, Athena?" Joe heard a woman's voice yell in the distance. "Someone calling for me? I heard you say my name just now."

"It may be, Mama. Just give me a second to hear what the man has to say." The woman turned her focus back on Joe. "I'm sorry, as you can see, she's not only alive, but she still hears pretty good, too."

"That's great," Joe said. "I wasn't sure whether this idea would pan out."

"Excuse me?" Athena said.

"Nothing, Ma'am. I don't want to take up too much of your time. Let me get straight to the reason for my call. Is your mother the same Ethel Wilkins who visited our town, Culpepper, Georgia, back in 1964? And might she have filled out a missing person's report on her son, Whitney Wilkins?"

"Oh, my Lord," Athena said in a shaky voice. "Lordy, Lordy." She didn't say anything else for a few moments.

"Can I take that as a yes?" Joe said.

"I can't believe someone is calling us about my brother... after all these years."

"So, he's still missing then?"

"Sadly yes, since way back then till now."

Joe figured as much, which really only meant one thing. "I'm actually part of a cold case squad recently created in our department. It's a fairly complicated story, how we came to pick up your brother's case, but we did. And I'm not even sure at this point, to be honest, if the case I'm working on will turn out to be about your brother's situation. That's really why I'm reaching out to your mother. I'm trying to confirm if these two puzzle pieces fit together."

"I don't think I'm following you, Lieutenant."

"I don't blame you. Like I said, it's a little complicated. But the main thing is, your mother's alive. Which means, she may be able to help me get some critical answers on this case. Would there be any way for me to talk with her? Not on the phone, but in person? I could drive up there tomorrow. Looks like you folks are about five hours away from me. I could leave in the morning, get there just after lunch."

"Well," she said, "I suppose that would be possible. I better ask Mama to make sure, though. Don't see why she wouldn't say yes. But this will come as quite a shock, so it'd be better if I talked to her first. Could I call you back in a few minutes?"

"Definitely." Joe gave her his cell phone number, thanked her and hung up.

Wow, what a break. The mom's alive, seems alert, even hears pretty good. Joe got up and grabbed himself a cup of coffee. By the time he'd fixed it and got back to his desk, Athena had called back.

"Hello, Lieutenant? This is Athena Wilkins. We just spoke a few moments ago."

"Yes, Athena. Thanks for calling back."

"You're welcome. I did speak with my mother. As I said, she was very surprised about your call. We haven't heard anything about my brother for, literally, decades. She had given up any hope of ever learning the truth about what happened this side of heaven."

"I understand. But...I want to be very upfront about this. I still don't know what happened to your brother, to her son. Something has come up, some new information, that may lead us to find out more. Maybe even lead us to the truth. But we're not there yet. My hope is, if your mother can confirm certain things and shed light on some other things, it may help me close that gap. That's why I'd like to drive up there tomorrow, if possible, and talk these things over with her. With you, too, if you can be there."

"I appreciate your candor, Lieutenant. I will explain that to Mama when I hang up. But we'll both look forward to talking with you tomorrow. Do you have our address?"

Joe gave them what he had, confirmed a few more details and said he'd probably be there around 2PM but would call when he got into town. He jotted down a few notes then made quick calls to Pendleton and Hank to brief them on his plans.

After Hank listened to what Joe said, he shared what he'd found out about the big stories making the front pages in June 1964. Turned out, Joe had been right. The biggest events that took place in the South that month had everything to do with clashes between the KKK, the ruling white majority, and civil rights protesters. Of course, Hank said, the stories had been covered in the local newspapers in a way that made the civil rights workers out as the villains. But he still hadn't found a single news story about a college kid gone missing in this area.

"Why am I not surprised?" Joe said. Especially since the kid was black.

44

The drive to Raleigh the next morning had pretty much gone as planned. Hank had wanted to come but was needed in town to help execute a search warrant on a suspected drug dealer. But he had to tell Joe before he quit for the day yesterday, he'd finished reading through all the Culpepper newspapers during the summer of 1964. Still, nothing about anyone going missing.

The five-hour drive gave Joe an opportunity to think through this case in more detail. A possible scenario was starting to take shape. Something had caused this black college kid, Whitney Wilkins, to drive down from where he'd attended college near Washington DC, around mid-June. But according to Hank, while there were all kinds of chaotic events in different parts of the South related to the civil rights issue, nothing had happened in Culpepper. So, why had Whitney driven down there? Hopefully, he'd have more answers than questions after talking with these two elderly ladies in Raleigh.

As promised, as soon as he got into town, he called Athena to let her know. She said they were all ready to see him. He followed the GPS instructions, which directed him to a small but mostly well-kept retirement community of duplexes. Athena had said look for the "old green Chrysler" parked in the driveway.

Joe pulled up next to it and got out. She must've seen him coming up the walkway. The front door opened before he rang the bell.

A well-dressed black woman probably in her seventies stood there with a warm smile, extending her hand. "You must be Lieutenant Boyd?"

"I am. You must be Athena...Wilkins, right?"

"Yes. Used to be Johnson. I reverted back to my maiden name ten years ago. A long story for another day. Come in, come in. Mama's waiting for you in the living room. We both are so curious and anxious to hear what you have to say."

Joe came in, followed her down a hall that opened into a small but cozy living room, overcrowded with furniture and knickknacks. Sitting in a recliner was a much older woman with an equally engaging smile. "You must be Ethel," Joe said. "May I call you that, or would you prefer Mrs. Wilkins?"

"Ethel would be just fine, Lieutenant. Pardon me for not getting up. I planned to but Athena said no."

"I'm sure you don't mind," Athena said.

"Not at all," Joe said. "Can I sit down?"

"By all means," Ethel said. "Can Athena get you something to drink?"

"No, I'm fine. Been drinking a Diet Pepsi for the last hour in the car. Well, I guess I should get right to it." He pulled out a copy of the missing person's report, set it down on the coffee table and explained to the ladies what it was."

"I do recall the police officer writing a few things down while I spoke," Ethel said. "But I got the clear impression he didn't take me seriously, nor did I really expect him to. Not just because I was a black woman talking to an obviously racist white officer, but I couldn't really say with certainty that my Whitney had gone missing in his town."

"I read that in the report," Joe said. "I guess you mentioned some of his college friends told you he was going there, to Culpepper?"

"Yes. He didn't tell me himself. I do know Whitney was heavily involved with the civil rights activity going on then. I was so afraid for him, because of all the things I was reading about and seeing on the news. But he was insistent it was the right thing to do. I think that's why he didn't tell me about his plans. He didn't want to worry me none."

"How certain would you say his friends were that he had driven down to Culpepper? And did they know why?"

"They were fairly certain. One of them was absolutely sure that's what he'd said. But it didn't have anything to do with the civil rights activity. He was helping a close friend, who I understand was white. They didn't know the young man's name, but it had something to do with helping him get away from his family, or something like that. I don't know why or what the problem was. All they said was, Whitney said he'd be back in a few days at most. But they never saw him or heard from him after that."

"And Lieutenant," Athena chimed in, "there's no way Whitney ran away or went off to start some new life some where else. That's what the authorities tried to tell us at the time. From their point of view, there was no crime. No evidence of foul play. They said it looked like just some college kid going off on his own to do his own thing. He was legally an adult, they said, so without any evidence of anything happening to him of a criminal nature, there was nothing they could do. But Lieutenant, there was no way Whitney would ever run off and leave his family like that. He just wouldn't. We were close, and he loved Mama more than life itself. He was in college, studying to become a doctor. He had everything to live for. I remember hearing him say on several occasions...the first thing he was going to do when he started making some real money was to buy all of us a big house to live in."

Joe noticed tears welling up in Ethel's eyes.

"That's the kind of son he was, Lieutenant," she said. "Whitney was a good boy. He'd never leave us like they say he did. Something happened to him. Somebody did something to him. I just know it. That's the only thing that would explain why he never came back to us."

Joe sighed. "Well, ladies, I know you're probably wondering what happened recently to bring this case back up again. What I'm about to share is going to sound pretty bizarre. But it will also be pretty difficult to hear. I can't say with a hundred percent certainty the things I'm about to read came from your son, but I'm starting to believe they very well could have." Joe went on to explain everything they had uncovered thus far about the mysterious message carved into the 2 x 4's found in Jack's lakefront house.

He ended reading the actual message, word-for-word. As much as they'd uncovered so far. Both women's eyes filled with tears as he did. It was obvious, they both believed those words had been carved into those boards by Whitney.

Before Joe left, the women hugged him and thanked him for driving all this way and for reopening this case. Joe promised to keep them informed of his progress. As he reached the front door, Athena rushed down the hall with a small book in her hands.

"I forgot to give this to you," Athena said. "We don't know if it will help any. It's a journal Whitney kept while he was away at school. He didn't write in it every day, like a diary. And it doesn't say anything about his trip to your town in Georgia. But maybe it will help you get to know him better. You'll see the way he thought about things and the way he talked about the future. It's one of the reasons we know for certain Whitney would never have run away. Somebody killed my brother, Lieutenant Boyd. And I believe it was somebody who lived in your town."

CAPTAIN PENDLETON HAD APPROVED for Joe to stay overnight at a hotel in Raleigh, drive back the next day. But Joe knew Kate hated sleeping alone. And considering how long it stayed light out, he figured he'd make it back to Culpepper before dark. Two hours into his car drive home, Joe got a phone call. He didn't recognize the number on the screen but, considering the nature of his work, he always picked up for anyone who called. "Hello, this is Lieutenant Joe Boyd."

"Hello, Lieutenant. This is Jim Hadley from Hadley's Hardware Store. I'm the elder Hadley. You first spoke with my son, John."

"I remember you, Mr. Hadley. We spoke about you

working for that construction supply company back in the early sixties, Dunn Brothers I think?"

"That's the one. You were asking about whether or not they delivered construction materials out to the sites themselves. You asked about the houses being built out by the lake during that time. I said Dunn delivered materials to the smaller companies, but the bigger ones often came and picked up their supplies with their own truck. I believe we spoke briefly about one of the bigger companies who built houses out by the lake, Rhodes Construction?"

"I remember, Mr. Hadley. You said that construction company went out of business back in the eighties, if I recall. As did Dunn Brothers, right?"

"Yes, the construction industry around here really took a hit during the Carter years. Anyway, I knew you were working on some kind of a crime from way back then. Figured it must be pretty important for you to come looking into things and seeking me out. So, last night I pulled out some old photo albums from that time in my life. You know, how looking at old photos somehow wakes up old memories you thought you forgot all about. Anyway, found this one picture my wife took of me when I worked at Dunn's. Wasn't so much what was in the photo, but just seeing it started turning on some lights, so to speak. Anyway, you asked me to call you should I remember anything from that time that might be relevant to your investigation."

"I did," Joe said. "Did you remember something?"

"I did, as a matter fact. Don't know how much it matters, but figured I'd call, let you be the judge. Anyway, I remembered being asked on a couple of occasions to help load building supplies onto a flatbed trailer owned by Rhodes

Construction. And sometimes I'd offload a pallet of materials directly onto Boone's pickup truck, if he didn't have too big an order."

"Did you say, Boone?"

"Yeah, Boone Rhodes. Back then their father, Judson Rhodes, owned and ran the operation. Boone kind of supervised construction projects for their company. The dad died a long time ago. Then Boone took over. Think he ran things until they went under in the eighties. They had an office here in town but also one in their big plantation house. It's an amazing place. Don't know if you've ever seen it. Goes way back before the Civil War. Think he and his brother still live in that place, if I recall."

"I haven't seen it, Mr. Hadley."

"Yeah, quite a place," he said. "I remember on one occasion driving out there to help offload a truck for a pretty big order. Way more than they could fit on the flatbed trailer. They asked me to come because I was certified to run the forklift. Boone was directing me where to lay all the pallets in their barn, which they'd converted into a little warehouse."

"Barn?" Joe said. "Did you say barn?"

"Yeah. It was just a regular looking barn on the outside. Pretty big one, as barns go. But they'd put a concrete floor down, big steel shelves, sturdy enough to hold wood pallets full of building materials. It's still there, I think. Course, I haven't been there in years, so maybe it's gone now."

"And you said this Boone is still alive?"

"Yeah, still comes into our store every now and again. He's an old guy like me. Maybe a few years younger. But he dresses pretty sharp. My son tells me the shirts he wears cost upwards of eighty bucks a piece, can you imagine? Who'd pay that for a pullover shirt? He's supposed to be quite the golfer, spends most of his time at the Culpepper Country Club. Then there's his younger brother. We never see him in the store, though. Strikes me as the kinda guy who hires people to fix things."

"Who's that?" Joe asked.

"I'm sure you've heard of him," Hadley said. "It's Mason Rhodes. You know, Councilman Rhodes?"

45

Joe hung up with Mr. Hadley and, in no time at all, his stomach got to churning. He knew why. That last thing Mr. Hadley had said pretty much sewed things up for Joe. He hadn't figured everything out yet, but all the corners and edges of the puzzle were now in place. And where this thing was heading? It was going to start getting messy from here.

He picked up his phone and called Kate. They should be done with dinner by now, the kids likely cleaning up the kitchen. It was nice that he could talk to her when working on cold cases. She loved a good mystery.

"Hey Joe," she said, "glad you called."

"A bad time?"

"For my man? It's never a bad time. You on the road?"

"For several hours now. Should be getting home right around when it gets dark. Thought I'd give you a call and fill you in on this crazy case I've been working on. You're pretty much up to date, right?"

"I think I am. Don't know how it went with those two elderly ladies you were meeting in Raleigh today. Did that go well?"

"Very well. Very sweet ladies. You could tell looking in their eyes, they both have a thousand different stories to tell. But they filled me in what they could about their missing son. Well, brother to the one. It's so sad. I'm about a hundred percent sure now that he's the guy that carved that message into the boards at Jack and Rachel's place. And that he was likely murdered shortly after. They talked to his school friends back in '64, just after he went missing. All of them said he was driving down to Culpepper with a white friend who lived there, to help him solve some problem he was having with his family. And that's the last anyone ever heard from him again. When the mom came down looking for him, she got absolutely no help from our Police Department. Which is no surprise, considering the state of things back then."

"Like that movie you and I rented before moving there?" Kate said. "What was it, *In the Heat of the Night*? Remember the one with all the racist cops, had Sidney Poitier in it?"

"Yeah," Joe said. "I remember it. Looks like that's pretty much how it was back then. They had no thought of investigating his disappearance. Acted like there was no suspicion of foul play. Sent her packing, saying he'd probably just ran off to start a new life on his own. Which was a totally stupid idea. This was a seriously bright kid, studying to be a doctor, who obviously had a close bond with his family. Had he been white, I'm sure they would have spent enough time with his mother to learn that, then would've done everything in their power to find him. Sadly, even if they had done the right thing, I'm afraid the search would've ended where ours is probably going to end."

"You mean...finding his body?"

"Yeah, that. But I haven't told you the bigger news yet. That came after I got two hours down the road." He relayed the contents of his conversation with Mr. Hadley about the brothers, Boone and Mason Rhodes.

After, Kate said, "You mean Councilman Rhodes?"

"The very one. And did you catch they've got a barn? Remember I said that was in the last message Jack uncovered, that the kid was chained up in a barn? I mean, there are very few barns in Culpepper to begin with. Then Mr. Hadley remembered, back then they used to deliver entire pallets of construction material to that barn, which would include, I'm sure, stacks of 2 x 4's."

"My gosh, Joe. Sounds like those guys are definitely involved in this. A City Councilman...can't imagine that's going to make Pendleton very happy."

"I know, right? Can you imagine the scandal when this gets out? That is, if we can prove everything. I've still got a bunch of things to nail down. But it's not looking too good for these...Rhodes brothers. Speaking of which, can you do me a favor, Hon? I know you're always looking things up on Google. If you could do this before I get home, I won't have to stay up doing it tonight. But I'm going to need to brief Hank and the captain in the morning. And especially for Pendleton, I'd really like to have a better handle on who my suspects are."

"What do you need me to do?"

"Something like a bio sketch for each of these brothers.

Since they're such a prominent family, I've gotta believe they've been in the local newspapers a bunch of times. See what you can find out for these guys, anything you think might be relevant. Maybe copy and paste whatever you find onto a Word doc. That way, I can read it over in the morning before I head into my meeting with Pendleton."

"Sure, Joe. I can do that. I think it'll be fun."

"Great. That'd be a great help."

"I'll get right on it. You drive safe and get home to me in one piece."

He said "love you" and hung up. He had half a mind to call Hank and fill him in next but then got a picture of him and his young wife cuddling on the couch after dinner. So, he let it drop.

But only for ten minutes. He decided, what the heck, Hank was a salaried guy like him, so he was expected to put in occasional overtime. But the bigger reason was how much he respected Hank's mind. Joe wanted to turn that mind loose on the new facts he'd uncovered, get him stirring all these things together between now and when they met in the morning.

This thing had suddenly become a big deal. He'd really rather have Hank up to speed when they went in to brief Pendleton.

Man, Joe thought. This thing could get ugly.

The next morning, Joe and Hank had agreed to meet at Joe's office to make sure they were both singing off the same sheet music before they went in to brief Captain Pendleton on the stunning new developments of the case.

Joe sat at his desk, grabbed his coffee mug and leaned back in his chair. Hank was sitting across from him at his worktable. "So, what do your instincts tell you, now that you had a whole night to chew it over?"

"That this case—which I thought at first had no chance of ever being solved—is all sorted out. I really didn't come up with anything new from what you shared last night. It's all circumstantial, at this point, but like most good circumstantial cases...you get enough pieces of factual information then tie them all together and they all point in the same direction? You know you're on the right track. We may not have enough to go to the DA yet, though I think we're close. But we've certainly got enough to go to Pendleton."

"Good," Joe said. "I didn't wake up with any doubts about any of it. In fact, I've already started making a list of questions to ask Councilman Rhodes when we interview him."

"You want to talk to him first before we talk to the older brother, Boone? Cause I'm thinking he's the more likely culprit, between the two of them. Unless you think they were in on this together."

"No, I'm not sure what the Councilman's role in all this was, but I'd be surprised if he played any role in the actual killing. Especially after going over the research Kate did for me last night. But I think talking to him first might pave the way for a more substantial conversation with Boone."

"Research?" Hank said. "What kind of research did you have Kate working on? Second question, why do you have your wife doing case research at home for no pay? When you got a partner here making top dollar who can do the same thing, and probably only take twice as long to do it?"

Joe smiled. "It was a one-time thing. Your job's still secure. I just needed the information before our meeting with Pendleton, and I knew you and I wanted to get together to compare notes before that." Joe held up a little notebook. "And see this thing here? It's another thing I did this morning, read over the last several entries in this journal."

"Journal? Where'd that come from?"

"I got it from the mother of the black kid who went missing, Whitney. Kind of like a diary he kept, only he didn't write in it every day."

"Did you get any good stuff from it?" Hank said.

"Yeah, I did. Something pretty significant. But I won't have time to go over that and the stuff Kate dug up before we meet Pendleton."

"Okay, so what did her research turn up?"

Joe slid three sheets of paper out from under the journal. "Got it right here, as a matter fact. It's basically a bio sketch of the two brothers. Everything Kate could find on the internet about them, mostly from newspaper articles over the last several decades. But to me, it's very telling. And when you put it together with the facts we've already uncovered, the fog lifts even a little more."

"Well, let's hear it."

Joe took a long sip from his mug. "Well, you already know their construction business went belly up during the Carter years. I didn't know this part, but the article said they went into full bankruptcy. Pretty much had to auction off all their equipment. But because of the way the father ran things, his name was Judson, he didn't tie the family property into the business in any way, even during the hard times. So, the family kept the plantation house and all the land along with it."

"Guess that was smart of him," Hank said.

"It was. Read another article written about a year later that interviewed the old man. He didn't go into any detail about this but, apparently, a couple of years before the bankruptcy he'd formed a separate real estate company to manage several different people who were leasing their land to farm on it. Things were tight, but they were able to keep afloat living on that. That's when Boone studied and passed the test to get his real estate license. The younger brother, Mason, had a bachelors' degree, but he went back to college to get a law degree."

"He definitely got it," Hank said. "I remember he had a law firm for a whole lot of years. Used to drive by a big old house they had converted into offices, just before you got into downtown."

"Yeah," Joe said. "Quite a few articles in the local news about him and his law firm over the years. Most of them were about him winning cases or getting awards for doing pro bono work for various African-American organizations in town. Lots of pictures of him shaking hands, holding plaques with a number of black folks...everyone all smiles, all dressed up. You could tell from reading the interviews, these people were friends. No trace of racism in that man that I could see."

"But let me guess," Hank said, sitting up. "His brother Boone wasn't in any of those pictures with him, was he?"

"No. His name never came up. There were a totally different set of articles about him that came out, from time to time. Some of them included pictures, too."

"And I'm going to take a wild guess," Hank interrupted, "there weren't any smiling black people in those pics?"

Joe shook his head. "Not a one. Smiling, frowning or doing anything else. Mostly rich white guys, if I'm being blunt. Quite a few on the golf course or in the clubhouse banquet room. Guess he wound up organizing some kind of charity golf tournament every year for a while. For the March of Dimes, if I recall. There were some stories about his real estate development company making some pretty sweet deals over the years. Some other articles about him getting married. I counted three times. In the third one, it mentioned he'd been divorced two times before. I don't know if he divorced the third one or she died. But I know he's not with her anymore. Mr. Hadley said he and Mason both lived together in the old plantation house now."

"Well, I do remember reading something a few years ago about Councilman Rhodes' wife dying," Hank said.

"Read that obituary, too," Joe said.

"If I remember, that was his one and only wife. Mason, I mean."

"Yep. That's what the obituary said. And they didn't have any kids."

"When you consider how their lives have gone," Hank said, "can hardly tell they're even related, let alone brothers."

"I know, right? Seems like an odd pairing, the two of them ending up as old men living in the same big plantation house they grew up in as kids."

"Yeah, it does."

Joe looked at his watch. "We've got to wrap this up in a couple. Supposed to meet Pendleton in five. But there's something else that emerged in my mind as I read more about these very different lives."

"What's that?"

"I may just be too cynical here, but I found myself wondering...was all of this extra effort, all these years the younger brother, Mason, spent helping out all of these African-American groups, really something he did out of a sincere desire to help his fellow man? Or..."

"Or," Hank interjected, "to assuage a deep-seated sense of guilt he felt about what his family did, or maybe what he failed to stop them from doing, to his black college friend way back in the summer of 1964?"

Joe was pretty sure he knew what assuage meant, by the way Hank just used it in the sentence. Both men looked at each other for a moment in silence. Joe nodded, then said, "Let's go see Pendleton."

47

Just before Joe and Hank stepped into Captain Pendleton's office, Hank stopped Joe and said. "So, Joe, tell me something. If you had Kate dig up all this information from the local papers on the internet, why did I have to go down to the library and spend all that time flipping through those old microfilm rolls? I didn't know the old local news stories were online. I could've just Googled the info, saved myself hours of time?"

Joe smiled. "You think I didn't tell you about it, because I like her more than you? I do, but that had nothing to do with it. Turns out, the library's old newspapers on the internet don't start till 1975. Guess they're slowly loading them up and that's as far as they got. Everything you looked into happened in the sixties."

"Oh. Okay." He opened the door, and they went in.

Pendleton's secretary pointed to his office door and said, "Go on in, he's expecting you."

Joe walked in first, took the office chair closest to the

wall. Hank sat in the other one. Pendleton had his back to them, reading something on his laptop. He closed the lid, spun around in his chair and said, "Okay guys, big cold case update time. Let me have it. Who wants to go first?"

"That'd be Joe," Hank said.

Joe set the journal and research pages from Kate on the edge of the desk. "Well Captain, we've made some serious headway in the last few days. Way more than either of us expected. In fact, I think we pretty much got it all sewn up."

"You're kidding? Wow, that is some big progress. But you know, we really need to have our ducks lined up in a row with this first one. It's definitely going to be in the news, whatever it is. So I want to make sure we've got a slamdunk on the conviction before we go to the DA. You think it's that solid already?"

"Almost," Joe said, "but not quite. We've got at least a couple more big interviews to conduct before we reach that point."

"Fine," Pendleton said. "If that's all you got left, why don't you split them up? Each of you take one, compare notes and get back with me then."

"Captain," Hank said, "don't you want to hear the case all laid out? The evidence we dug up so far?"

"Do I need to? I trust you guys. You know how to do your job."

"I think you're going to want to hear this, Captain," Joe said. "Especially when you hear who the two guys are we want to interview next."

"Okay...who are they?"

"See Cap," Joe said, "here's the thing...this case has kind

of taken a crazy turn. In a way, we're almost here to ask permission to do these interviews with these two guys."

"Permission?" Pendleton said. "Since when do you need to ask my permission to interview people for a case?"

"When one of them is a very well-known and well-respected sitting City Councilman," Joe said.

"And the other one is his brother," Hank added.

"What? City Councilman? Who? Who are you talking about?"

"Councilman Rhodes."

"Rhodes," Pendleton repeated. "Why do you need to talk to him?"

"And his brother, Boone," Hank said.

"Okay, why?" Pendleton sat up straight.

Joe did, too. "I guess the best answer would be...that's where the evidence is taking us."

"You think Councilman Rhodes can somehow help you solve this case?"

"It's a little bit darker than that," Hank said. "We're saying Rhodes is directly involved in the case."

"What?"

"It's a little more complicated even than that, sir," Joe said. "We do think he's involved. His older brother, probably a lot more."

Pendleton shook his head in disbelief. "I can't believe this." He leaned back in his seat. "Joe, I was hoping for some good publicity for this new squad out of this first case. Not a scandal. What are you telling me?"

"Well, Captain, if you give me a couple of minutes I'll share with you what we turned up so far. You might not like this little twist here we've just dumped on your desk, but we came by it honestly. We're not making this stuff up. It's where the evidence brought us. If you give me a minute, I'll show you how. And if you think we're jumping the gun, you let me know. Fair enough?"

"Yeah, fine. Show me what you've got."

"Well, for starters, I've already told you about the carved message Jack Turner found in the walls of his new place. Think you're up to date on the latest we have on the message itself."

"You mean about the guy saying he's chained up in a barn," Pendleton said.

"Yeah, that," Joe replied. "Which, at first, threw us a curve, because we don't have too many of them in Culpepper. Guess which property has one of the very few in town? That would be the Rhodes plantation."

"Well that's not very conclusive," Pendleton said. "It could be—"

"Wait, Captain, there's a lot more. We pulled the permit on Jack's lake house. Built by Rhodes Construction back in the summer of 1964. At first, we didn't think this was such a big deal. We figured the kid who carved the message was chained up against a whole stack of 2 x 4's, which meant the crime must've happened at the building supply warehouse."

"Makes sense," Pendleton said.

"Right, it does. Only thing is, as you might imagine the only building supply business operating in Culpepper back then went out of business years ago. But you know Hadley's Hardware Store downtown?"

Pendleton nodded.

"Well, Mr. Hadley, the father, used to work at Dunn Brothers, the building supply place. Back in the sixties when he was twenty-something. He distinctly remembers that Rhodes Construction routinely took deliveries of entire pallets of material, including 2 x 4's, at the plantation house. Apparently, they had converted their barn into a mini-warehouse for just that purpose."

"Which means, Captain," Hank said, "the kid who got killed, the one who carved that message into those boards, was likely chained up in that barn at the Rhodes plantation, not in some faraway warehouse."

Joe looked at Pendleton's face. They weren't there yet, but he was starting to see it. The fight was leaving his face. "And it gets worse for them, sir. I checked our records in the basement for the summer of '64. A missing person's report was filed right around that time. It never went anywhere. Looks pretty obvious that the officer who filled it out didn't give it any serious thought, let alone any effort. But he did take down some of the details. The woman who came in was a black lady whose college-age son, Whitney Wilkins, had gone missing. I don't know if you remember the history of that time, but during that summer in particular, a major upheaval was taking place in the civil rights movement. Lots of violence, lots of black churches being bombed, KKK crosses set on fire, lots of lynchings."

"Now," Pendleton said, "I don't think we had anything quite that bad happening around here."

"I'm not saying you did, sir. But that was what was taking place all over the South back then. And in that setting, you have this black college kid driving from the DC area where he went to school, down here to Culpepper with a white college friend, supposedly to help him out with some family problems he was having."

"And you know for sure that kid, that black kid, came down here to our town?"

Joe nodded. "We do, Captain. The mother said so. Several of his friends said that's where he was headed, to Culpepper, Georgia. And that's the last thing they ever heard from him. Ever again. He drove down here with his white friend and never returned. His mother and sister, they're the ladies I spoke to in Raleigh, convinced me. Something very sinister happened to him. He was a med student, with a close family and a bright future ahead of him. He had no reason to just run off like that. It doesn't make any sense, unless something very bad happened to him once he got here."

The captain's face dropped. Joe could tell, his cop instincts had finally taken over. He was seeing it.

"And you think this black kid's white friend is..."

"I don't think, sir, I know who it is. It's Mason Rhodes, the Councilman." Joe reached over and lifted the journal. "This thing proves it, makes the connection crystal clear. This was handwritten by Whitney Wilkins, the missing black kid. His mother let me borrow it. She'd gotten it from his college decades ago. They sent it to her with his other things when he never returned. This morning I read over the last several entries he'd written. He didn't write anything on the day or two just before he made the trip down here to Culpepper. In the days before that, though, he writes quite a bit about all the civil rights work he was involved in during the summer of '64. And his last entry is about this big bus ride he and his friends were about to make down to Mississippi, to help register more black people to vote in that state. He writes about how excited he is, and nervous he is. Things like that. But then he writes several paragraphs, one of them kind of a

long one, about his good friend...Mason Rhodes. He talks
about how amazing it is that a white kid like Mason, who's
clearly from a totally racist family, one that actually ran a
plantation and owned dozens of slaves, is now so completely
committed to their cause. And he also said Mason was
keeping all of this a secret from his family, and that he was
hoping to find a way to help Mason find the courage to break
free."

"Wow, Joe," Hank said.

"Yeah. This is the thing I told you about, that we didn't
get to this morning before coming in here." Joe looked back
at Pendleton. "Sir, we've got to be able to talk to Councilman
Rhodes. Everything that happened points directly to him."

Pendleton looked down, rubbed his forehead, then
looked up again. "So, what role do you think he played in
this?"

"I don't know, sir. But I believe he knows exactly what
happened to Whitney Wilkins. And my hope is, after I share
all these things with him, he will clear up this mystery once
and for all."

48

Joe and Hank were driving together to the downtown office of Councilman Mason Rhodes. It was a few minutes before 1:30PM. After the fairly tense meeting with Captain Pendleton, Joe called the Councilman's office and spoke with his secretary, informing her that they needed to speak to her boss on a "matter of urgent police business" and that they preferred to speak with him as soon as possible. Joe also mentioned, to give the message a little more clout, that Captain Pendleton had authorized and agreed with the need for this interview.

The secretary was clearly a bit shaken by the call but handled it professionally. She called Joe back in less than five minutes with the afternoon appointment time.

Joe looked at his watch, turned to Hank, "Think I'll give Jack a quick update before we get there."

Hank looked at the dashboard clock. "Think there's time?"

"Jack's a busy guy in the middle of the day. It'll be quick. I may not even reach him." He pressed the number.

Jack picked up after a couple of rings. "Hey, Joe. How you doing? Anything new on the case?"

Joe laughed. "Actually, a good bit. In fact, I think we may have solved it."

"You're kidding? Wow, that's some serious progress."

Joe quickly filled him in on the latest info, ended with, "We're just pulling up to the Councilman's office as we speak."

"To arrest him?"

"No, just question him, see how he reacts to all this information. Hopefully, he'll cooperate. If he doesn't, I may need more help from you and Rachel."

"You mean us tearing down some more walls, trying to find the rest of that message?"

"Yeah, that. I mean, when you read what we've already uncovered, it seems like the vic was just about to identify himself and maybe the killer, too. I think we know both of those names now. But having those boards on hand that actually say it..."

"I get it," Jack said. "I'll talk to Rachel about it, but I already know she'll agree. If you need that info to close this case, I'm sure we can make that happen."

"Great," Joe said. "And hey, listen, I can probably get authorization to have you hire someone to do that work, if we need it for the case, and to do the repair after. Get it back to where it was before."

"That would help, but hey, whatever you need, just let us know."

"I will. Okay Jack, we're here. Gotta go. Talk to you soon."

Joe turned off the car, grabbed his brief bag. He and Hank headed in through the glass doors of the upscale downtown office building. All of five floors. And that was tall for downtown Culpeper. Another reason Joe was glad he didn't have to leave this place. A receptionist informed them the Councilman's office suite was on the second floor. In no time at all, they were in his lobby greeting the gal Joe had spoken with earlier. He registered the anxious look on her face. He wished he could ease her mind but wasn't altogether sure she didn't have a good reason for concern. She buzzed the Councilman on the intercom, and he said to let them through.

The inside of Rhodes' office was just about what Joe expected. Big mahogany everything. Plush burgundy drapes. Brass lamps and fixtures. Nice view of the downtown city park. Not a bad gig at all.

Too bad it was all about to go away.

"Come on in detectives, have a seat. Can we get you anything? Coffee, tea?" Big smile on Rhodes' face. Still had most of his hair. Pure white, like his mustache. Fine, polished southern accent.

"No, thanks," Joe said.

"I'm good," said Hank.

"I must say, you've got us quite curious about the purpose of this visit. Can't imagine how I can be of any help with your urgent police business, but I'll try."

"Thanks, Councilman. So I don't take up too much of your time, I'll get right to it. I'm sure you've heard, Captain Pendleton recently established a cold case squad here in Culpepper. Hank and I were asked to be the charter members for it, I guess you could say."

"I've seen some television shows about that sort of thing," Rhodes said. "I get the general idea."

"Right," Joe said. "Well, we're actually pursuing leads on our very first case. And believe it or not, your name...well, your family name, has entered into the picture."

"Really?" the old man said.

Joe looked at the expression on his face. No change. "So, I have a few questions to ask. Maybe you could help clear some things up for us. I've learned that your family, even the plantation house property you own, goes back several generations."

"That's true. It predates the Civil War by several decades in fact. And, I'm sad to say, my family were avid slaveholders during that sad chapter of our history. Of course, I've never believed in that or defended it in any way. I've spent the better part of my professional career doing everything I could to level the playing field between the races, so to speak."

"I've read about that," Joe said. "I'm only in this town a little more than four years, and I'm sure you can tell, I'm not from the South."

Rhodes smiled. "I could tell."

"Anyway, I understand that before your involvement in local city government, you had an established law firm in town. And before that, before the Carter administration, your family ran a fairly successful construction company."

"You've obviously done your homework, Lieutenant."

Joe noticed the first furrowing of his brow. "Can I ask, what was your role in the company? I believe back then, both your father and brother were involved, as well."

"You are correct. I was actually something of a junior

partner, being the youngest in the family. My father was the owner and president, and ruled the roost right up until the day he died. My brother would have been second-in-command, mostly in charge of field operations. Overseeing the actual construction projects themselves. I was more involved in the commercial side of things, especially when we got the contracts to build several new wings on the University campus."

Joe pretended to take some notes. "Speaking of the University. You didn't actually attend the one here in town, correct?"

"No, I graduated from Georgia Tech. That's not where I got my law degree, but—"

"But didn't you attend the University of Maryland your first year?" Joe asked. "And weren't you also pretty heavily involved in the civil rights movement back then, especially during the summer of 1964?"

Rhodes' face instantly changed, as if Joe had just slapped him.

"Why, uh...yes, that's actually true. May I ask where you got that information? I don't believe that part of my story has been published anywhere. Not that I'm ashamed of it, but—"

"Well, if you're not ashamed of it, Councilman," Hank said, "why has it been left off your public biographical profile? Nothing wrong with the University of Maryland that I know of."

"Well no, you're right. There isn't anything wrong with that school. Actually, I omitted that part of the story out of deference to my father. But I really should have made it part of the picture after he passed away."

"Why is that, sir?" Joe said. "Why would you need to do

something like that out of deference to your father? See, I did some looking into it. Was it because back then, during the year you went to that school, you got involved in this civil rights activity, something you clearly cared deeply about, but you did it *secretly*, behind your father's back, and when he found out he was very angry?"

Rhodes sat straight up. "Lieutenant, where are you getting this information? I don't understand. The things you're talking about are not public knowledge."

"No Councilman Rhodes, they're not."

"So, where did you get all this from?"

Joe bent over, pulled Whitney Wilkins' Journal from his brief bag, held it up. "I read them in here."

49

Joe looked right at Rhodes as he held up the journal. Clearly, he recognized it. "You remember this, don't you? From way back, during that first year of college in 1964. I'll bet you saw your good friend, Whitney Wilkins, writing in it a time or two, didn't you?"

"Whitney?" Mason said feebly. He looked down at his desk. "I haven't heard that name in..."

"I imagine you haven't heard his name spoken much since that night when your father and brother chained him up in your barn."

Mason's face turned white. He looked almost about ready to faint. "How... how do you know about that? Whitney couldn't have written it in there."

"No Councilman, you're right. He couldn't have written it in here."

"But why do you know that, sir?" Hank added. "How could you know that?"

Mason didn't answer.

"Is it because you knew," Joe said, "that Whitney didn't live to see another sunrise after that night? Did he?"

Hank leaned forward. "And since he was chained up in your barn during his last few hours, he couldn't possibly have written anything more in the journal."

Mason's face looked like death. He glanced at Hank, then at Joe, then at the journal. He exhaled a deep sigh, then looked down. "Whitney, I'm so..."

Joe knew he was just about to say the word *sorry*. He didn't want to give him too much time to ponder. "Councilman, my partner asked you a question. You just said, correctly, that Whitney couldn't have given me that information by way of this journal. My partner asked, how you could possibly have known that considering that we both know what happened to him that night in the barn."

A long pause. Another deep sigh. Mason looked up. "I know he couldn't have written it, because I was there. The last time I saw him he was sitting in our barn, his hands chained to a pillar, leaning against a stack of lumber." A single tear rolled down his left cheek. He didn't wipe it away.

"Would that stack of lumber happen to be 2 x 4's?" Hank said.

"Probably. I'm not totally sure."

"We know it was," Joe said.

"How do you know all these things?" Mason said. "The only people who knew any of this were in my family. And I know none of them ever said a word to anyone, and they certainly never wrote any of this down."

"And as you said," Hank said, "Whitney couldn't have written these things in his journal." He looked over at Joe.

Joe let a moment hang in the air, then said, "But Whitney

did tell us, Councilman. In fact, he's the reason—the entire reason—we're here talking to you today."

Councilman Rhodes just sat there, staring at Joe, dumbfounded. Joe went on to explain to him, play-by-play, everything that happened leading up to this moment. Jack and Rachel's surprising discovery hidden behind their walls, the message Whitney had carved into that stack of lumber. He even read to Rhodes the lines of the message they'd uncovered thus far:

HELP
ME. I'M CHAINED UP
IN THIS BARN
VERY DARK. HARD TO
SEE. MY NAME IS

IF I GO MISSING
I AM PROBABLY DEAD
MY KILLER WILL

Joe told him about the original permit he had found for Jack's lake house which led to their family construction firm. The missing person's report filed by Whitney's mom, the interview Joe had with her and Whitney's sister, the ache they've carried in their heart for all these years never knowing why he disappeared. The things Whitney had written about his good friend, Mason, in his journal.

When Joe got to that part, Mason began to sob. First quietly, then he buried his face in his hands and didn't even try to restrain it. Joe looked over at Hank, who made an expression that suggested he didn't see that one coming, meaning Rhodes coming clean like that.

Joe had a feeling he might. We're talking decades of guilt-written community service here. But no amount of external do-gooding could erase that kind of a stain on a man's soul. Joe knew firsthand, that kind of thing required a come-to-Jesus moment. Literally. He looked around, saw a box of tissues sitting atop a mahogany file cabinet. He walked over, snatched it and set it on Rhodes' desk near his elbow.

Mason heard the sound, lifted his head. "Thank you," he said, pulled out several tissues. After he regained some of his composure, he said, "I can't believe Whitney had the presence of mind to carve a message into those boards. I was so terrified that night. I'd never seen my father or brother so angry."

"So, is that what happened?" Joe said. "You kept your mouth shut, because you were afraid they were going to kill you?"

Mason sighed. "I wish it were something as noble as that. No, I kept my mouth shut because I was a coward. A first-rate coward. I don't think my father would have let my brother kill me. But make no mistake, though I didn't see it happen, I have no doubt my brother, Boone, did this thing. He killed Whitney that night. They locked me up in my bedroom the entire night, after giving me a pretty decent beating. But I was there in the barn when they caught Whitney and I together. He had actually come there to rescue me. I was supposed to just sneak into the house, gather some of my things—including three thousand dollars in cash that I'd saved—and get out. They caught me, Boone and my dad, and locked me in the barn."

"They locked you in the barn?" Hank repeated.

"At first, yes. Tied me to a pole. It was just supposed to be a punishment. Something they used to do when I was younger, if I did something really bad. But when I didn't come back to our rendezvous point, Whitney got worried and came looking for me. He found me in the barn. I had just given him the money, told him to go back without me, use the money for the cause. But he didn't want to leave me there. Then the barn doors opened, and there they were. Boone saw Whitney holding the box of cash and accused him of stealing. So they untied me and chained him up in my place, against that stack of lumber. Unfortunately, Whitney made the mistake of telling them he'd go to the FBI, bring them up on charges of kidnapping."

"Why was that such a mistake?" Hank said.

"You've got to understand how different things were back then," Mason said. "Whitney knew he couldn't go to the local police or County Sheriff. Like most of the law enforcement in the South back then, they were sometimes the worst perpetrators of racial injustice. He thought invoking the FBI would get my dad and brother to wake up to the crazy thing they were doing and let us go. But I knew, even then, knowing Boone, knowing my dad...Whitney just sealed his fate saying that."

"So, what did they do to him?" Joe said. "Or should I say, how did they kill him? What did they do with his body?"

Mason looked down at his desk again, rubbed his forehead a few times then looked up. "That's not part of the story I can help you with. As I said, they locked me up the entire night. But I'm totally certain they discussed how they were going to dispose of Whitney. Boone did the dirty work. I have no doubt of that. He would've reported back to Daddy when all was accomplished, and that was the end of it. All Boone said that next morning was, *That friend a-yours won't be giving us no more trouble. I made sure of that.*"

"He said that?" Joe said. "You heard Boone say those words?"

"Yep. I'll never forget it."

"So," Hank added, "Your father and brother are the last people on earth to ever see Whitney alive, and the last thing your brother says on the subject is, *Your friend won't be giving us no more trouble. I made sure of that?*"

Mason nodded yes. "We never talked about it, ever again. Daddy said something that morning about giving me one last chance to be the kind of son he'd raised me to be. I knew perfectly well what he meant. And as any true coward would do, I got in line from that moment on and behaved myself." Another deep sigh. "And I've been paying for it ever since."

Joe thought about what should come next. This was about as full a confession as one could hope for in a moment like this. "It sounds as if you are genuinely sorry for what happened to your friend, and to his family...not knowing what happened to him for all these years."

Mason looked at him. "I am. And you needn't read me my rights, Lieutenant. I don't know all the nuances of criminal law, but I don't think I've committed any crimes. On the other hand, I've been about as bad a friend to my friend, Whitney, as a person could be. And I will testify to everything I have told you in court, against my brother. In fact, after the conclusion of our time, I plan to draft a complete statement spelling out everything I've said, and anything else that comes to mind that might be relevant. After that, I'll be creating a press release announcing my resignation from city government, effective immediately."

"That would be helpful, sir," Joe said. "And can I ask you a favor? Would you not mention any of this to your brother before we are able to secure a warrant for his arrest? I don't know if he's a flight risk, but I know you're both fairly wealthy, and I'm concerned—"

"I won't say a word to Boone," Mason said. "You have my word on that."

50

J oe and Hank made their way back out to their car, parked at the curb near the Councilman's downtown office. Joe's head was spinning at the speed at which events were transpiring.

"I did not see that coming," Hank said, as he got in the car.

"Yeah, I figured eventually he'd come around, if I kept appealing to the issues I knew he felt guilty about. But I didn't expect all his defenses to come tumbling down in one sitting." Joe got in, turned on the ignition. "I better call the Cap, give him a heads up."

"I wonder how this will play out in the local press," Hank said. "You can tell Pendleton's a little nervous about it."

"It'll be a big story," Joe said, "but if Mason Rhodes communicates things with the kind of contrition, if that's the word, we saw in there, it might not be so bad. Might even be kind of refreshing. Since when do you ever hear a politician take full responsibility for their actions without any spin or excuses?"

"Yeah, I didn't think about that. The press won't know what to do with him. Be interesting to see how the black community responds, once they hear the news."

Joe picked up his phone. "Better call this one in." He waited a few seconds for Pendleton to answer.

"Okay Joe, I've been waiting for this call. What are we looking at?" Pendleton said.

"We're looking at a rock-solid case, sir. It's not just circumstantial anymore. Things could not have gone any better with Councilman Rhodes just now." Joe went on to explain everything that just happened.

When he finished, Pendleton said, "My goodness... that's...amazing. Guess the old guy was sitting on a ton of baggage. He really said all that? Just...admitted to everything? Just like that?"

"Just like that," Joe said. "So, you okay with us making the arrest right now? Of Boone Rhodes? I don't think we'll get any grief from the DA, do you?"

"Not at all," Pendleton said. "Bring him in. I'll get with the DA as soon as we hang up. I have a feeling he's gonna love this case. Since our meeting this morning, I've been thinking it over. I'm not so worried about the publicity anymore. I think we might come out looking pretty good on this, especially now that the Councilman's cooperating. Have any idea where the brother is?"

"We got a pretty good lead. I asked the Councilman before we left where we might find him. He said at this time of day he's almost always hanging out with his buddies at the country club café. Guess we'll head on over there now."

• • •

IT TOOK Hank and Joe about twenty minutes to reach the Culpepper Country Club. It was on the outskirts of town, and they had stopped first to put gas in the car, get a refill on their coffee. The elderly guard in the gatehouse let them through quickly once he saw their badges. "Here on official business fellas?"

"Afraid so, sir. Here to make an arrest," Joe said.

"Oh my," the guard replied. "I was only kidding. I don't think we've ever had an arrest out here before."

"Guess there's a first time for everything," Hank said, as they drove past.

They followed the signs to the clubhouse, parked in one of the guest spots. The parking lot was filled with an array of the finest cars money could buy.

"You ever golf?" Hank said.

"Look at these cars, Hank? You really need to ask? I don't think I could afford to eat a burger in this place."

Hank laughed. They both got out of the car, headed toward the clubhouse door. Hank got there first, opened it for Joe. "Whatta you say we go ruin an old murdering racist's day?"

Joe smiled. "I say, let's do it."

The clubhouse café looked like a mid-sized fancy restaurant. Even from the front, it was hard not to appreciate the view. The entire back wall looked out over the golf course through a series of plate-glass windows. And of course, the lawn and landscaping were picture perfect. Joe had actually golfed a few times with some buddies at a cheap city course back in Pittsburgh. The only fun he had was driving the cart.

It took a few moments for his eyes to adjust to the lower lighting of the room, but a loud outburst of laughter drew their attention to a group of men gathered around some tables on the left.

"I think I see Boone," Hank said. "Guy in the middle with the white hair, light blue pullover shirt. Recognize him from the pictures."

"I see him." Joe headed in that direction, Hank right behind him. "You got the cuffs?"

"In my hand," Hank said.

They reached the group of tanned, nicely dressed elderly men and stood behind the guy at the head of the table. Joe didn't say anything for a moment. One by one, the men stopped talking and laughing and turned to face Joe and Hank.

"Can we help you gentlemen?" one of them said. "This is a private club. Don't think I've seen either one of you men here before."

"We aren't members," Joe said. "This won't take long." Hank started making his way around the table toward Boone Rhodes.

"What's going on here?" another one said.

"We're with the Culpepper PD," Joe said. They showed their ID badges. "Boone Rhodes," Joe said sternly. "Please stand. We're here to arrest you for first-degree murder."

Boone began to stand, said, "Murder? What are you talking about? This is outrageous."

Hank quickly pulled his arms behind him, snapped on the cuffs.

All the men began to protest loudly, offering their varied opinions at the absolute absurdity of what was taking place.

"We're arresting you," Joe said loudly, "for the murder of Whitney Wilkins, a young African-American college student back in the summer of 1964. Remember him, Mr. Rhodes?"

"You've got to be kidding," Boone said. "No, I don't remember him. I've never heard that name before in my life, ever."

Hank began pulling him toward Joe, and toward the front door.

"Go ahead and read him his rights," Joe said to Hank.

Boone turned to one of the men. "Bill, call my lawyer. Have him meet me at the station." He looked at Joe as he walked past him, "You're going to regret this, young man. I'll have your badge for this."

"Don't think so," Joe said, smiling. "Keep walking." He turned to the rest of the men. Some standing, some sitting. All of them visibly distressed. "Sorry to ruin your little afternoon get-together, fellas. Don't think you'll be wanting to keep Mr. Rhodes in your little club here, once you get the drift on what this is all about. Have a nice day." He turned and followed Hank and Boone Rhodes toward the front door of the clubhouse.

As they drove through the parking lot, Boone continued breathing out threats and protests. Joe was tempted to let him have it but kept his peace. There would be time for talk once they got him in the interrogation room and laid out the now very-solid case they had against him.

Hank and Joe were surprised once they got past the guard house to find a reporter they both recognized from the local newspaper there to greet them. He had his camera out, so Joe slowed the car down just long enough for him to get some very decent pictures of an angry Boone Rhodes swearing from the back seat.

"Guess we don't need to wonder who called him," Hank said.

Joe smiled. Pendleton was already working out his new PR plan.

51

W hen Hank and Joe arrived back at the station with Boone Rhodes, they noticed a small crowd gathering by the front door, so they went around to the back.

"Think they're reporters?" Hank said.

"Probably," Joe said. "Maybe I should've just gone through the front door, let them have at it with this jerk."

"I heard that," Boone said from the backseat. He'd been pretty quiet the last ten minutes.

"That's why I said it. You want me to turn the car around, go back and face the press?"

"Just keep talking like that," Boone said. "More ammo for my attorney."

Joe pulled the car into the parking space. "We're not even a little intimidated by you, Mr. Rhodes. We know what you've done and, worse, what you are. When everything comes out, your attorney is likely going to want to drop you like a rock."

That shut him up. They all got out and walked up the handful of steps. Joe held open the back door for Hank and Boone. Once inside, they walked through the halls toward interview room one. As they rounded the corner, all three of them saw Mason stepping out of Captain Pendleton's office into the hallway. Pendleton was right behind him.

Boone said, "So, that's what this is all about. Are you kidding me? After all these years, you finally decided to rat me out?"

Mason just stood there, looking at him, didn't reply.

"What, now that big house isn't big enough for both of us? So, you come in here thinking you can get rid of me? After all this time? Well, you won't succeed little brother. You didn't see nothing, and you don't know nothing. Hear me, Mason? Big Mr. City Councilman?"

"Get in there," Joe said, shoving him into the interview room. Hank came in too, closed the door behind them.

"Have a seat," Hank said. "And for the record? Your little brother saw and heard plenty."

Boone sat on the padded steel chair. "I ain't saying a word until my lawyer gets here."

"Fine," Joe said. "That's your right." He looked at Hank. "I'm going to go check in with the Captain. Be right back." Joe stepped into the hall. Mason and Pendleton were still standing near the captain's doorway.

"After you left the Councilman's office," Pendleton said, "he wrote out his statement, emailed it to me. It was pretty extensive and detailed. I read it over and asked him to come down, so we could get his signature on it. Though he didn't actually see his brother kill his friend, everything else he heard and saw, particularly what Boone said to him the next morning, should be enough to persuade Boone to consider a guilty plea. Especially when you put it all together after laying out the circumstantial case you and Hank created."

"Even more than that," Joe said, "from everything you've told us, Councilman, it sounds like your brother was a full-on racist back when this crime was committed."

"Oh, he was," Mason said. "He and my father both. They never spoke of a black man unless they referred to him as boy, darkie, or their favorite term, the N-word. Which they must've said a couple dozen times a day. They had absolutely no respect for minorities, or anyone else for that matter, unless he was white and Protestant."

"Well," Joe said, "I would imagine your brother has gone to great lengths to reform his reputation from those old racist days, hasn't he?"

"Oh sure. Like most of the old white racists of that era. They won't own up to it anymore, except the real diehards. But Boone tried harder than most to cover things up, especially when he learned how bad his racist views were for his real estate business."

"I see where you're going, Joe," Pendleton said. "Even more ammo we can use to persuade Boone to plead guilty. All that ugly racist stuff Boone used to live by would all come front and center, on full display, if this thing goes to trial."

"Gentlemen," Mason said, "my brother and I have almost nothing in common, but I do know a little bit about what makes him tick. He is not going to want all his friends, and all that effort he's put into crafting his reputation, to come crashing down around him. He'd be left with nothing and no one. When he sees all the evidence you've already put together, and reads my statement, and realizes I'm all done propping up the phony family legacy, and that I will talk plainly in court about what he and my father were really like...he will be willing to make some kind of deal. I don't see this case going to trial. Now, if you'll excuse me, I'm going to make a quick statement to the press who've gathered out front. I'll leave my brother in your capable hands."

"That would be fine," Pendleton said. "We'll be in touch, Councilman."

"And please, Captain. You can stop calling me Councilman. I've already turned in my resignation. I don't deserve that title any longer. I'm not an honorable man."

"I don't know about that, sir," Joe said.

"Well...if you'll excuse me." Mason started walking toward the front door.

After he got halfway down the hall, Pendleton said, "Joe, go listen to what he says to the press. I go out there and they'll be all over me."

"Okay, sir." Joe hurried down the hall after Mason Rhodes.

Joe walked outside and maneuvered around the dozen or so reporters and stood back behind a couple patrol cars.

Mason Rhodes stood on the steps and said, "Ladies and gentlemen, I have a brief announcement to make. A very serious matter has come to my attention today, which has made it abundantly clear to me I can no longer serve as a City Councilman in this great town of ours, so I have turned in my resignation to the Mayor, effective immediately."

"But Councilman," one of them yelled, "This isn't the Mayor's office. We're at the police station. Does this have to do with some kind of criminal matter?" A number of other reporters yelled out similar things.

"All I will say now is, meet me at this same time tomorrow outside the Mayor's office, where I will make a more complete statement about what has happened, and why I've made this decision. I can't say anything more just now. Thank you."

At that, he walked down the steps and headed toward his car, followed by every single one of the reporters, stretching smartphones and digital recorders in his face and yelling out things.

52

Joe had to admit...yesterday was pretty amazing. Don't get too many days like that in the police business. Kate could hardly believe the story when he'd shared the details with her after dinner, once the kids were upstairs and out of earshot. Then he'd called Jack to let him and Rachel know how things had turned out.

Today though, might end even better.

He and Hank were driving to the mayor's office, at Pendleton's instruction. Things had gone better than expected during the negotiations between the DA, Boone Rhodes and his defense attorney, earlier in the day. Once the extent of the case against his client had been presented, the attorney was able to persuade Boone to do the right thing. Maybe not for the right reason, but that didn't matter. The results would still be the same.

"You clean up pretty good," Hank said.

"You don't look half bad, either," Joe replied. The captain

had asked them to look their best. He planned to market this moment for all it was worth.

When they arrived at the mayor's office, a little bigger crowd had gathered around the stairs of the police station than had shown up yesterday. This time the local TV news was there, as well as dozens of curious onlookers who'd read the story in the morning news. As they got out of the car, Joe saw the mayor, Captain Pendleton and Mason Rhodes come out of the glass doors and stand in front of a temporary podium outfitted with microphones. Pendleton saw the two of them and pointed to his side.

"Guess we're being beckoned," Hank said. "Think we'll get a medal?"

"Doubt that, but this may help solidify that raise we both just got."

They walked around the crowd and up the side steps, stood next to Pendleton.

The mayor spoke first. "Okay folks, I have a few comments to make as we get started here. I'm sure many of you have heard by now that Councilman Rhodes has tendered his resignation, as of yesterday afternoon. He and I have talked at some length about the reasons why, and I have accepted it. I could say more about this, but I don't feel the need to, since Mr. Rhodes is here himself. In a moment, he'll explain what this is all about. But first, I want to ask our police chief, Captain Pendleton, to come up and share some of the significant events that led up to this moment. Captain Pendleton?"

Pendleton stepped up to the mic. "Good afternoon everyone. Some of you may have read a story in the local news about a new Cold Case Squad we've recently set up here in

Culpepper. Actually, the events that took place yesterday and today are the first-fruits of that decision. Due to a rather bizarre crime tip submitted by a concerned citizen, who's asked to remain anonymous, our new cold case unit began investigating what has turned out to be a ruthless and senseless murder that took place in this town back in June of 1964. Those of you old enough to remember, or those who know their history, might remember that was an era of great unrest throughout the South. Great sweeping changes were underway in the area of civil rights. Sadly, it has now become clear that Culpepper played an unfortunate role in that dark chapter of history. Yesterday, we arrested Mr. Boone Rhodes, a long-standing resident of this town, on a charge of first-degree murder in the shooting death of a young African-American college student named Whitney Wilkins."

"Will any charges be brought against his brother, Councilman Rhodes?" a reporter yelled out.

"Not at this time, no," Pendleton replied. "But please, let me finish my statement. In a plea deal struck a few hours ago, Mr. Boone Rhodes agreed to plead guilty to the charge and to lead us to the victim's remains, so that the family of this young man could experience some measure of closure in this tragedy. As I said, this rather extraordinary case was solved partly through the efforts of a concerned citizen but especially due to the fine investigative work of our new cold case detectives, Lieutenant Joe Boyd and Sergeant Hank Jensen."

After an awkward pause, a few onlookers clapped. Joe didn't care. It really didn't seem like the kind of thing to applaud. He knew what mattered the most was happening:

Pendleton was getting the publicity he'd hoped to get for the department.

Pendleton continued, "And now Mr. Mason Rhodes has a statement he'd like to read."

He stepped aside to allow Mason Rhodes to come up to the mic. It looked to Joe like the man had aged a decade in the last twenty-four hours. And his eyes looked all puffy, like he'd done a fair amount of crying.

"Hello again everyone. I better just read this, if I have any hope of getting through what I need to say this afternoon. As you've already heard, my brother is pleading guilty to a murder committed on our family property back in the summer of 1964. That's a very long time ago but, in some ways, the memories are as fresh to me as what I did last week, maybe more. Back then, I had just finished my freshman year in college and, unbeknownst to my family, I had joined hundreds of other white and black college students who came down to the south in buses, specifically to try and get more black citizens registered to vote. Because of severe racial intimidation, only a fraction of them ever dared go near the polls. Sadly, my family totally supported suppressing the black vote back then. Many of you know, my family owns a historic landmark on the edge of town, the Rhodes Plantation. Up until that summer, and for many years afterward, my family continued to hold a deep-seated racism against blacks and other minorities. A racism which I had come to despise. That summer, I finally decided to take a stand."

Mason took out a handkerchief and wiped the sweat off his brow. "But before you mistake me for an honorable man, you need to know, I am not. As it turns out, my family learned about my secret allegiance to the cause. They forbid me from having anything more to do with the civil rights workers. However, a very good friend of mine, a black college student about my same age named Whitney Wilkins, knew I was serious about wanting to break this long-standing pattern of racism in my family. He agreed to take a secret trip to my house, where I could get my things together and head back up north, where I could start my life over, free of this legacy of hate. But we got caught by Boone and my father. I was beaten and threatened with being cut off financially forever. But my good friend, Whitney..." Mason's voice began to falter. Tears welled up in his eyes. He reached for the handkerchief again and wiped them.

"Well, my father and Boone decided to kill Whitney that night, basically to silence him. I was locked up in my room, and at some point after, Whitney was taken somewhere on the outskirts of our property and shot by Boone. I was so terrified by what happened and knew that coming forward with this information would fall on deaf ears. The police in this town back then, as in most southern towns, were very sympathetic to the violence being committed against black people. So, I said nothing. I did nothing. I tried to go on with my life, as if I could put all this unpleasantness behind me. And as many of you know, I've dedicated my life since then to doing everything I could to bring about racial reconciliation. While those efforts were all done sincerely, nothing but God's mercy can erase the stain on my soul for my failure to stand up for my friend, or at the very least, to let his poor family know what happened to him. So to that end, I am also announcing today that I've instructed my accountant to do an inventory of all my assets and will give half of whatever that figure turns out to be to Whitney's family and loved ones. He was an amazing young man, and a wonderful friend." Mason paused, sighed, wiped his brow again.

"The saddest part of this, to me, is that the world will never know the incredible contributions Whitney could have made to society, had he only been given the chance. I'm deeply sorry for all the pain and shame my family has caused, and that I've caused by failing to come forward about this before now." He picked up the papers he'd been reading from the podium, folded them in half and slid them into his suit coat pocket. "Well, that's all I have to say." He stepped away, turned and headed back into the mayor's office, as reporters yelled out one question after another.

Joe looked at the onlookers who'd gathered to watch the spectacle. Most wore stunned expressions, as if unable to process what they'd just heard.

The mayor stepped up to the mic. "That'll be all for now folks. Thank you."

Pendleton looked at Joe and Hank. "Great job guys. This couldn't have gone any better. I wouldn't be surprised if one of those real-life cable crime shows gets wind of this story and comes looking to do an episode on it. Nobody will be thinking a bunch of bumpkins live around here if that happens, will they?" He turned and headed inside the mayor's office.

"Well," Hank said. "Guess the show's over."

"Yeah," Joe said. "Let's get out of here before any of those reporters come after us."

53

Hank and Joe had just driven out from the police station through the winding country roads that connected the town to the lakefront area. Every few seconds, Joe glanced in the rearview mirror to make sure the car they had been escorting was still close behind. It was.

"I'm amazed that woman, Ethel, could even make the trip at her age," Hank said. "She's in her nineties, right?"

"Yeah," Joe said, "but her mind is sharp as a tack." He put his turn signal on early. When they reached the dirt road leading to Jack's place, he turned left. Good, they were still behind him.

"Is the guy driving Ethel's grandson, or the other woman's?"

"Her name's Athena. It's her son William, so that makes him Ethel's grandson. Seems like a nice guy." Joe guessed William to be in his late forties, early fifties. He had driven the ladies down here from Raleigh in a rented, decked out black Cadillac. Apparently, Ethel's son Whitney had promised her as soon as he became a doctor, besides buying her a house, he was gonna trade in her old rust-bucket for a brand-new black Caddy. William wanted to give her a fore-taste of what was to come. Apparently, Mason Rhodes had already forwarded fifty thousand dollars to Athena's account, as they awaited the exact amount to be tallied up. Pendleton had whispered to Joe yesterday that the mayor thought the liquid part of Mason Rhodes' estate was easily worth ten million or more. And the Wilkins family certainly had a great civil case to make against Boone Rhodes, if they wanted.

"The road's coming right up on the left," Hank said, looking at the GPS screen.

"I see it." Joe was still old-school, preferring his own eyes to technology unless he was completely lost. He made the turn. Now they were only a few hundred yards away from Jack's place.

"I wonder if this is gonna be kinda creepy," Hank said. "I guess if I was them, I'd be curious and want to see it. But still..."

"Yeah, I know what you mean."

When they reached the clearing on the left, Joe saw Jack's car parked in front, then Jack and Rachel standing on the porch. He'd called to let them know they were on their way when he'd left the station. One more glance in the rearview mirror to confirm William was still behind them, then he pulled in beside Jack's BMW.

The black Caddy pulled in beside Joe. Jack and Rachel came walking out to greet them. Joe made all the necessary introductions. The Wilkins family couldn't have been more gracious, hugging Jack and Rachel like they were close relatives. Both Ethel and Athena made an instant fuss about Rachel's big belly. Everyone else paused as they talked baby talk for the next few minutes.

It was William that got everyone back on track. He took his grandmother's arm and helped her onto the porch steps. He offered to help Athena, but she swatted him away. "I don't need help getting up a few porch steps."

Before they walked inside, Ethel asked, "Now my boy never actually went in this house, right?"

"No, Mama," Athena said. "Remember what I said, he died near that plantation house we drove by yesterday? Remember what they said? He was in that barn and carved that message into that stack of lumber. That lumber was then used to build this house."

"Okay, now I understand." She looked at Jack and Rachel. "And you were the two who found the message my son wrote?"

"Yes, Ma'am. That was us. We were just doing some remodeling, wanted to take down some walls to make it feel bigger, and—"

Jack was interrupted by Ethel giving him a great big hug. Then she started crying, so he just held her. After a few seconds, everyone got a little teary.

When she started to regain her composure, she said, "I'm so sorry. It's just...I...I never thought, after all these years, I'd ever find out what happened to my boy. If it weren't for the two of you, I still wouldn't know to this day."

"Well, I'm glad we could help," Jack said. "Though really, we only got things started. It was really Lieutenant Boyd and his partner, Hank, who sorted this all out."

"I know that." She looked at Hank and Joe. "They have

been just so wonderful. When Lieutenant Boyd came to my house a little while ago, I could hardly believe it. After being so completely ignored all this time, he not only started checking things out in your town, he drove all the way to Raleigh, just to talk to me and Athena. And you men not only figured out what happened to my boy, you brought the man who did it to justice. We will always be grateful." She walked over, gave both Joe and Hank a hug.

Her grandson William walked up, took her gently by the arm. "We best go inside now, Gramma."

Joe noticed Jack and Rachel had everything all tidied and swept. On one side of the living room, they had stacked up the 2 x 4's so that the carved words could be easily seen. "What's the TV for?" he asked. A large flatscreen TV had been set up on a folding table.

"That's so they could see the boards that are upstairs or still attached," Jack said. "We took pictures of those and left the boards in place. But they're kind of hard to read on the tablet. When you blow them up on the TV, you can read pretty well."

"Good idea," Hank said.

Jack walked over to the stack of 2 x 4's. "Mrs. Wilkins..."

"Please, call me Ethel."

"Okay, Ethel. These boards here were the first ones where we noticed the carved letters." Jack bent down and pointed them out. "I'll shine a flashlight on them to help them stand out better, if you want to come over and get a better look."

All three of them came closer. As Ethel traced the carved letters with her finger, Athena read the message out loud. She got choked up as she finished.

Joe noticed tears rolling down Ethel's cheeks. "My boy

wrote these words. The very last words he said on earth."
She paused, took a deep breath. "We heard you, Whitney. We
finally heard what you wanted to say."

Hearing that got to Joe. He quickly wiped the tears away.
But it felt very good inside to be able to give this fine woman
this precious moment while she was still alive.

Jack got the remote and turned the TV on. He walked
over and tapped his tablet a few times, swiped a few more
times, then the pictures of the other boards with carved
letters appeared. "Here's the rest of the message Whitney
wrote," he said.

Ethel, Athena and William came over and stood in front
of the screen. Again, Athena read the words aloud.

"I guess there are still a few more boards with words
carved on them," William said.

"It would seem so," Joe said. "When you put the words
together, between the ones in the stack over there and the
ones on screen, it was enough to get us to this point. But
yeah, obviously it's incomplete."

"It looks like," William continued, "there must be boards
with my Uncle Whitney's name, as well as the killer's. The
way this message reads, he must have identified them."

"We think so too," Jack said. "We had just offered to rip off
the rest of the wallboard, see if we could find those other
carved studs. But then the killer confessed."

Everyone stood there in silence for a few moments.
William said, "You still want to go visit with that lady Uncle
Whitney spoke to last? Maisie, I think her name is."

"If it won't be too much trouble," Ethel said.

"No trouble at all, Gramma. I think she's expecting us."

They made their way to the front door. After they got out

to the porch, Ethel said to Jack and Rachel, "Thank you so much for meeting us out here today. I am so glad we came."

"It was our pleasure," Rachel said. "And really, it was an honor to meet you. All of you."

"You want to follow us to your next stop?" Joe said to William.

"I don't think that'll be necessary, Lieutenant. I have Maisie's address, and that car has a very nice GPS system. We should be okay, if you want to head back to the station."

"You sure? We won't mind."

"No, I'm sure we'll be fine. But you remember, we'll be in town a couple more days. My grandmother insists you let her treat you and Sergeant Jensen to lunch in the finest restaurant this town has to offer."

"Oh, I remember," Joe said. "You'll get no arguments from me."

They stood there on the porch waving as the black Caddy drove off back toward town.

"Well, that was pretty interesting," Hank said. "But, I guess we should be getting back." He started walking toward the car.

"I'll be right there," Joe said. He looked at Jack and Rachel. "How you two doing? I'm guessing this has been kind of an emotional time for you."

"We're doing okay," Jack said. "Certainly helps that the older brother confessed, saved all of us from everything getting all dragged out through a long trial."

"Well, if you want some help getting this place put back together, let me know. I'm pretty good with a hammer, or we can hire someone, get the city to pay for it."

Jack and Rachel looked at each other and smiled. "You want to tell him?" Rachel said.

Jack stepped back into the house a moment, came out holding a sign. He turned it around, showed Joe what it said.

"For Sale by Owner," Joe read aloud, then laughed. "Guess I can't blame you."

Jack walked the sign out about thirty feet, positioned it so that it faced the road. "Yeah, Rachel and I decided just last night. Maybe we're not supposed to have a place on a lake after all." He started hammering down on it with a mallet. "Maybe we'll be making our family vacation memories the same way as you and Kate. Get us a real nice pop-up camper and take it on the road."

Joe smiled. "I know we love ours. And the best part, at least for you guys, you get a new one and there's virtually no chance anybody died in it."

Jack and Rachel laughed. Then Rachel said, "Just to make sure, I'm going to make sure the salesman puts that in writing."

WANT TO READ MORE?

If you haven't read any of Dan's other suspense novels, you'll be happy to learn *If These Walls Could Talk* is actually a "**Sequel Series**" to Dan's bestselling 4-Book Jack Turner Suspense Series. The events and mysteries unfolding in these 4 books take place in the years just prior to this book (**see the links below**), and include many of the same characters and places.

All of Dan's 20 other novels are similar in genre and style to *If These Walls Could Talk*. Except half of them (including his 5 Christmas novels) feature more heart-impacting, spiritual themes, and some have a stronger romantic thread.

As of now, his novels combined have received over 7,000 Amazon reviews (maintaining a 4.6 Star average). They've won multiple national awards and received rave reviews from publications like USA Today, Publisher's Weekly, Library Journal and RT Book Reviews magazine.

Here are some quick links to a few of *Dan's other novels*:

The Jack Turner Suspense Series (*over 1,800 Amazon Reviews, 4.6 Star Avg*)

When Night Comes - http://amzn.to/1xNat4G

Remembering Dresden - http://amzn.to/1RO7WvN

Unintended Consequences - http://amzn.to/2pvSvmG

Perilous Treasure - https://amzn.to/2HOgpl7

THE FOREVER HOME SERIES (*Dog Rescue Series - over 1,800 Amazon Reviews, 4.8 Star avg*)

Rescuing Finley – http://amzn.to/1Hnovrg

Finding Riley - http://amzn.to/2c7xdWY

Saving Parker - http://amzn.to/2g9vKkA

You can check out all of Dan's other novels by going to his Author Book Page on Amazon. Here's the link:

http://amzn.to/2cG5I90

WANT TO HELP THE AUTHOR?

If you enjoyed reading *If These Walls Could Talk*, the best thing you can do to help Dan is very simple—*tell others about it*. Word-of-mouth "advertising" is the most powerful marketing tool there is. Better than expensive TV commercials or full-page magazine ads.

Leaving good reviews is the best way to insure Dan will be able to keep writing novels full time. He'd greatly appreciate it if you'd consider leaving a rating for the book and writing a brief review. Doesn't have to be long (even a sentence or two will help).

Here's the Amazon link for *If These Walls Could Talk*. Scroll down a little to the area that says "**Customer Reviews**," right beside the graphic that shows the number of stars is a box and says: "**Write a Customer Review**."

https://amzn.to/2XDJfOi

If you'd like to contact Dan, feel free to email him at dan@danwalshbooks.com. He loves to get reader emails and reads all of them himself.

SIGN UP TO RECEIVE DAN'S NEWSLETTER

If you'd like to get an email alert whenever Dan has a new book coming out or when a special deal is being offered on any of Dan's existing books, click on his website link below and sign up for his newsletter (it's right below the Welcome paragraph). Also, **every first-time member can choose to receive one of Dan's bestselling novels for FREE** (see the Tab for the Free Book in the Menu).

From his homepage, you can also contact Dan or follow him on Facebook, Twitter or Goodreads.

www.danwalshbooks.com

AUTHOR'S NOTE

If you've never heard of Ashburn, MS, there's a good reason. Ashburn, MS is a fictitious town I created to represent some of the things that happened in a number of smaller Mississippi towns during what is historically known as *Freedom Summer of 1964*. Actually (and sadly), the kinds of things I've shown in my story pale in comparison to many of the horrible things done by southern white racists to blacks and even many white people who helped to abolish these civil rights abuses.

Most of my childhood was spent in the North in the late fifties and early sixties. Thankfully, I was raised by parents who despised the way these civil rights workers were treated in the South, as well as the way blacks were treated in general. I have vivid memories of seeing many of these things depicted on the nightly news then seeing and hearing my parents' reactions. Although we are white, we were also Irish. Our ancestors never owned slaves and, like most Irish immigrants, were often themselves the object of severe prejudice and scorn.

I personally remember watching Martin Luther King, Jr's "I Have a Dream" speech given on the steps of the Lincoln Memorial in 1963. I've watched it dozens of times since. To me, it was one of the most inspiring public speeches ever given. How I wish, as a country, we'd fully embrace those ideals. I especially love the idea Dr. King mentioned, that we should be judged on the content of our character, not the color of our skin. I long for the day when this might be true, not just for blacks and whites, but every other race, as well.

I do have a living hope that I will see such unity one day. The apostle John observed this in Revelations about Heaven: "*After this I saw a vast crowd, too great to count, **from every nation and tribe and people and language,** standing in front of the throne and before the Lamb. They were clothed in white robes and held palm branches in their hands. And they were shouting with a great roar, 'Salvation comes from our God who sits on the throne and from the Lamb!'*"

ACKNOWLEDGMENTS

There is really just one person I absolutely must thank for helping to get *If These Walls Could Talk* into print. That's my wife, Cindi. Her editorial advice and input on this book was indispensable. I also want to thank my proofreading team: Patricia Keough-Wilson, Debbie Mahle, Jann Martin, Terri Smith and Rachel Savage.

Dan Walsh

ABOUT THE AUTHOR

Dan was born in Philadelphia in 1957. His family moved down to Daytona Beach, Florida in 1965, when his father began to work with GE on the Apollo space program. That's where Dan grew up.

He married Cindi, the love of his life in 1976. They have 2 grown children and 4 grandchildren. Dan served as a pastor for 25 years then began writing fiction full-time in 2010. His bestselling novels have won numerous awards, including 3 ACFW Carol Awards (he was a finalist 6 times) and 4 Selah Awards. Four of Dan's novels were finalists for RT Reviews' Inspirational Book of the Year. One of his novels, *The Reunion*, is being made into a major full-length feature film.